Rampaging Lovers

Rampaging Lovers

"The key lies not in Pretoria but in London."

B. B. Dandekar

GYAN

ISBN : 978-81-212-1334-9

Price : ₹ 980

First Published, 2016

Published by

Gyan Publishing House
5, Ansari Road
Daryaganj, New Delhi-110002
Phone: 9811692060
E-mail: books@gyanbooks.com

Printed at: G. Print Process, Delhi.

Cataloging in Publication Data—DK
Courtesy: D.K. Agencies (P) Ltd. <docinfo@dkagencies.com>

Dandekar, B. B., 1938- **author.**
Rampaging lovers : "the key lies not in Pretoria but in London" / B.B. Dandekar.
pages cm
Novel.
ISBN 9788121213349

1. Suspense fiction, American. I. Title.

PS3604.A53R36 2016 DDC 813.6 23

PROLOGUE

July 11, 1980

She sat in a soundproof room at the back of the house watching the tapes run in front of her, hearing their voices in her headset. Farnsworth had put in the room as an addition to the master bedroom into which it opened, almost as a walk-in closet. Tiny. No other exit or entrance except through his bedroom. Barely room for the table and the chair and the electronic equipment that cluttered it. Lined with six-inch thick sound insulation that isolated her from everything except the voices in her headset. Not much of a room, except that it sat directly above the study where the three men were talking.

Farnsworth was speaking, the clipped British accent, gruff when he was aroused was soothing to her ears. She could picture him below, bald and rotund, with military whiskers that curled away and upwards, the shrewd eyes seemingly closed beneath bushy eyebrows. Sitting in the padded armchair, passing his hand past his forehead and over the back of his bald head when in doubt, trying to appease the other two.

Saul, too, she could recognise. The South African accent was unmistakable, carrying a dangerous edge when raised in anger. As now. She had seen Saul once at the house; the ruggedly-built bronzed body had caused her eyebrows to arch in appreciation. Farnsworth had sent her away, but the memory lingered. Beautiful, wavy-blond hair, open shirt stretched tight by the muscles underneath, clean shaven chin and upper lip, devastating smile. Even at her age, she could have capitulated.

The third man she did not know. The soft sing-song accent, almost inaudible at times, gave him as being Welsh. Or quite possibly one of those foreigners, Farnsworth was forever dealing with. She wished he'd speak up a little. The microphone she and Farnsworth had wired into the overhead lamp above the study table wasn't picking him up too well. She'd begged Farnsworth to have a peephole in the ceiling, but he'd turned her down.

All he wanted was a complete record of the conversations.

They seemed to be having some sort of quarrel—Saul and the Welshman—with Farnsworth adjudicating.

"Now, now, gentlemen," Farnsworth said, "I'm sure we can settle this to everyone's satisfaction. Come now, Donaldson, there must be another way out?"

"You're not listening to me Farnsworth. He made it so plain, the papers on his table jumped clear of it. He wants Slagter. No compromises. No alternatives. Either he has Slagter or he knocks off six of our best in Eastern Europe. Mainly in Poland. He knows them all. Smithy, Vincent….."

"Quite! Quite! You've made your point, Donaldson. Well, if he has to have him, he has to have him."

"That's impossible," Saul said, the voice rising higher, an edge creeping into it. Even a touch of fear. Her hand reached for the volume button.

She couldn't turn it down too low, or she'd never pick up Donaldson.

"And why?" Donaldson asked softly.

"Because, Goddammit, Donaldson, nobody knows who Slagter is! Not even National Intelligence! He's a freelancer. They call him in when they need him. Through an elaborate, foolproof system of communication that leaves him faceless. And he communicates with us in much the same way. I've been tailing him for five years, Donaldson, and I couldn't even get near him. Nowhere close. He covered his tracks the way you wouldn't believe it. Andropov can understand that."

"No, he can't. I tried to tell him. You think I don't know about our friend Slagter? Andropov's argument is very simplistic. If South African National Intelligence uses Slagter to interrogate Russian agents, and then ends up butchering them, they ought to at least know who he is. That's the way Andropov looks at it. And seeing what Slagter did to Vladimir, I can't blame him for feeling the way he does. I have the autopsy reports on Vladimir here. He insisted I take them. Do you want to see them?"

She heard the thud of the briefcase being placed on the table; the click of twin locks.

"No, thank you! No one believes Russian autopsies anyway. Cooked! Through and through." Saul gave a little laugh as if he'd taken care of that little problem.

"He was willing to ship the body to East Berlin and have our people take a look at him there. I told him that wouldn't be necessary. No one could possibly cook up a report like this one. He was cut up with some sort of African machete. There were places where the meat was carved off the bone. Shall I go on?"

The tape would around silently without voices on it. There was a drumming noise, but that was Farnsworth tapping on the table. The drumming stopped as Donaldson continued: "Andropov feels—and quite rightly if you ask me—we have overstepped our bounds this time. Either he has Slagter or we lose six in the Eastern theater. Not just South African either. British and American too. Our American friends aren't going to like that too well. I have to admit, the stance he's taken surprises me. It isn't usual for the KGB to get sentimental over the loss of one of their agents—even under these grotesque circumstances. Maybe they're becoming like us?"

"Cut out the crap, Donaldson, and stick to the point, will you?" Farnsworth said.

She smiled delightedly. He'd done that to her often enough before, cutting her short even in front of his patients with a wave of his hand, the ferret-like eyes closing in on her.

"Perhaps we can work out some sort of compromise. A deal! As our American friends would say. We give them, say, some classified stuff on the Chinese front. Sensitive to them but which we don't particularly care about. We have a lot of that stuff filtering in through our people in Hong Kong. Stuff they'd dearly love to have."

"I tried that, Farnsworth," Donaldson said.

She had to admire the patience in his voice. As soft and low now as it was at the start. She couldn't say that for the other two. A peephole would not have helped. All she'd have seen would be the tops of their heads. Until Donaldson moved to the door as he was leaving the room.

"Well then, Donaldson, damm it, at least we need more time to come up with Slagter. Andropov can understand that. The bloody fool! God! These bloody Russians think all they have to do is call—and we come running. We need more time."

"I talked to him about that. Without committing MI-6 to anything of course. Two weeks. That's what we have."

"Two weeks? That's absurd! Is it possible, Saul?"

"The whole idea is absurd!" Saul's voice, raised in anger, battered her in the ears, and she winced in agony as she raised her hands, instinctively, to the headset. He was fumbling for words. Frothing most likely too.

"And just how do you propose to flush Slagter out in two weeks? I couldn't flush him out in five years. The man's wily and a damn good agent. And the South Africans aren't going to give us any bloody help either. He's one of the best."

"And cruel too. But I think we can land him this time. This time, God, we've just got to get him."

She heard the scrape of the chair and the soft pad of his light footstep. It was very like his voice. Barely heard. Hardly felt. Yet she knew he was there. Inspite of the silence. No sound. No voices. No movement. She heard the slight crackle of the bug as if it had been accidentally touched.

"You will forgive me, Farnsworth," Donaldson said, "if I set you back a few pounds on this one? The light does so hurt my eyes."

She heard the muffled, scrambled sounds as the lamp above the study table was yanked from the socket in the ceiling.

Then the headset went dead.

There wasn't any point in sitting up there any longer. She removed the headset, throwing back her head to straighten the tousled hair that was normally kept in place by her nurse's white cap. She backed into the bedroom, wasting a few moments to straighten her white dress and stockings in front of Farnsworth's dressing table mirror. The double chin was showing a bit. She patted it up without much emotion. At her age, it could be forgiven. It was even expected of her. Not many could avoid it at forty, she told herself.

She pinned the cap back on to her head; then moved silently down the backstairs to the kitchen. Now she was not in a soundproof room, and they were all master agents in there. Every footfall magnified into danger around them.

For a rather stockily-built, thick-set nurse, she made remarkable time, noiselessly, out the back door and round the side of the house to the hedge that bordered the driveway. There was only one car in it. Saul's car. She recognised it. They must have come together. Saul and Donaldson. They must know each other well.

She eased herself into a comfortable position beside the hedge, parting the twigs and leaves silently to get a good view of the front door, through which they would leave. Then she'd have to go back and index the tapes. But that could wait for a while.

Twenty minutes later she heard the front door open. Saul came through. He appeared to be talking to someone inside the door. She waited. Saul took a few steps backwards, and Farnsworth appeared at the door. She couldn't hear them at that distance. Donaldson was behind Farnsworth, no doubt, or perhaps he had hung back to gather up his notes?

Saul and Farnsworth shook hands. Saul turned to leave, stopped, half turned back, changed his mind and strode to the car.

Alone.

She slapped her thigh in anger, as she backed away from the hedge and raced to the rear entrance of the house. She heard the door slam shut as she turned the corner, but the study jutted out and the fireplace blocked her view of the back. She kicked off her shoes, sliding past the wall to the corner that commanded a view of the vegetable garden at the back and the path that led to the wicket gate at the bottom of it.

She was too late.

All she saw was the back of a figure in a long overcoat that vaulted the wicket gate, into the field behind it, and disappeared from view.

Chapter 1

January 11, 1965

The little Indian sat cross-legged on the dry sand, fully dressed even to the green batik tie which the wind had whipped carelessly over one shoulder. He seemed to sit within the hollow of the sand and emerge from it, the one upstanding object in the expanse of golden beach that stretched for a mile in each direction.

She would be late in coming. He was sure of that. The thought brought a faint smile to the light brown face, arching the black eyebrows past the line of the heavy turtle-shell frame that gave him a scholarly look. No dismay. No loss of patience. She had always been late in all of the times they had met this way, on this deserted stretch of beach of the South Coast, twenty miles south of Durban and eighty miles to the north of Margate.

It was a safe enough spot. The road from Durban to Margate took a sharp bend at that point, separating itself from the beach with a shoulder covered over with undergrowth and overgrown with palm trees that hid the beach from the road.

There was only one steep, sandy path that led from the shoulder down to the flat beach, and it, too, was difficult to find overgrown from disuse.

Joshua had pulled the car off the road on to the shoulder. He found it without difficulty because he knew precisely where it was; then he cleared the entrance to the path so that Laura might find it easily too.

Otherwise she would shout to him from the shoulder above—as she had done the last three times—petulantly demanding that he come and get her. He had run up the path to bring her down, clawing at the brush on either side to quicken his progress to the top.

That she came at all made her very special to him.

He had an unreasonable fear that one day she would not come.

But she always did.

She dropped on her knees, onto the sand in front of him, but when he reached forward to kiss her she rocked back out of his reach.

"Is that all you ever think of, Joshua? Just kissing and fondling. I came here to talk to you, and this time you're going to hear me out. I mean it, Joshua!"

"I'm sorry," Joshua said. "Did I offend you? If it makes it easier, I know what you want to say."

"Oh, Joshua! Please don't make it harder than it is. Please. Why can't you get angry, like other men? Or say something stupid and hurtful? God! This is going to be awful. Why do I feel like I was fifteen years old, like a silly schoolgirl, when you look at me through those large glasses of yours?"

She leaned forward and slipped them from his face. Then she put her hands round his head, drawing his face to her, and kissed him on the lips, lingering to kiss him again as they drew away.

"There now. Will you listen to me, Joshua?"

"Have I said a word? Except to say I know what it is you want to say. I can spare you the agony of saying it."

"No," she said. "I'd rather say it myself. Help me choose the right words, Joshua. They're so important."

She stood up to face him. His eyes lingered over her. The ash blonde hair floating with the evening breeze across her beautiful mouth and cheeks. Large lips. The blue in her eyes unmatched even by the blue of the sea. Or so it seemed to him, as they entranced him with their brilliance whether they were angry, or sad, or in love. He would never forget her eyes, now searching his face, wiping away the hurt she knew would come. She brushed her hair back from her eyes, now begging to be understood.

"I came to tell you, Joshua, I can't come to England with you tomorrow. This is all over. I can't ever meet you again, here or anywhere else. There! I've said it. Please don't be hurt."

"I'm not hurt. Perhaps it was too much to ask. It was madness to think you might even consider it. Leave home and friends and country, and come away with me. I was unreasonable—and I see it now. Thanks for setting me straight. May I ask a question?"

She looked around to the water's edge before she nodded. The waves, flecked with the shimmer of the evening sun, pounded the beach with one last thunderous roar before racing up the sands to within a few feet of where he was sitting. Never reaching him. Shouting their discontent in a hiss that saturated the sand at the water's edge.

"Have you been truly happy? While it lasted?"

"Oh, Joshua! How can you doubt that, my darling! It has been so exciting. Meeting you out here. And in that little café in Grey Street. I will sit at that table in the dark corner away from the window, and see your face across it each time. Long after you've gone. How can I tell you, Joshua? It was not all a game. There was fun, and laughter and excitement."

"But no love?"

"I don't know, my love. I truly don't know. But there was trust."

"That is not enough," Joshua said. "For me, that has never been enough. I, sometimes, trust my enemies. Even my servants. Is that all it has been—just fun and laughter and excitement?"

She threw a quick glance up and down the beach. The sands glittered for miles in both directions, catching the sunlight in waves of blinding light that followed the curve of the beach. They could have been the only two people in the entire universe. Certainly they were the only two people on that beach.

And behind them was the steep shoulder of the cliff, overgrown and desolate. Barely twenty feet away. Rising menacingly with an overhang that was hidden by the brush and the undergrowth.

"I have a gift for you," she said.

It surprised him to hear her say that. She had given him gifts before—and some were expensive ones—but this time it was different. He had seen her run down the path, and she had not been carrying a parcel.

Perhaps it was small and hidden on her person. She was wearing a light-green dress, with a slit to her knees. No pockets of any sort. The neckline was the curve of a boat that displayed the slender white neck, but little else. No place one could conceal a small gift. The arms were short, loose sleeves that bared her almost to the armpits.

"Will you take it, Joshua?"

"It will be a pleasure and a joy," he said. "I'm only sorry, I haven't brought anything for you. And now I see how wrong it was of me not to have brought something for you. I knew we would be parting in this way. It was thoughtless of me. Will you forgive me? But I will always treasure what you give me today. More than the woollen cardigan and the silk tie. Or the gold cuff links."

She stood before him and undressed.

She dropped the light-green dress with the boat neckline and the short sleeves, reaching behind her back to unzip it, the tearing sound of the zipper magnified by the sudden silence between waves.

And between them.

The bra opened in front, releasing from captivity the delicate, perfectly formed breasts which swung free. She hesitated for one brief moment before she dropped her panties, stepping clear of them at her feet. Flared hips. Strong thighs. Ash blonde hair. He should have guessed. No woman could hide the colour of her hair. But at eighteen, he hadn't seen any live, naked women. She was his first.

The composure with which he had sat, cross-legged, on the sand deserted him. He was no longer the still, calm person, she thought him to be. The turmoil within him showed as his eyes wandered over her, lingering for precious moments as if to imprint her shape and form and colour and curve and texture in his mind. She seemed to sense it, because she stayed perfectly still, following his eyes over all of her, feeling the searching desire in his gaze on her breasts and hips and thighs.

She took pleasure in his pleasure. With a touch of sadness at the thought that it had taken so little, and she had waited so long.

When he dropped his gaze, as if ashamed of himself, she knelt before him.

"Joshua, my darling, I am eighteen years old. And a virgin. And though my entire body rebels, and against all my own desires and feelings, I am a very moral person. Will you believe it is the only reason I hold back?"

His reply was almost a whisper.

"I can understand," he said, still avoiding looking into her eyes. "You have been kinder to me than I could ever have dared to hope. I will always remember you—this way."

She leaned forward to kiss him. Her hair, swept in light, whipping flutters, now caressed them both, blowing across his face and hers, ruffling their cheeks, then dropping to her shoulders before blowing once more to engulf them both.

He was the passive one. Her lips searched his out and played with them. His hands hung stiffly by his sides.

She leaned back away from him. He did not understand. Her hands reached out to his clenched fingers, unclenching them, stroking each palm until the soft touch of her fingers relaxed the stiffness in them. He thought she would carry his hands to her cheeks, perhaps slide them one by one across her open mouth and kiss them.

She carried both hands to the sides of her breasts.

"Another time and another place, Joshua my love, if it makes you feel any better to know it, you would have been the first."

Above them on the shoulder, hidden within the brush, Saul watched them make gentle love on the sand. At that distance he did not need the pair of binoculars that lay on the grass beside him.

He had deliberately slowed down at the junction, two miles away in the direction of Durban, to give her time to make her way down to the beach. The last time, in his impatience to keep up with her, he had arrived to find her waving to Joshua, demanding he come up and get her. So he had driven straight on for another mile before returning.

This time Joshua had done a better job of clearing the entrance to the path, and she was already on the beach when he parked his car almost directly behind hers. He would be gone before she came up the path. He had no wish to confront her. It had all been innocent enough in the past.

The superbly built, bronzed body lay perfectly still in the undergrowth watching, without alarm, the girl alternately stand and kneel before Joshua. There was no alarm because Joshua was leaving for England, and the whole silly little affair would come to a natural end. Laura would turn to him and the life he had to offer.

Women sometimes found excitement in loving the esoteric. That was what Joshua was to her. An esoteric, rather degrading little interlude. A diversion. Women needed that sometimes.

What it had meant to Joshua, he preferred not to think. It was not his affair.

He would be able to forgive her. And him too. It would not damage his friendship with Joshua. They—he, Joshua and Jomo—had been friends for almost six years now. Ever since boarding school in Britain. He was genuinely fond of the both of them. Their leader too. In matters that required the use of muscle. Like the time they'd thrashed the dorm bully in the eighth form for picking on Joshua. They'd always turn to him for help when they were in trouble. That caused him a great deal of amusement. Gave him pleasure too. In the end they needed him. Like the time they were being interrogated by South African National Intelligence for being suspected members of the African National Congress.

He had laughed out aloud at such an outrageous idea; his old buddy Parker in the Internal Section had been almost offended.

"You're wasting your time, Parker! They may pretend to be important, but those two are bloody harmless, they are. Now go round up Jomo's brother, Boko, in the Ciskei. There you'll have something to get your teeth into. Instead of playing with little minnows in the village pond."

He allowed himself to think about Jomo. She was still talking to him down there on the beach. Superbly built, the black, rippling body had been pure delight. At least he and Jomo had that in common. But Jomo would be waiting for him in Durban. First he had to keep a watch on Laura.

Almost a watch for Laura.

Trust her to do something foolish. Like meeting Joshua down on a deserted beach at this time in the evening. At least she could have waited until it was dark. There was a curio shop a mile up the road towards Durban, and tourists often stopped there. Occasionally they stretched their legs on the beach. Even if they walked only a few hundred yards picking up shells, they could see for miles.

But that was Laura. Impulsive! She would grow out of it; he was sure of that.

He saw her stand up and face him. She looked up and down the deserted beach.

The interview was over.

She had told him what she had come to tell him, and she would now go for a swim in the warm waters of the Indian Ocean.

She had done that to him once before, and it had signalled the end of her visit. Joshua did not swim. He knew how, but perhaps he was ashamed of showing his thin body. He would sit on the sand and guard her clothes while she gamboled in the surf.

Her laughter had caused Joshua to smile. Saul too.

He had touched her clothes once. The last time. An unusually fierce roller broke through, sending a strong wave that surged up the beach. Joshua saw it coming and gathered up her clothes, holding them close to his chest, retreating hastily to higher ground. Laura, seeing it, laughed in merriment; Saul only frowned. It wasn't personal clothing, he told himself. Just the short, printed skirt and matching top that tied in front underneath her breasts, both of which she'd worn over her purple bikini.

He saw her unzip the light-green dress and drop it at Joshua's feet. Like the last time.

She was wearing a white bikini. Must be a new one, he thought.

He'd seen the four she had when they'd frolicked together on the South Beach in Durban or walked on the Marine Parade, and none of them was white.

Could she have been buying it that afternoon, when she'd told him abruptly she had to leave? She hadn't been herself at all. Tense, worried, nervous, snapping at him without plausible reason. In such a state, to calm themselves, some women bought hats. Maybe Laura bought a bikini. He knew that Joshua was leaving the next day, and she would be upset. It was understandable.

He told himself, over and over again, in the years that went by, that there was no way he could have stopped her. By the time he had fumbled for his gun she was already standing naked before Joshua, and when his rage closed his fingers around the trigger, she was kneeling in front of him, and he would have killed them both.

"God!" he moaned to himself. "The bloody bitch! The dirty bitch!"

He put the gun aside and fumbled for the binoculars in the grass. And when he could no longer watch, he put his head into the undergrowth, covering his ears with his hands so he might not hear their laughter that floated to him on the shoulder above.

"One day, Joshua Samuelson," he said, screaming the words out in his mind, "one day, I will kill you for this! And you will die like nobody else has ever died before! Screaming your guts out!"

It seemed, to him, to last forever.

Mercifully she was now hidden from his view, by his hands that clasped her at the sides. But he could see Joshua, now on his knees on the sand, leaning forward towards her. And behind them the waters of the Indian Ocean.

She stood up, still naked, to enter the water, facing Joshua—not him—and for the second time he fumbled for the gun in the grass beside him. But she was not an easy target, as she walked backwards, urging Joshua with one last plea to enter the water with her, and failing that, blowing him a kiss as she turned around and raced into the waves.

He saw Joshua, still sitting cross-legged on the sand, tending her clothes.

He formed a perfect target. Slightly drooping shoulders. Thin body, the narrow waist almost disappearing into the leather belt that kept his trousers up. With such a small waist, he had to have a belt. Fully dressed, even on a deserted beach. If Joshua turned around, he would see his tie. Saul was sure of that. Even at boarding school, Joshua was the only one who always wore his tie, when he didn't have to.

Saul put the gun away. Friendship didn't die that way he reasoned. He had known Joshua long before either of them had known or met Laura—at a birthday party at Saul's house. They were home from boarding school for the vacations. Joshua was invited because his father and Saul's father had been at school together in England. Jomo was not invited. In any case, he could not have come because he spent his vacations with his family in the Ciskei.

That first time, they had both been ill at ease. Gawky sixteen years old. What did they have in common with girls? Saul had cracked some dirty jokes about her to Joshua, which had met with polite disapproval. Joshua had been more impressed with her. At first, Saul had not cared. But the next year, when they were back from school for the vacations, she was one month over seventeen and a woman, and suddenly it had all changed.

They had lived in the same dorm—he, Joshua and Jomo. There were a lot of memories in just living together. He would have to kill them first. Nothing would ever be the same again, but at least friendship had earned Joshua a lease on life. Not a bullet in the back.

That would be too easy a way to kill Joshua. She would then spend her time grieving over him, and that would never do.

Saul worked his way back through the undergrowth to his car. He would not follow either of them. He knew precisely where they were headed. Laura would return to the Marine Parade in Durban, and Joshua would return to his mother's house in the Chatsworth area. He would wait for Joshua there.

He talked constantly to himself on the drive back to Durban, taking all sides, pleading all causes—without assuaging the hurt within him. It was memory that haunted him and images that insisted on dancing in front of him, though all that lay in front was the road, which he did not see, naked images. And if they were before him, must they not dance even more vividly before Joshua? Her wind-whipped hair had hidden her eyes from him, and sometimes her mouth, but nothing else. The rest of her had been fully and frontally exposed to his view.

And Joshua's.

For the second time he screamed in agony. This time aloud. Beating his head against the steering wheel, his screams merging, with the continuous, raking cry of the car's horn which he did not hear; beating his clenched fists into the dashboard; beating himself, while the car lurched from side to side like a drunken animal on the road back to Durban.

Jomo! He needed Jomo. Only Jomo could soothe the hurt within him, as no one else could, not even Laura. Least of all Laura.

He hated her. God! How he hated the both of them for being what they were. And as he drove along the road back to Durban, for the first time since he'd become a man, he wept.

Chapter 2

Saul was wrong.

Joshua did not drive back to the Chatsworth area of Durban. True, he followed Laura for a short distance as they started off, but she drove very fast, as usual, and soon she was only a microdot in the fast fading light. He idled the accelerator, and at the junction about a mile up the road at the corner with the curio shop, he swung right around to drive towards Margate.

He drove long, and fast, without much visible emotion. Yet he was being haunted in much the same way as Saul. He, too, did not see the road but a still life image. And if he closed his eyes, he felt the softness he had held in his palms, and it hurt just as much.

He had lost her for good.

On the right, and to the north, the Drakensberg range, with mountains in colours of grey and blue, threatened him. He would not be crossing them. He would cross them only if he had to, and this time it could be avoided. His road to the south ran along the coast. He saw the sugarcane fields, covering the rounded hills in sharp contours, and the roadside littered with the hibiscus flower, which seemed to grow everywhere without ever being planted.

He avoided Margate. It was a seaside resort, and though it was most popular in June and July with up-country folk trying to escape the inland cold, the season extended all the year round even into the summer months.

It was nearing midnight when he entered the Xhosa tribal lands, first the Transkei and then the Ciskei. The road crossed the Bashee river, flowing with its own idiosyncratic twists and turns down to the Indian Ocean, meeting with the railway line at Idutywa. To his relief, the town had shut down for the night. Only then did he relax, for the first time, when he saw the last homestead disappear in his rear view mirror, settling himself comfortably for the short run to Butterworth and then on to the Great Kei river which demarcated for a considerable part of its inland ramblings the extent of the Ciskei.

The land had changed. Now he was in flat rolling hills dotted with the flowering mimosa tree; the smell of corn and the cortizone plant, the leaves of which Joshua had seen being used to bandage the circumcised initiates to manhood in the abakwetha ceremony. He had never been convinced it did much good to the initiates, but the elders certainly seemed to think so.

He left the main road, turning off towards the village he knew so well.

A feast was in progress. An ox had been slaughtered, being first made to bellow so as to call the ancestral spirits to attend the feast at which it was being sacrificed.

Joshua shuddered at the thought of the last time he had seen such a sacrifice. Never again, he had sworn to himself, would he subject himself to it. But he could not wipe away the memory of the only one he had seen. And at times like these, it was impossible to prevent it from surfacing.

The feast, then, had been to celebrate Jomo's return from abroad. Joshua had been invited and went. Saul was not invited, but he could not have gone anyway, because he was spending his vacations with his family in Durban.

Boko had offered the ox from his herd. He would do the sacrifice himself, he said, to celebrate the joyous return of his younger brother Jomo from foreign lands. But first the animal had to be made to bellow to call the ancestral spirits—or the sacrifice would serve no purpose.

Joshua closed his eyes and tried to wipe out the memory of it. And failed.

The sweat was dripping down Boko's face and neck, then pouring down the front of his bare chest, and still the animal refused to bellow. He threw away the assegai, in disgust, and demanded a sharper one.

How could a man be expected to sacrifice an ox with a blunt assegai?

The ox, with its feet trussed up, lying on its side in a pool of its own blood, would not bellow.

Boko tried everything the medicine man had taught him. All the sharp thrusts into all the weak and sensitive areas of the animal, twisting the instrument for effectiveness.

But no bellow.

Not a cry, not a whisper, not even a snort that would hurriedly have been construed as a bellow. Nothing! Boko tried to look into the large, limpid eyes of the ox, and dropped his gaze. He consulted the medicine man, whose official opinion it was that, for an occasion such as this, the animal to be sacrificed should have been a goat, not an ox. The sacrifice of an ox was reserved for far more important occasions with larger gatherings—such as a wedding, for instance. If Boko merely wanted to celebrate the return of a dear brother from foreign lands, a goat was more appropriate to the occasion.

The ox was released, hobbled out into the fields under its own power, but being unable to eat, died a week later under the broiling sun. Since both its throat and its vocal chords had been cut, it did not make a cry.

Then the goat was brought into the ring.

Joshua felt the small hand slide into his. He could have kissed its fingers for the comfort it gave him. She patted him on the cheek, sprawling herself across his back and whispering in his ear.

"You don't really have to sit and watch, Uncle Josh. I can't bear to watch it either. Come and play house with me. You can be Father this time. I'll be Mother."

They stole away from the back of the circle.

Ewa had chatted, non-stop, to the hut, where her dolls sat in a circle in the far corner, away from the entrance.

"You will have to talk to the children today, Father," she said severely. "They have been very, very naughty! Haven't you children?"

He had plunged into her game with an enthusiasm that surprised and delighted her. He chastised the children with a tone of anger so intense that, finally, Ewa came to their defense, conceding that, perhaps, they had not been that naughty after all.

Joshua parked the car as close to the village as he could, but the ground was soft and he dared not leave the road, or what passed for road, in case his wheels got stuck. There were rut marks that told him heavy vehicles had churned through not too long ago.

A fire had been lit in the open space between the huts of the kraal. The villagers wrapped in their red blankets sat around in an irregular circle, passing the gallon can of brewn beer and the long stem pipes, while the children, those who were awake, picked at the roasted meat.

His eyes searched the gathering for Boko and Jomo. He would have to look hard. Jomo, wrapped in a red blanket, with a doek on his head and beads on his chest, would look a little different than the Welsh schoolboy with suit and cap and tie.

They ignored him. The feasting had begun in the early afternoon and was in progress for several hours. No one cared that a stranger passed by them. Besides he wasn't a stranger. Some would have recognised him. He had sat with them on other occasions, that did not involve a sacrifice, drinking beer from the gallon can, wiping the mouth clean before passing it on to Jomo. The beer went down real smooth. He enjoyed it. He refused the pipe; it made him sick.

He worked his way past the line of huts close to the fire, towards Jomo's tribal hut.

The round hut, plastered with mud, showed some of the tree branches intertwined between the vertical posts forming the framework of the hut, the rafters in the conical roof projecting through the thatching at the top.

Ewa sat in the far corner, her legs beneath her, a short skirt round her waist. Joshua sat on the ground and lifted the weeping child into his lap. She put her arms around him and sobbed.

"Where's Jomo? And Boko? Have they left already? Why did they call me here, if they weren't going to be around? What are you doing here alone?"

She held him so tight, he could hear the thumping of her heart on his chest. "There, there, Ewa," he said, patting her bare back, rubbing her shoulder blades and spine, rocking her gently, kissing the curly hair, until slowly she released him from her grip.

"I'm so glad you're here, Uncle Josh! Oh! I thought you'd never come. Never!"

"Is that what Jomo told you? That I would come?"

"Yes."

"And? What else did Jomo tell you?"

"Don't you know? That you'd take me away of course."

"I would? Where would I take you away?"

She looked at him in surprise, pushing herself away from him to look at him. "To your house in Durban of course. Where else?" She laughed and dug her head into his ribs. He closed his arms around her.

"Is that what they said? That I would take you to my house in Durban? Are you quite sure, Ewa? We can be in awful trouble otherwise."

"I'm sure. Quite sure! Jomo told me to be sure I told you. He said, and I repeat……"

"Never mind, never mind, Ewa. I quite understand. Well, if we must, we must. But we'll have to be quick about it. It's a long way to Durban."

"I'm packed."

"Packed? Where?"

She pointed to the red blanket on the ground in which she'd tied her cherished things. Mainly Enid Blyton books. Girls' stories set in English boarding schools. No clothes of any sort.

"Don't you have anything to wear?"

"I have a skirt on. And I'm only eleven. And if I'm not married, my breasts are bare. Not that I have much there," she said, examining herself by the light of the lamp that circled them both.

Shrouded by the darkness outside.

"Thank heavens for that! I'm going to be in one hell of a pickle if they catch you with me in Durban."

Her laughter was infectious. Even Joshua smiled.

"It's all very well for you to laugh, Ewa, but I do wish Jomo and Boko had taken you with them when they left. When did they leave?"

"This morning. They had to leave in a hurry. Didn't I tell you? We had people from East London here today. Later in the morning. They searched the place thoroughly. Especially the hut. And they asked me a lot of questions. Stupid questions about where Jomo and Boko had gone. As if I'd know? I kept telling them they'd never leave me and go. And I wasn't going anywhere. They wanted me to go with them, but I kicked up such a fuss they thought the better of it. But they took my clothes away. So I couldn't leave in a hurry, I suppose."

"Did they find anything in the hut?"

"No. Boko took all of it away."

"What did Boko take away?"

Ewa was silent. Her black eyes searched his face as if in doubt.

"He told me not to tell you," she said. "But I will, Uncle Josh. Papers and maps. Papers mainly. Oh, Uncle Josh! I do wish I was back at school in England. The girls there must be so wanting me back. I'm their star hockey forward. Can't we go now? Please!"

"How would you like to wear a vest?" he said, taking off his shirt and stripping off his vest. "The latest in women's wear on Bond Street. King's Road in Chelsea style. Imported from an Indian village in the Punjab!"

She giggled with girlish impunity at the vest that, surprisingly, fitted her very well. He wasn't a big man, and she was not too small a girl.

Then she took him by the hand, knowing the land better than he did, working their way out unseen, from behind the huts of the kraal to the parked car.

The house was in total darkness when they reached it. Ewa slept for most of the journey, which was fortunate for him because her drooping head was below the level of the windshield. If there were any roadblocks they weren't being manned at that time of night. At Idutywa he thought he saw a sleepy man rush out of the Police Station and try to wave him down, but he was late in signalling and Joshua drove on as if he'd missed it.

Durban was deserted at that time in the morning; nevertheless his face relaxed and the tension eased as he entered the Chatsworth area of Durban. Now he was on more familiar ground. Or so he thought.

The house was set in the hillside, above the level of the road, with stone terraces leading up to the front porch. The striped awnings above the windows had been unrolled to ward off the summer heat. His mother had insisted on that before she'd left for England. The house was almost shut up. Joshua was to follow; the real estate agents would move in the day after.

There was no light on the front porch. At night, this spoke of the house being unoccupied.

He should have remembered to leave the porch light on.

On second thoughts, he had left the porch light on!

It told him, he had a visitor.

Or perhaps the bulb had burnt out. He must remember to replace it.

He gathered Ewa in his arms and mounted the steps that led to the front door. She stirred in her sleep, passing her hand into his shirt to feel ribs at the side of his chest. It seemed to comfort her, the touch of his body, because she went limp again. She was heavy. He had not realised that girls of eleven could weigh so much. Ewa had always looked slender to him. Classical features with large lips and curly hair, the broad nose setting off the beautifully alive black eyes that laughed so much, and sometimes could never stop giggling.

As when she'd worn his vest.

The room, taking its cue from the house, was in darkness. Joshua did not reach for the light switch inside the door. Instead he crossed over to where he was sure the sofa was positioned, feeling it with his legs, before depositing Ewa into it. She turned over into its depths.

"You may put on the table lamp," the cultured African voice said from the armchair across the room. It was a friendly suggestion. "I have taken the liberty of drawing the curtains. Very careless of you, Joshua, to have left them open."

"And very careless of you to have switched off the porch light," Joshua said.

"Did I? Yes, that was thoughtless of me. I thought you might need the darkness while carrying Ewa up the steps. Not that any of your neighbours are awake at this time in the morning. Or that they particularly care if they see you carrying her in. But I couldn't be sure."

Joshua switched on the table lamp; then he walked across and shook hands warmly with Jomo. Jomo and Ewa had a lot in common, Joshua thought, looking at the powerfully built African fitting with remarkable grace in the oversized armchair. Joshua saw the massive shoulders, with the arms folded across the chest, straighten up in relief as he heard Ewa mumble in her sleep. A load seemed to roll off them. It had been hard, at least for him, to leave her behind, and the handsome face broke into a warm smile of appreciation; the lips parted to display snow white teeth within the ridged lips.

He had a scar down each cheek, that spoke of some tribal custom, but the scars seemed to accentuate the cheekbones, not disfigure the face.

The room was as he had left it. The furniture draped with cloth in anticipation of his departure, looking like somber, seated figures in the shaded light. Indian paintings, some highly erotic with naked Indian goddesses flaunting themselves for the viewer's delight, looked down on a grand piano, which too was draped and muted. The nine-armed Menorah on the mantelpiece gave the only indication it was a Jewish home.

"How did you get in?" Joshua asked. "I'm almost sure I locked up before I left."

"That would be telling. Never mind how I got in. If you must know, the front door was open. So much for the security of your house. May I thank you, Joshua, for bringing Ewa here?"

"And that's another thing. Is that why you called me to the Ciskei? I thought I was invited to a feast in your honour? I am happy to have helped, but you could at least have told me. I feel used."

"I'm sorry, Joshua, I really am," Jomo said, the face reflecting genuine contrition, the long, black, bony hands stretched out towards him. "We did not know until early morning they were coming for us, and we had to move in a hurry. I tried to call you from East London late in the afternoon, but by then you had left from here. Where were you?"

Joshua made no reply.

"Come on, Joshua! You know me well enough to know I wouldn't have deliberately misled you."

"Except at Saul's bidding."

"Yes. But it was not at his bidding."

"And where is Boko?"

"That, too, would be telling."

Joshua's eyes flickered around the room. Carelessly.

"I can tell you he is not here. Not in this house. Does that make you feel better? I will also tell you he is in Durban. Not too far away from here. Why don't you like Boko? He is my flesh and blood brother. You love Ewa and me; why can't you just like him?"

"He isn't like you Jomo. Much less like Ewa. You are, both, peaceful, gentle people. The gentlest I have ever known! But he? He is violent and often deliberately cruel."

"It is for a cause. A just cause."

"No cause can be that just."

"He would say you have no courage. And no stomach for it. I am only saying what he would say, you understand."

"I understand, and I feel sorry for you. And for Boko. How long will you live this way? Hunted like wild game. And what about Ewa? Doesn't she matter anymore?"

"Of course, she does. That is why we sent you for her. We could not possibly leave without her, could we?"

"Leave? South Africa?"

"Yes. Didn't I tell you? Boko and Ewa and I are leaving on the STAR OF DURBAN later this afternoon for England, from Pier Seven. Come and see us off."

"You must be dreaming," Joshua said, sinking into the sofa. Ewa stretched out promptly and put her feet in his lap. He rubbed the thin legs in endearment. "Do you know, you need passports to leave the country? Or were you just planning to sort of go up to the purser of the STAR OF DURBAN and say: 'My brother Boko and I are members of the African National Congress. This country's getting too hot for us, so we thought we'd skip on your ship.'"

They both laughed. Ewa showed her annoyance at being disturbed by snuggling deeper into the dream-filled, fractured, button-tufted feel of the sofa, turning around and digging her knees into Joshua's chest.

"If I were to say that," Jomo said, "I would not fail to mention, we were leaving behind one of our Indian brethren, who was planning to flee the country on the EMPRESS OF BRITAIN."

"Hey! Hey! That's not true. Not at all. I'm not running away from anything. I'm going to study medicine in England. That could hardly be termed as 'fleeing the country' now, could it?"

"Please yourself, Joshua. You could have gone to school here—and you didn't. You could study medicine her—and you aren't. A certain pattern wouldn't you say?"

Joshua straightened Ewa's legs across his lap.

"We're talking about you; not me. You can't get out of this country without passports. I have mine. You aren't likely to get any."

"True. Very true. But they're there. Lying on the piano beneath the gaze of your nude goddess, who never fails to amaze me with her pose each time I look at her. Tell me, do I worship her with lust?"

"She will accept your worship any way you wish, Jomo," Joshua said, gently setting Ewa aside and rising from the sofa.

There were three passports on the piano. Genuine enough, it seemed to him. In the names of Boko Mbangeli, Jomo Mbangeli and Ewa Mbangeli, presently residents of the Ciskei, complete with photographs, officially signed and sealed with the stamp of the South African Government, and issued by their central passport office in Pretoria.

"Rather nice photographs, wouldn't you say, Joshua?"

"I think I'll go to bed," Joshua said wearily.

He felt drained, even confused by the events of the day. The long drive to the Ciskei and back, all in one night, hadn't helped. He would think about it in the morning. After a good night's sleep, answers to himself would be more forthcoming. So he thought.

Jomo bounded out of the armchair with the trained agility of the hunter in the field. Or the hunted in the bush. For the first time that morning—and the glow had begun to appear in the East—Joshua saw signs of agitation in Jomo. The superbly built, African body trembled as it blocked the way to the stairs leading up to the bedroom.

"There is something I have to tell you, Joshua. Something important."

"Can't it wait until later? I feel dead all over."

"No. It can't wait. We have taken the liberty of appropriating your bedroom upstairs. There are no beds in any of the other rooms. I checked. But this sofa does open into a bed, doesn't it? Perhaps you and Ewa can share it for the remainder of the morning?"

"We? Who is we?"

"My friend and I. We may not see each other for a long time, and we could not let this night pass without spending it together."

"Do I know her?"

"Yes. You know him. Poor Joshua! Does that shock you?"

"No. Is it a debt you are repaying? For the passports?"

"No! No! How can you say such a thing? There is a genuine, loving feeling. Which you wouldn't understand. You have never really understood."

Joshua tried to manage a smile and failed. He would grow a moustache and a little beard in England, he decided. Maybe it would make him feel older. He felt so young before all of them—Laura and Saul, Jomo and Boko. Not much older than Ewa.

"Thank you for telling me," Joshua said. "It must have been difficult for you. Please feel free to use my bedroom upstairs."

He heard Jomo climb slowly up the stairs, and heard the bedroom door as it shut behind him. His ears did not strain for the soft murmur of greeting that reached him down the stairs before the door closed on Jomo.

He lifted Ewa off the sofa and propped her in the armchair Jomo had vacated. She stretched herself, with her hands in his face and yawned luxuriously, watching him convert the sofa into a bed.

"Come on, little one," he said. "This bed's now big enough for the both of us."

On that day, January 11, 1965, some six thousand miles away, at six in the evening, the eleventh Earl of Bromfield sat down with his granddaughter, Lady Julia Rayburn-Spencer, for dinner, in the formal dining room of the Elizabethian mansion that was his estate in Bromfield, some twenty miles to the north of London.

His daughter, the child's mother, had died six years before, and he had grown very close to the eleven-year-old clear-complexioned, little girl with long brown hair and deep brown eyes sitting beside him at a table designed to serve forty. Her governess hovered behind her. The butler stood, respectfully, behind him.

And the lady Julia, firmly, but without raising her voice, refused to eat her pudding.

"It's tasteless, Grandfather," she said, pushing away the bowl and wiping her mouth with her napkin. "You try it. Let Emma try it. And Tomkins too."

"What? I try it? And ruin the taste of my brandy? Nonsense, child! It's perfectly edible, I'm sure. Now do finish it off, Julia, and let's get away from this table. Come, there's a good girl."

"Wouldn't you like me to be honest, Grandfather?"

"Yes, of course."

"Always?"

"Goes without saying. We Bromfields have the word 'honest' in our motto: For truth and honest judgment before God and Man."

"Well then, the pudding's tasteless. It tastes like sawdust. I know. I fell into a pile of sawdust once, and it tasted just like the pudding."

The eleventh Earl had a spoonful and choked on it.

"Tomkins! Take away this rubbish. I wouldn't even feed it to the horses. And Emma you'd better have a word with the cook. That is if she wants to continue with this family—as her mother and grandmother before her. By gad! You're so very right."

The eleventh Earl patted his granddaughter appreciatively on the head, smoothing back the brown hair that had settled on the forehead.

"Bring me the brandy in the study, Tomkins. And a glass of milk for Lady Julia as well."

"Would you like me to read you some of my stories, Grandfather? Julia asked. "In the continuing adventures of Bimbo the Clown?"

"That would be nice, Julia," the eleventh Earl said, pushing back his chair, while Julia neatly slid out of hers. "I enjoy your stories. I showed some of them to the Editor of the Times, and he said you had a very lively imagination. Gave him goose-pimples, you did sometimes, he said, with the way you said things. Where has the circus reached now?"

"India. And Bimbo isn't getting any laughs from the children."

"No bloody sense of humor, these bloody wogs!" the old Earl growled with a twinkle in his eye.

"But it'll soon change. When he does what he has to do."

"Oh? And what is that?"

Julia dropped her voice conspiratorially.

"He's going to paint himself. Right there, before them. That'll start them giggling. And once they start they'll never be able to stop. Children can never stop giggling once they start."

"Don't I know that," the eleventh Earl said, rolling his eyes to the high vaulted ceiling of the massive dining room. "It all sounds frightfully interesting!"

The eleventh Earl and his granddaughter, holding hands, passed through the solid oak door from the dining room into the corridor that led to the study.

The eleventh Earl sipped his favourite brandy, swirling it in the crystal glass with the long stem, savouring the aroma with every sip. He was a man at peace with himself. Julia drained her glass of milk, wiped her mouth with the back of her hand, felt the wetness on it, looked around for a napkin and couldn't see one, glanced at her grandfather who looked away hastily, and wiped the back of her hand on the side of her dress.

Then Julia cleared her throat, to draw her grandfather's attention, opened her notebook on page one and started to read.

Chapter 3

July 16, 1980

William Farnsworth watched the girl come up the driveway. She parked the car at the edge of the gravel path, almost on the closely cut grass, thirty yards from the house. Then she walked.

He moved the curtains of the bedroom window to see her more clearly. So young. So very pretty.

But could she kill when the time came?

The brown hair glinted in the sunlight. It was thrown back at the forehead; cut short at the shoulders. Not much else he could see at that distance.

Fifty feet from the house, she stopped, deliberating, indecisive, whether to proceed. She opened her handbag and had a quick look; then she snapped it shut, slung it back on to her arm and strode briskly towards the house.

He could see her clearly now, no more than thirty feet away. Fine figure. Full too. And the height to go with it.

The clinging dress hugged her body, setting it out strongly. It was pulled in sharply at the waist, mushrooming pleasantly above and below, without being outrageous. Strong thighs. Farnsworth sighed.

She stopped again before the front door. Did not ring the bell. Not immediately. She adjusted the belt around her waist, tightening it a notch, slid her hand into her blouse that opened in front, straightening the shoulder strap, easing the cut of it into her back and sides. Now he could see her quite clearly. Clear complexion, a touch of makeup visible only to the discerning eye, except for the glow on large red lips, half open when in doubt. As now. Brown eyes that reached with sensitivity for the doorbell. Before her long, slender fingers, with the red fingernails cut short, actually touched it. Farnsworth allowed the curtains to fall into place as he hurried downstairs. He motioned her to silence, with his fingers to his lips, as he opened the door to her. "The old battle axe hasn't left yet," he said. "She will fuss so. I've told her you're the daughter of an old army friend of mine, so act the part will you? When she's around."

"Do I call you Uncle Bill?" she asked with a straight face that could barely hide the amusement in her eyes.

He saw the large lips, glowing with wetness, tremble in the softly formed face and mouth. She had taste and it showed.

"Over my dead body, Julia!" Farnsworth said. "He was a very, very old army friend. One generation too old."

He touched her bare arm, and she felt his fingers slide up to her shoulder.

"I thought I heard the doorbell, Dr Farnsworth," Nurse Timmons said, coming in from the surgery. The short, thick-set woman smiled in a friendly sort of way with just that touch of middle age distrust. Of the youthful. "So you must be Julia."

"Yes. Uncle Bill heard I was in London and invited me down for the morning. He does look well, doesn't he? You must take very good care of him."

Nurse Timmons glowed, "I try, Julia, I try! He won't always let me. Take his clothes. Isn't it warm? We've been having a real Indian summer. Makes all your clothing cling to the body. So I told him to go in for some of these newer fabrics. Newer styles too. Look young. But does he ever listen to me? Wears a three-piece in this weather."

Farnsworth passed a hand over the bald part of his head. The portly frame quivered, trembling with the impatience that showed in the half-closed eyes. What bothered him more, he realised, was not Jane Timmons's overbearing concern for him, which he had learnt to ignore, but Julia's obvious enjoyment of it.

"Jane you are a nurse. Not my housekeeper or my nursemaid. I pay you to be a nurse. You've locked up the surgery for the morning. May I suggest, you now go home."

"Don't mind him, dear," Nurse Timmons said. "He isn't always such a bear. He can be quite nice really. If it wasn't for me, he'd go hungry all day. Would you like some tea?"

"No, thank you," Julia said. "I'm just fine. Really I am. It will be almost lunch time soon. Thanks awfully though."

They watched her, in the white uniform with starched cap and black stockings, go down the driveway. Farnsworth closed the door. Julia did not see her turn the corner, as she doubled back to the rear kitchen door. They did not see her let herself in, holding the lock back so that it wouldn't click; then climb the stairs softly to the closet behind the master bedroom, above the study.

"Come into the study," Farnsworth said, showing her in. "Be comfortable. Kick off your shoes. It's going to take some time."

Julia slipped off her shoes. She wasn't wearing hose. It was too warm for that. She had painted her toenails, like some of the Indian and Pakistani women she'd seen, in their colourful saris, walking down Fitzjohn's Avenue past her London flat in Hampstead. Only the feet showed from beneath the sari. In the summer they wore open sandals, and the toenails had always been painted. She'd rather liked it. The eleventh Earl was a trifle dismayed when she showed up with them the first time. Not quite knowing whether to be pleased or upset by them. And that too at a formal reception he'd thrown in Bromfield for the Lord Mayor of London. But they had looked appealing—I never thought feet could look appealing he confessed to her later—so he let the matter pass. She was his hostess for formal receptions in Bromfield, and she could do no wrong. Since then many of the younger women in Bromfield had taken to painting their toenails. Major Ormsby had distinctly mentioned that Mrs Ormsby was going to follow suit.

Julia suppressed a smile as she recalled it.

"Did I say something to amuse you, my dear?" Farnsworth asked, with a touch of annoyance Julia shook her head.

"I was looking at my toenails," she said.

Farnsworth threw up his hands. He'd never understand women. "Would you like some sherry?" Now that he understood.

"Sherry will be fine," Julia said.

Farnsworth settled himself in the round-armed, leather-backed chair opposite to her, drawing her up to the table, beneath the overhead lamp that was socketed into the ceiling. Donaldson had made an awful mess of it. Repairing the ceiling had been a horrid expense. Donaldson had brought chunks of plaster down with the wiring. He balanced his sherry on the rounded arm of the chair. She held hers close to her waist in her lap.

"Nice house you have, Dr Farnsworth," she said.

"Thank you. I'll show it you some day. It was specially designed for Military Intelligence. During the war, in the early forties, London wasn't a very safe place then. It's a little out of date now, so they let small fry like me have it."

"How do you keep her from knowing?"

"Jane? That's easy," he said, leaning towards the table and lifting his head slightly as if looking towards the lamp. She saw him smile and didn't understand why.

"She isn't very bright really," he said, a little louder than was necessary. "She's a good nurse and takes her duties seriously, but otherwise she's thick in the head. Stupid! You know what I mean? But let's not talk about her. She thinks I'm only a doctor—which I am to my patients. It's good to have a profession. It takes the tension away from being what we are—small fry in a large organisation."

"I'm small, but I've heard it said you're quite high up really."

"You mustn't believe everything you hear," Farnsworth said drily, wiping the sherry off his military moustache.

He opened the file on his lap.

"May I start by saying I'm sorry I've ruined your vacation. I really am. But it had to be you."

"I'm flattered. Of all the agents MI-6 has, it has to be me. And just when I was getting a nice tan on the French Riviera. Do you know how difficult it is for me to acquire any sort of tan? Any sort at all?"

"I'm sorry, my dear. I really am. You have a clear, healthy, beautiful complexion—if I may be permitted to say so. I can't really understand all this fuss about getting a tan. Maybe I'm getting old? I'm sorry, Julia, to have dragged you back from Nice. How was it? Your vacation, I mean?"

"What little of it I had, you mean. Heavenly! Just lying on the sand, doing absolutely nothing. Not even thinking. After a year of this sort of thing, I thought I'd earned it. Quite obviously, I was wrong."

"You've earned it and more, my dear. And I promise you, when all this is over—in about two weeks—I'll have MI-6 pay to fly you back to Nice. I promise. Does that seem fair? I'll send off the requisition today. For an open-dated ticket."

She nodded.

Farnsworth continued. Without looking at her.

"You knew Saul Prentiss, didn't you?"

"Yes. A little."

"He's dead."

Julia drained the sherry, placing the glass on the table beside her, grateful for the touch of warm oak.

"He was in Nice last week," she said. "I saw him on the public beach. Casual like. Then he disappeared."

"He didn't tell you anything, did he?"

"Like what?"

"Like anything of importance. Like why he would be murdered three days later."

"No."

"Well, he's dead. For sure."

"Is that why you brought me down here? To break the news to me gently? All right. So I knew him. As a friend. Perhaps a little more. Nothing serious. I'm very sorry he's dead. I'd be upset if anyone I knew had died."

"Aren't you going to ask me how he died? Or who killed him?"

"Aren't you going to tell me?"

Farnsworth leaned his bald head against the top of the chair, lifting his sherry to gaze into it, not very happy with it. "We don't know," he said, finally. "There's a lot we don't know."

"Who's we? Or may I not ask?"

"Well, it really is more a matter for Scotland Yard. We don't know where he was killed, but his burnt out body was found in an abandoned building in Clapham. There was an almighty explosion and fire that brought the building down. The fire department people thought it might be a broken gas main, until they found the charred body in the rubble. So they called in the police. Identification wasn't easy, I can tell you, but the dental charts identified the body as being Saul's. That brought us in automatically. They couldn't very well proceed without us, now could they?"

"Any doubts? About it being Saul?"

"I'm afraid not."

Julia uncrossed her thighs; looked down at her feet. There were some things Farnsworth could not possibly know. He was only playing with her. Either that or he was fishing. And either way she didn't like it. It felt uncomfortable.

"I'm going to take you into my confidence, Julia," Farnsworth said, speaking so low she had to strain to hear him. "Did you know he was a double agent?"

Julia's eyes opened wide. Farnsworth noted they were even prettier when they were surprised.

"I have to tell you. You need to know all the facts or you aren't going to be able to do much. It's all in these files." Farnsworth tapped the file on his lap; pointed to two more on the study table. "More sherry?"

"No thanks. One will be quite enough. I'm driving back to London this morning. I had no idea that Saul was a double agent!"

"You haven't been with us long, Julia. A year? You would have found out in time. As others did. Don't let that worry you. We'd known for a long time he worked for South African National Intelligence. They recruited him long before we did—when he was only eighteen. He infiltrated the banned African National Congress, only to find that some of the most radical members were his close school friends! It has to be said to his credit that loyalty to his friends won out, and he finagled them out of the country. That was way back in 1965. But it didn't go down too well with the authorities, so they transferred him from the Internal Section to the Foreign Section and shipped him out of the country. Stationed him in London. Which suited him nicely, because one of the black nationalists was also his lover."

Julia raised her eyes, saw Farnsworth awaiting her reaction, and folded her hands in her lap.

"It's all here in the files. You can go through them presently. But that's when we recruited him. When he came to London. And generally speaking, we didn't mind. South Africa is a friendly country. It's not as if he was working for the KGB."

"Perhaps they killed him. The South Africans I mean. When they found out he worked for us?"

"No, my dear. That won't wash. They knew that already. In an unofficial sort of way, he was a form of liaison between them and us. For unofficial transfer of information. Things we wanted them to know without having to tell them. Things they wanted us to know without going public with it. That sort of thing. Oh, no! That couldn't have been it."

Julia was silent.

"To be perfectly frank, Julia, we're much more interested in why he died than who killed him. Or how. Agents die in the field sometimes. Sometimes they disappear. I don't mean to sound callous, but these are the hazards of our profession. We live by the excitement it brings into our lives—and then sometimes, we pay for it. But why? At least we owe him that much. To find out why?"

"Wouldn't hurt us either. To know why?"

"Precisely. You do understand." Farnsworth reached for a cigar from his outside pocket. Unwrapped it. Reached for a light. And stopped. "Do you mind if I smoke?"

Julia assented silently.

"Another sherry?"

Julia declined.

"Will you permit me to have another? The old battle axe thinks I drink and smoke too much." Farnsworth lit his cigar. He reached for the sherry bottle on the table and refilled his glass, going through the ritual of inhaling the aroma before sipping it with deep satisfaction. He blew a puff of smoke in her direction. "Saul Prentiss was South African by birth. But very British. Educated in one of the finest public schools that side of the Welsh border. We suspected he might have connections with MOSSAD, but that was never proved. At least not to my satisfaction. Six days ago he comes back from Nice, where to all accounts he is having a nice time. We don't know why he came back. We thought you might be able to tell us."

Julia opened her arms, throwing back her shoulders in a gesture of dismay.

"Quite obviously, you can't," Farnsworth said, without looking up from the file on his lap. "We think he went to Paris, and from there, instead of going back to Nice, he comes to London. Why? Then we lose him for about three days until his burnt out body—burnt beyond all recognition—turns up in a house in a rather seedy area of Clapham." Farnsworth blew another ring of smoke, riveting his eyes on her face, trying, and failing, to penetrate the mask of innocence that had descended on it.

"It seemed a simple enough matter," Farnsworth continued. "One of our agents attached to the South African desk of MI-6 gets himself murdered. A private killing? Another woman? We could live with that. But if it is our business, we want to know. If it isn't we don't probe any further. Let the London police handle it. Then it doesn't concern us."

"Standard Service Regulations."

"Precisely."

"Yet you must think very strongly it is our business—or I wouldn't be here."

"You're very perceptive, my dear. Saul sent a message before he died. Here's the point that bothers me, Julia. He didn't send it to us and he didn't send it through us. He sent it to his opposite number in South Africa, coded, new code too. They change it every month. They changed it seven days ago, so he must have been passed the new code by South African agents operating out of Marseilles.

He didn't pass the code on to us—as he should have. He didn't send the message through our regular operating channels—as he should have. Instead he uses a post office in Hampstead, on Finchley Road. That's very close to your London flat, isn't it?"

No answer.

"We intercepted the message, and I've spent four feverish days bringing in our South African agents, trying to break the code."

"Well?"

"Well, we struck lucky. Our man in Paris was having it off, shall we say, with a lady of doubtful reputation and a varied list of clients. Politicians, generals, agents too. Some of the names on that list would make your pretty eyes open wide. I won't go into all the sordid details, my dear, but she had the code for him in twenty-four hours. He flew in yesterday, and we spent the better part of last night deciphering it. He sat in that very chair you're sitting in." Farnsworth reached into the file and handed her the message. She noted, with quick disappointment, that the code used to decipher it was not on it. It read:

ASSEGAI MAKE SAMUELSON TALK AT ONCE EXCLAMATION. HE IS THE ONLY ONE WHO WILL KNOW EXCLAMATION. ASSEGAI MESSAGE ENDS.

"I don't understand," she said. "Assegai?"

"It would have surprised me considerably if you had," Farnsworth said, puffing at his cigar. "The word ASSEGAI used before and after the message is our form of RED ALERT! The words change every month, so we couldn't know at first. The code itself wasn't too difficult. But we had to know the importance of the message to them—and it is a RED ALERT! Had one of our agents in Eastern Europe, say, sent us such a message, the cabinet would have been in an emergency session. The P.M. would gave been on the line to the President. Especially if the agent sending the message then gets himself murdered. Pretoria must sleep uneasy tonight."

Farnsworth got off the chair and walked behind her, standing close with his hands on the headrest, his fingers barely touching her brown hair.

"That makes it very intriguing, Julia. So very intriguing. Because there is nothing in the message to mark it out as a RED ALERT. That is used by them, and us, only when national security is threatened in some way. Say the assassination of a prime minister. Or invasion by a foreign power. That sort of thing. Top priority! With such a message?" His voice tailed off.

"Who's Samuelson?"

"Ah! Now that does surprise me. Very much."

"It does? That I don't know who Samuelson is?"

He could not see the deep brown eyes reach back into themselves, withdrawn and intense. Standing, as he was, behind her. "The only Samuelson I know is Dr Joshua Samuelson who shares a practice with Dr Clayborne on Finchley Road."

"Precisely."

"It can't be. What would he know about all this? On second thoughts, he did know Saul didn't he? And he is from South Africa, isn't he?"

"You're right on both counts. Tell me, he's your doctor, isn't he?"

"Not really. I go to Dr Clayborne. Who started it first. Dr Samuelson joined him later. I've absolutely nothing against Indian doctors, you understand. Heaven help us, the National Health Service would go under if it wasn't for them! But I'd been a patient of Dr Clayborne long before Dr Samuelson joined him—since I was eighteen—and I saw no reason to change."

"Of course."

"What do we know about him? My—our—Dr Samuelson, that is."

"Quite a bit actually. Research did a good job on him. And on the others too. It's all here in the files for you to read. But what do you know about him?"

"Very little, I'm afraid. I've met him a few times in the surgery. While waiting for Dr Clayborne to be available. Mild-mannered, polite, gentle sort of chap. Not too tall, slim build. Sports a moustache and a goatee beard that makes him look a little older than he is. Wears glasses. The sort of fellow you could easily lose in a crowd."

"Is that all?"

"Let me see. What else do I know about him? He's a bachelor. Never married, I've heard. Has a certain reputation with women—purely hearsay that! Mid-thirties. Not much to go on, I'm afraid."

"On the contrary," Farnsworth said, "You've told me quite a lot. Most importantly—that you know him."

"What does all this have to do with him? He's a doctor who shares a practice in Hampstead. There are hundreds of Indian doctors in the country. What could he know?"

"That, Julia, is precisely what you're going to find out. What is it that Samuelson knows that is of sufficient interest to South African National Intelligence that he must be made to talk? Important for Saul to send a coded RED ALERT message to Pretoria? Without telling us too. And then getting himself murdered? Not very nice, would you say?"

Julia did not reply.

"So now you see, my dear, why we had to have you and no one else. You knew Saul. A little. You know Dr Samuelson. A little. Sufficiently well enough for you to establish contact. With a new agent, we'd have to plant him in a suitable way, and that can take an awful long time. You're ideal for us to use."

"Thank you."

"I didn't mean it that way, Julia. In some ways we are all being used. I like to think we're doing something useful."

"Like getting information from him."

"Like keeping him alive! If what he knows is of interest to South Africa, it must be of interest to others as well, like ANC agents here in London. This country has always been a hotbed of radical politics—that don't concern us. It's the price we pay for being the most liberal democracy in the world. We've always tolerated radicals. Marx and Trotsky. Even Freud. The Bangladesh liberation movement started here in a pub down in Belsize Park. Look what they did? Started a war between India and Pakistan for their freedom. Got it too. The leaders of half a dozen African States were educated at the London School of Economics. God help us. We must take some credit for the mess they're in."

"So I have to play nurse-maid to an Indian doctor?"

"Only until we find out what we want to know. What it is he knows? And why Saul was killed for it?"

"And then?"

"Then let him take care of himself. It has nothing to do with us. South African National Intelligence and the bloody African National Congress can do what they bloody well want with him."

"Drop him? That way?"

"Well, give him a tip to get out of the country. Fast! If that makes you feel better, by all means. That's fine with us, but not until you've found out why Saul died."

"I don't suppose I could turn down the assignment, could I?"

Farnsworth tried very hard not to smile. When he was on the point of failure, and he knew he wouldn't be able to help it, he turned away from her, hoping she hadn't noticed. He did not chastise himself for being unable to keep a straight face when he needed to. He told himself he was an agent—not an actor.

"I suppose you could, Julia," he said. "I could cover up for you. The South Africans will use Slagter to interrogate Samuelson. They can't afford to fail on this one, so they'll use the best. And he is the best. In the light of that, I could suggest to London you weren't the most suitable person for this assignment. We might take a day or two to find someone to replace you, but we'd do it. Use another Indian, perhaps. Would you like me to do that?"

He saw Julia stiffen. Her body quivered. The brown eyes became angry. He had expected it. She looked even more beautiful than before, when she was angry. The heaving breasts and the clenched fists pressing hard into her thighs said so much for the hurt within her. Surfacing only through the eyes. The voice was still as soft as ever, and controlled, as she said:

"I'll be very happy to help in any way I can, Dr Farnsworth."

"I'm having second thoughts about it, Julia," Farnsworth said, looking into his empty glass, tinkling it with his fingernail. "Revenge isn't a suitable incentive for what we do. Never is! Colours our judgment. Makes us take chances we wouldn't normally take."

"I would like to help. Dr Farnsworth, please!"

It pleased him to have her beg in this way. He ought to make her do it more often.

"Why must you be so bitter about it? Slagter was only doing his job. It just so happened you were involved. These things happen all the time, all over the world. Do they hurt you in the same way?"

"Vladimir died one horrible death because of it!"

"He was a KGB agent, Julia. Stationed in a hot spot. Mozambique! He knew the risks he was taking when he went out there. He knew the price he would pay if the South Africans got hold of him. Why can't you accept, it wasn't your fault. Or mine."

"He died because I was too naïve."

"Is that what hurts? You could hardly have expected the British Government to condone immorality. Officially that is."

"I don't wish to discuss it any further, Dr Farnsworth," Julia said quietly. "If you don't mind."

"Not at all, my dear. Best forgotten. May I offer you some more sherry. You could do with it."

"Thank you, no. I'm all right. Really. Don't let me stop you though."

"Yes, I think I'll have another," Farnsworth said, unwilling to arouse himself to reach for the bottle. "Pour me out another, will you? If Jane were here, she'd confiscate the bottle. Bad for me, she says. After you've gone, I'll stretch myself on the sofa and snooze until lunch, and I won't touch another drop until after surgery. I promise."

Julia poured him out a very small one. He pulled a wry face at her miserly effort; then settled back to enjoy it.

"We are not concerned with Slagter," Farnsworth said. "I do want to make that quite clear. You do understand that? But I've received reports he's already on his way here. If he hasn't slipped into England already. We'll obviously try to stop him entering the country, if we can. I doubt it, though. Saul trailed him for years without discovering who he was. Every time an agent was killed by him during one of his interrogations—really butchered—Saul was sent there to check it out. And came away empty. And they were all trained agents. Samuelson isn't even an agent. He'll spill his guts within two minutes when our friend gets to him. That's why I had to get you back from Nice. Fast."

"I'm so glad you did," Julia said fervently. "Who's looking after him now? We may have lost him already. I'll need a back-up."

"I've got a chap called Donaldson keeping an eye on him. Nice fellow, Donaldson. Do you know him?"

"I don't think so."

"Bit of a free-lancer. Very reliable though. We use him for odd jobs. Like trailing people. When we can't spare one of our own on a twenty-four hour basis. He's supposed to call me once a day, and the next time he does, I'll tell him to start calling you too. Don't be fooled by him. He sounds a little simple-minded over the telephone, but he's very good really. You can trust him."

"May I look at the files?"

"Yes, of course. You can't take them with you. Service policy. But take your time with them over here. I know. I could do with a pot of tea. Let me make some. Inspite of what my old battle horse has led you to believe, I do know how to boil an egg. Or make a pot of tea. Will you have a cup of tea, my dear?"

"That would be nice," Julia said, throwing her shoulders back and straightening herself. She had not been slouching in the padded chair, but she shifted slightly so that she was now leaning towards the table, her elbow resting on it.

"That would be nice," she repeated. "Perhaps I can look at the files in the meantime?"

Farnsworth unlocked the filing cabinet in the corner of the room. She had to turn a little to see him do it. He used a key that dangled from a key chain he produced from his inner pocket. There were only two keys on it so she presumed they were not house keys.

"Let me see now. You'll need the file on Saul. And we've put together a file on our Dr Samuelson. Very hurriedly I'm afraid, so it won't tell you much. You probably know more about the man than the file does. The file I'm searching for here is the file our people put together on ANC agents and their activities in England. Ah! Here it is." Farnsworth drew out the file.

Julia moved her hand, now on the table, towards the sherry bottle. Within easy reach.

Farnsworth jerked the drawer, which slid noisily in its tracks back into place. Julia's hand hit the sherry bottle, sending it first on its side, then rolling towards the edge, sherry sloshing in low gurgles on to the table top.

Farnsworth who had raised his hand to drive in the lock of the filing cabinet, turned around.

"I'm dreadfully sorry," Julia said, rising out of the chair. "So terribly sorry! Oh, dear!"

She stood the bottle upright; looked pleadingly at him for a cloth or paper towel.

"Nothing to worry about, my dear," Farnsworth said, disappearing into the bathroom for a box of paper tissues. "They say sherry's good for table tops. Fortunately we don't seem to have spilled any on the carpet, or I'd never hear the last of it from the old battle axe. God help me! This is my house. Why do I live constantly in fear of her?"

Julia mopped up the sherry on the table.

Farnsworth watched her. Cleverly done that, he thought. Very cleverly done. Perfect timing.

"Here you are," he said, handing her the files. "Let me get the kettle going. I won't be long."

Julia waited until she heard his footsteps die down the corridor that led to the kitchen in the rear regions of the house.

It didn't take her long to find the file she was looking for. SLAGTER. It was three inches thick. Documentation on every case he'd been involved with. All the interrogations he'd carried out on enemy agents. Six in all. All over the world. Much of the documentation consisted of photographs of the victims. She felt sick looking at them. Most had been hacked before death occurred. All had been stripped naked. No sexual mutilation in any of the cases. And each case had Saul's detailed reports attached to it. Reports he'd sent back from the cities the interrogations had taken place in—Tangiers, Miami, Bombay, Haifa, Paris, and the last from Johannesburg. That one she knew well. Poor Vladimir! She could have saved him from such a death, and each time she thought of it the hurt and the anger was still the same. That was the last case; the one she found most difficult to look at. But she owed him that much to study his case too; the photographs of his stripped and mutilated body, after Slagter had finished with him.

This was not the time to agonize. She had to read what she could. As fast as she could. She heard the kettle whistle in the kitchen. Farnsworth wouldn't be long in returning, though, fortunately for her, he seemed to be taking his time over it. Perhaps because he didn't make his own tea often enough. Somewhere in that file there were clues that would lead her to Slagter. Above all, she wanted to get close to him; form a picture of him in her mind. The way in which he operated. She had to enter his mind, feel with him, almost be one with him; then only would she know him. Such killers, she decided, were made not born.

Saul had been on the trail for five years, according to the file in her hands, and he hadn't even come close to him.

The first report was dated five years ago. From Tangiers. Abdul had been working with Saul on a difficult case that involved arms being shipped, illegally, into South Africa. They had been together. Then Abdul disappeared, until Saul found him again.

The last report was dated only one month before. Vladimir in Johannesburg. Saul had been sent down from London, after it was all over, to report on it. He was furious he wasn't in Johannesburg when Slagter interrogated Vladimir. What good did it do to be on the scene so many days later?

There was no pattern to any of the others either. The ones in between. All had been men except the American agent in Miami. She had been a young woman, twenty-five years old, and she had been treated by Slagter in exactly the same way. Stripped naked and cut up badly before being murdered. No sign of sexual mutilation there either.

She heard the door of the refrigerator. That would be Farnsworth reaching for the milk. Not much time now.

She put Slagter's file back into the filing cabinet. In its exact place. Idly she looked for Spencer under S. It was a very thin file. She could easily have taken offense. They didn't have much to report on Julia Rayburn-Spencer. It made interesting reading. Her eyes opened wide, in amusement, at some of the research reports filed on her. She could barely restrain herself from laughing at their description of her. They had been very thorough where it mattered though. Such as under 'sexual preference'.

Heterosexual. Not a virgin.

They were accurate in their research. She had to give them credit for that.

She slid the drawer back softly; did not lock it. Then she settled herself back into the padded chair, brushed her hair back from her forehead, and opened the files Farnsworth had given her. She would need the information in those files too, if she was to find out what Dr Samuelson knew, and why Saul died. There was more on Saul than there was on Joshua. Even less on people they knew so well or were intimately involved with—like Saul's wife Laura or their friend

Jomo Mbangeli. Even less on Jomo's brother Boko. Nothing at all on Ewa.

Except the mention of a sister to the other two.

They were all from South Africa. There were brief biographies, with photographs of them all. Except Ewa. Saul she knew. The tall, handsome, blond body looked back teasingly at her. Bronzed and powerful. The muscles seemed to come alive. The face, with Grecian features, mocked her.

His cover had been a small, novelty shop in South Kensington. Buying gifts abroad and selling them in London. It was a perfect cover. It allowed him to travel all over the world in search of novelty items.

Joshua, too, she recognised. He was small—a hundred and twenty pounds perhaps—with black hair and black eyes. The trim moustache curled downwards to meet a short goatee beard. The heavy, turtle shell glasses gave him a doctorly look. Quiet sort of a chap. Self-effacing, the biography went on to say, but she knew that already.

He was handsome, she decided, in his own gentle sort of way. Quite unlike Saul's rugged handsomeness. He was born in Durban of Indian Jewish parents who had emigrated from India to South Africa more than fifty years before. Educated in Britain, with a medical degree from London. He had gone back to India for a while—almost five years—but the report drew a blank on his activities there. Presumably he had practiced medicine. He was now an MRCP and licensed to practice in England. He had joined Dr Clayborne about three years ago. And she knew that already. He lived in an expensive flat on Fitzjohn's Avenue. He was barely three houses away from her. That she did not know. The surgery was located on Finchley Road, just minutes away.

Julia's eyes opened wide as she read on. So it was all true what they said about quiet Dr Samuelson!

His brother Joe and he were both bachelors. They had a reputation for picking up au pair girls—those who would allow themselves to be picked up, that is—at the Evening Star, a pub they frequented regularly, throwing late night parties, after closing time, to coax the girls home. The parties were financed largely by Dr Samuelson, since Joe, who worked with a furrier in the East End, was not too well off.

Success was estimated at one in ten. So the file speculated.

Julia laughed out aloud.

"Yes, it is a trifle funny, isn't it?" Farnsworth said, coming in with the tray and stopping behind her chair for a moment to peer over her shoulder into the file. "He's a respectable doctor—and to all accounts a good one. But in the evenings he seems to acquire a different personality. Lecherous! I found it amusing too. He and his brother seem to run riot with all these foreign au pair girls in London. Thank God, English girls have more sense!"

"I don't know about that," Julia said. "With English girls you just have to work harder that's all."

Farnsworth noticed that the filing cabinet was unlocked and locked it. Julia poured the tea.

Saul and Dr Samuelson, she knew a little; Laura she did not know at all.

The photograph showed an extraordinarily beautiful woman in her early thirties, with ash blond hair and blue eyes. Long eyelashes that had been held from a flutter by the clicking of a button. She looked so vulnerable, Julia could see how men could go for her. The shoulder length hair framed the face as in a portrait; yet the wrinkles around her eyes gave her a tired look.

A certain sadness too in the face, even though the eyes were smiling.

Julia was about to open the file on ANC activities in London—and on Jomo and Boko Mbangeli—when the telephone rang in the living room.

Farnsworth frowned.

"Excuse me, my dear," he said. "That must be Donaldson. Keep at those files, while I get rid of him."

Julia waited until she heard him close the living room door; then she tiptoed swiftly down the corridor, until she was opposite the living room door.

No sign of Jane anywhere. She was thankful for that. It would be hard to explain what she was doing in the corridor outside the living room door, in bare feet.

He had closed the door behind him, but he had not locked it. She turned the knob silently; then pushed the door gently with her bare toes. Just sufficient for his voice to come through.

The door moved noiselessly. The merest crack to let vision through. His back was turned towards her. But all she wanted was to hear his end of the conversation.

He had lowered his voice. His normally strident tone was muted, but snatches of sentences still came through to her behind the door. Especially towards the end of it when he got excited.

"She's already here, damm it!"

Donaldson at the other end must have had quite a few things to say, because there was a long, fuming silence, broken by attempted interruptions which were ignored. She heard him pound his fist on the telephone stand as if to cut off Donaldson who would not be interrupted.

"Well, I don't see how that changes anything. I don't see how we can change anything. We'll just have to go ahead with Canard. She's willing and she'll just have to do."

She heard Farnsworth swear into the telephone. Words that made her eyes open wide. Words she'd never heard him use before. Somehow she didn't think middle-aged, bald men even knew such words. They poured out of him in disconnected sentences that made her blush.

"No! No! God, yes! But is she capable of it? How the hell can I be sure? Now you, look here, don't give me that..."

Donaldson had cut him off again, because she heard him fume some more and swear some more.

Another long silence. This time Donaldson must have insisted on having himself heard, because she heard Farnsworth mumble as he was forced to listen to what was being poured into his ear from the other end of the line. A string of Welsh bludgeoning no doubt, Julia thought, as she marveled at Farnsworth's silence. Except at the very end.

"Damm it, Donaldson! I don't give a damn camel's whisker what you bloody well think. Or what the bloody Agency thinks. Now you call her, or the whole deal's off. Do you hear that?"

And Farnsworth slammed the receiver down on the telephone.

Julia darted back to the study. She straightened the clinging dress over the curve of her thighs; opened the handbag, examining the face in the small mirror of the powder compact it held. Satisfied with what she saw from an angle or two, she settled back to wait for Farnsworth.

He wasn't long in coming. The blood had rushed to his face and his lips trembled.

"That was Donaldson," he said, as evenly as he could. "Reporting on our quarry. Apparently Samuelson is sitting at this moment in a little Italian restaurant off Oxford Circus. Not a care in the world. So Donaldson says. Maybe he's waiting to have lunch with someone. That's what Donaldson thinks. He can't be sure. He's across the street keeping an eye on him. I told him he's to call you at least once a day and fill you in with what he's got. He has to follow your instructions implicitly! I made that quite clear to him. He's a good sort, Donaldson. You'll like him, but don't take any of that Welsh crap from him. The fellow can be an absolute bastard!"

Farnsworth watched her walk down the driveway to the car parked at the edge of the gravel, almost on the grass. And sighed again. Her shoulders were thrown back; she walked briskly. Her heels clicked on the stones. This time, going away, she did not hesitate. As when she had approached the house. Not even breaking step as she searched for the car keys in the handbag. Not looking around though she knew he was watching her from the upstairs window.

The more he thought about it, the more he was convinced he was right and Donaldson was wrong.

She would be able to kill when the time came.

He went back to the study. Switched off the microphone in the lamp above the study table.

But he did not snooze on the sofa until lunch. Instead he poured himself another sherry, a large one, leaned back into his favourite chair and thought intently.

Chapter 4

Donaldson had been right.

Her quarry—or more correctly, the man she had been assigned to protect temporarily—was sitting in Romano's Italian restaurant, just off Oxford Street, not too far from Oxford Circus. Outside, the London traffic ground its daily honks, and bad language, past the striped awning of the restaurant, the aroma of fresh bread intermingling with the spicier smells of Italian sauce. There was an Indian restaurant next door that put even spicier, and exotic, smells into the London street via the open door, and Joshua alternated between them with the mood of the moment. But today he was meeting Laura, and since she didn't care too much for Indian food—it was like gulping fire with every morsel, she said—today it would have to be Italian cuisine.

Joshua sat at the table near the plate glass window, and looked out into the street. The red buses that rumbled past the window blotted out his vision beyond the narrow sidewalk, clearing suddenly to reveal the shop windows of the shoe store across the street.

Joshua saw the man leaning against the shop window, enjoying the sunshine.

After a while of watching, he was oblivious to the frenetic activity in the street. When several minutes had passed, he looked, occasionally, at his watch or at the grandfather clock in the entry foyer, near where his coat was hanging. They were only cursory glances. She would be late in coming. As always. He was in no hurry. He wasn't due back in the surgery that evening. He'd done his stint looking after the sick, and the not so sick, people of Hampstead, while Clayborne was on his vacation in Nice; now it was his turn to take the day off. Clayborne, reliable as ever, had returned that morning, telephoned Joshua to confirm it, and hung up. He seemed worried, old Clayborne did, Joshua thought. Maybe he ought to look in on him? Perhaps later that evening he'd do just that.

Now his mind was on lunch. And Laura.

The Italian girl wiped the table clean for him, bending over as she did, giving him a clear view into her large, plunging breasts, nestling in the not too tight bra. In the warm weather, freeing them a little made for more comfort.

She was not a bad girl. The friendliness was reserved only for her favourite customers like Dr Samuelson. People she felt comfortable with. Not just as customers more like family. He had eaten there more times than she could remember. He had no family of his own, except for a brother of whom he was very fond and of whom he spoke glowingly. So if she fed him all the time, she had a little more responsibility to him than to just take his money from him. So she reasoned.

What had attracted her to him the first time around, though, was the outrageous tip he left for her? And many times after. But in later months, she refused to take his tips anymore.

It was people like him that made the place what it was, not their tips, she said, as she sat beside him one day when business was quiet and folded the money back into his hand.

So he stopped leaving money for her when he came alone, remembering her birthday instead with a rabbit fur coat he'd bought off Joe.

She was a pretty girl, a little on the heavy side because she wasn't too tall, with a sensuous Italian face, the long, black hair tied in an enormous bun at the back of the head. Once, after a couple of beers, he had asked, hesitatingly, to see how long it was, and after a quick glance around—the only other customer was the old Colonel in the booth and he had his back to her—she removed the pins deftly, allowing it to cascade behind her. He felt the softness of it. The old Colonel turned around to signal Lysa for his coffee, so she'd gathered up her hair in front of her, and disappeared into the kitchen. The old Colonel had winked at Joshua.

Lysa finished wiping the table.

"Would you like to order, Dr Samuelson?" she said.

"May I wait for a while, Lysa? I'm expecting company. The widow of an old friend of mine, Mr Prentiss. You knew him? We came in here sometimes together."

She paused to talk to him, one hand inside her apron.

"Oh, yes! I read all about it in the papers. So sad! Nice Mr Prentiss. To think it could happen to him? One hears about gas explosions happening only to strangers."

"Perhaps I'm blocking a table," Joshua said. "Would you prefer me to wait in the entry foyer until she comes? I'll be happy to do that."

"Oh, no! Dr Samuelson! How can you say such a thing? Sit here as long as you want."

She reached into the pocket of her apron, drawing out a 'Reserved' sign, leaning over to place it in the centre of the table, brushing her breast against his shoulder.

He felt the touch of her thigh on his leg.

"Thank you, Lysa. You're a very good girl. Perhaps I can take you out for a drink sometime?"

"Lysa!" Mrs Romano called out. "You're wanted in the kitchen. When you've finished with Dr Samuelson, of course."

Lysa arranged the table napkin in front of him. It looked like a white bird.

"I would like that very much, Dr Samuelson. I'm not so sure, Papa would."

"Think of me as an old friend. To talk to. A beer or two. I'll see you home safely too."

She turned towards him, blocking the view of her arm from the other occupied tables in the room.

He slid his hand around it, in between the arm and her breast.

She closed it, almost instinctively, to her side. He felt the breast yield forgivingly as the back of his hand plunged into it.

"I have to go," she said.

"I understand."

"About that drink. I'd like that. Where? And when?"

"I drink regularly at the Evening Star. It is a fine, cozy pub on Finchley Road. Between Finchley Road and Swiss Cottage tube stations. On the other side of the street.

Between eight and eleven most evenings. Definitely on weekends. If I'm not there, ask for my brother, Joe. He'll know where I am."

He ran his hand down the soft side of her body to the bone of her hip. She nodded and disappeared towards the kitchen.

Laura watched from the door.

He looked up to see her standing there, and arose from his chair to greet her.

"My dear," he said, "how nice to see you. I got a reserved table for us. Lysa was very nice about it."

"I'm sure she was," Laura said. "Fine girl, isn't she?"

"Only a child. Let's talk about you. I'm so dreadfully sorry about Saul. I really am, Laura."

He reached for her hand, holding it in his own, fondling it with caresses to her palm and fingers, until the tension in her face relaxed, gradually, and she started to cry.

"It must have been a terrible shock. I know it was to me. If there's any way I can help, Laura, you've only to ask."

"Don't make it more difficult than it is, Josh," she said. "You were always very good at that. I'm crying, but not for him. I got over crying for him ten years ago. The whole goddam marriage ended ten years ago. You knew I was making a horrible mistake. And, yet, you just stood by and watched."

Lysa came to take their order, curtsying mournfully to Laura in silent sympathy. Joshua ordered for the both of them. He looked out of the plate glass window. The shoe store was bathed in sunlight.

The man in the felt hat still leaned against the window of it.

A passing red bus blocked him from view. When it passed, he was still there.

"I always thought you two were very much in love," Joshua said. "At least during those early years in Durban. You made a perfect couple. At the wedding, everyone said so. What else could I have done, but stand and watch?"

"He wasn't right for me, Josh. He was always away somewhere or the other. I don't know what he was into. Certainly a lot of women. All over the world. Used the novelty shop as an excuse to be away from me. I tried to be with him when I could, but it wasn't always possible."

The tears trickled past the pale cheeks on to the tablecloth. He could only hold her hands and let her cry. Not much else he could do for her.

"You must be charitable, Laura. He had a novelty shop; he had to buy novelties for it. It seemed to be doing well. He always kept you well provided for money, didn't he? Give him credit for that."

"Too well! That's what is so strange. I knew nothing about the things he did. And I lived with him for fifteen years. Is that possible?"

"He's dead, Laura. Let him be."

"He was killed! I know it!"

"I thought he died in a gas explosion in Clapham. Though what he was doing in an abandoned building down there beats me!"

"Meeting a woman more likely. Or a man."

"Come now."

"Don't tell me you didn't know? He took them all. I wouldn't be at all surprised if he's had you too."

"I'm not bisexual," Joshua said quietly. "Saul was. I'm truly sorry you had to find out."

"You knew. And you didn't warn me? Oh, Joshua! You could have told me."

"Would you have believed me?"

"No."

"And even if you had believed me, would it have made a difference?"

"I suppose not. I had to find out. I found it out years ago. He was into other things too, Joshua. You have to believe me."

"What other things?"

"I don't know. There were phone calls to the shop. He answered them most of the time, and when he wasn't there that bitch Shari took the messages for him. But sometimes the phone would ring when the shop was closed, and I answered it."

"Well?"

"They never left any messages with me. Said they'd call back. Or just hung up. Why, Joshua? I was his wife."

"My dear, I don't know. To be honest, I think you're seeing shadows that aren't there. You never told me all this when he was alive? So why do you keep thinking that way now he's dead?"

"He was murdered. That's why! They killed him and now they're after me too. I'm terrified, Joshua!"

"Come now, Laura. I'll admit he died under rather strange circumstances. That I grant you. The police are investigating. We don't know all the facts as yet. Or the details for that matter. The results of the autopsy will be available soon from the coroner's office. And as his doctor, they'll send me a copy. That'll tell us how he died. But why should you be afraid?"

"Because they're following me. That's why! Every where I go, there's this man after me. Won't let me out of his sight. Doesn't even bother to hide himself. There, look! Across the street. He's just waiting for us to finish our lunch. Why are they following me, Joshua?"

"I don't know, my dear girl, but I am sure as hell intend to find out."

She saw him leave Romano's. He waited for a break in the traffic; then darted across the street. The man in the felt hat, leaning against the window of the shoe store, straightened up, but did not run. She saw Joshua's gesticulating arms wave wildly; almost heard the angry stamp of his foot. It brought a faint smile to the tear-stained face. He had always been so emotional in everything he did. So typically Indian!

The man tipped his felt hat to Joshua, and sauntered away.

"Well? What did he have to say for himself?" Laura asked.

"Says he doesn't know you from Adam or Eve. Says he's enjoying the summer sunshine leaning against the window of a shoe store. Watching the traffic go by. But if it bothers you, he says, he'll go somewhere else. I felt sorry for the poor bloke. Spoke with a heavy sing-song Welsh accent. Come to think about it, I'm surprised he didn't insist on his rights and punch me in the nose."

"Joshua, I'm so afraid! I really am! That's why I asked you to meet me here. Darling, will you come and stay with me for a few days? Please! Just a few days. It'll make me feel so much better."

So different now than it was fifteen years ago, Joshua thought. The face was a little different; more tired and sad. Still with the same vulnerable look, he had found irresistible. The ash blond hair framing the softly molded nose and chin. The same blue eyes, more hardened now than they had been at the beach. They had been innocent that day. There was no innocence in them anymore. Is that what fifteen years of marriage did to you? And her body? Had that changed too? She must look a lot different now.

"What are you staring at, Joshua?" she demanded. "You seem to be somewhere else. Here I am telling you how afraid I am, and you're not even with me!"

"I was, my darling, I was."

"Well then, will you move in with me for a few days? Younger people seem to be doing that all the time. And if they can, why can't we? Is that too much too ask from an old friend?"

"No, of course not."

"Then you will?"

"If you want me to."

"I do, Joshua. Oh, I do! My poor faithful non-lover. Don't let that hurt, Joshua. I'll make it up to you tonight. I promise."

"It may be too late, Laura. I'm thirty-three years old. A confirmed bachelor."

"And a very lecherous one. Don't think I haven't known about all the women you've had. Or that it hasn't hurt each time."

"There may be no magic left any longer."

"But we can try, can't we? And you will find out why I'm being followed in this way?"

"Well, I'm a doctor, darling, not a detective. But one of the patients on my list is a police sergeant at Hampstead Police Station. He's pretty healthy, but he's constantly in with one of the kids. I was going to drop by and have a look at the child anyway. I'll talk to him about it. But I have to know a little more from you. What shall I tell him? Maybe if we knew why Saul died, we'd be nearer the truth. And how did he die? If it wasn't the explosion, what was it? They say the body was pretty burned up. Maybe we should just wait for the autopsy first?"

Laura put her fingers to his lips.

"The way you talk, Joshua, is enough to drive anyone insane. Will you just listen?"

"I thought I was, my darling."

The hurt look didn't stop her continuing. "Saul came back six days ago from Paris."

"I thought he came back from Nice? That's where he'd gone, you told me."

"No. He went to Nice first—I know he had a woman there—but from Nice he went to Paris."

"All right! Nice! Paris! What difference does it make?" Joshua said heatedly. "It's all France!"

"You're so right. What difference does it make? He had a woman in Paris too. The bastard! He had a woman wherever he went to comfort him. But from Paris, instead of going back to Nice, he comes to London. Why?"

"You're telling me there's something odd about his coming back to London? He was coming home to you."

"Oh, Joshua, how can you be so naïve? He came back in a hurry. Not in the usual tired way. He seemed excited. As if he'd stumbled onto something big. He was on an emotional high. Nearly drove me crazy, these ups and downs of his." She paused for a moment to look outside the window. The man in the felt hat had moved on. She craned her neck to see whether he had crossed the street or was anywhere near the Italian restaurant, but she couldn't spot him. Perhaps he was waiting in the Indian restaurant next door? She resolved to peek into it when they left.

"You could see the level of excitement, he was trying so hard to suppress. He closeted himself with Shari—store accounts, he said—and while they were in there he had a phone call from someone called Donaldson."

"You answered it?" Joshua sat up in his chair.

"No. Actually I didn't. He has called several times before, but each time I've answered the phone, he hangs up without speaking. So this time, I let Saul answer it. Hung around outside the door. He dropped his voice, but I heard enough to know he'd been called away the next day to an important meeting somewhere."

"Where?"

"I don't know."

"Didn't you ask him?"

"I stopped asking Saul questions like that a long time ago. He went to his meeting."

"And then?"

She did not answer him immediately.

"He'd changed, Joshua."

"Changed? When he came back? How?"

"He was withdrawn. Drained of all emotion. I'd never seen him so low before. In all the years I've known him, as on that evening.

His eyes were glass, Joshua, I swear it! He frightened me. He looked like a hunted animal."

"What was the meeting about?"

"He wouldn't say. I asked him about it. He said it was with two other people. A British importer and a Welsh dealer."

"Novelty items?"

"I don't know. I suppose so. But he was so different, Joshua. He took me out to dinner that night. An expensive place in Soho. Valentino's. Champagne and all. Dancing afterwards. Close too. He hadn't done that in years. I was even fool enough to think, maybe, we were having a new start."

"Perhaps he was trying, Laura."

"But half way through the evening, he changed again! How can a man change so completely? Hardly a cause for it. It couldn't be a new beginning when he almost left me stranded on the dance floor. More like he was saying goodbye? One last gesture before leaving?"

"I see."

"The thought struck me, it was the end," Laura said, putting her hands to her cheeks and looking into Joshua's eyes. "I'm not that dumb. I thought he was going to leave me. For some other woman. Maybe the one he had in Nice. But I kept hoping. I could do that, can't I?"

"Go on."

"That night he disappeared. I waited up for him, thinking maybe I could talk it over with him. Try to reach an understanding, but he never came home. Not the next night either. And on the third day, I read about the explosion in Clapham and the charred body in the rubble. How could I have known it was Saul? I went to a movie that evening. A comedy at the Bijou. When they identified him, the policeman on the beat came in with the Inspector and broke the news to me very gently. And then, ever since, this horrible man has been following me around everywhere! Wherever I go, he's there. Scaring me to death!"

"You poor dear," Joshua said, patting her hand.

They held hands for a while, dropping them while Lysa cleared away the dishes. Joshua ordered rhubarb pie for dessert. And hot tea with milk and sugar. None of this iced tea for him, even in the hot weather.

"What did he come to see you about?" Laura asked, stirring the pot, peering into it as if she could read the leaves.

"Me?"

"Yes. He came to see you, didn't he? That morning?"

"No"

"No?"

"I just told you. No. Why would he come to see me? What makes you think he came to see me?"

"Oh! I thought he came to see you that morning. After he came back from Paris and before he went off to that meeting of his."

Joshua clanged the saucer with the teaspoon in annoyance at being disbelieved.

"Well, you thought wrong!"

"Why would he tell me he was going to see you that morning, if he wasn't?" Laura asked, spreading out her hands in dismay at him. He brushed them aside.

"Is that what he told you? That he was coming to see me? Well, he didn't. I was in that morning, but for surgery. Clayborne was away, so I was in."

"No, no, Joshua. Not in the surgery. At your flat in Hampstead. Before his meeting. Oh, you are being thick and obstinate today! First you don't believe me when I tell you I'm being followed, and now you won't even admit he came to see you."

Joshua's brow cleared. The wrinkles in his forehead disappeared. He smiled sweetly at her.

"Did you say my flat in Hampstead?"

"Yes. That's where he was going to meet you."

"Then that explains it. I wasn't home all morning. In fact, I wasn't home all night. At a friend's. So Saul missed me. That makes me feel much better, though I don't know why? Do you think I'm obstinate?"

"So, then, you didn't see him that day?"

"Well, I did actually."

"Oh? When?"

"That evening at the Evening Star with Jomo. They were having some sort of argument. I bought them a round. They stopped talking when I went up with the drinks, so I took the hint and sat with Joe instead. And a little later, when I turned around, to see if they wanted another round, they'd left."

"What time?"

"Time?"

"What time did they leave, Joshua?"

"I don't know. Would you keep a note of times people come in and out of a pub?"

"I probably would. But then I observe people; you just look at them. Think hard, Joshua. What time?"

"I left—with Joe—at closing time. So it must have been before that. No wait! It was much earlier than closing time, because I bought Joe a round, and when I went up to the bar to get it, I had to pass them, and they weren't there."

"And you never saw Saul after that?"

"No."

"Did he call you? Drop you a note?"

"No! No! No! How many times must I repeat the stupid word?" Joshua fought hard to regain control of himself. And succeeded, because when he spoke again, he was his gentle self again. "You're just blowing up this thing out of all proportions, Laura. You must see that. Until the results of the autopsy come in, we don't even know he was murdered. And the fellow across the street could be someone quite harmless. Who he says he is. Doing what he says he is doing."

She leaned back into the padded bench of the booth. The lunch hour was almost over. The restaurant had emptied itself. Romano was counting the takings for the afternoon. Soon he would be off to the bank to deposit them. Lysa was nowhere to be seen.

"So you think I'm worrying unnecessarily about you? That you're not in any danger?"

"Me?" Joshua said, in some surprise. "I thought we were talking about you. I'm not involved in this, am I?"

"I think you're in great danger, Joshua," she said very softly. "I think we are both in great danger. Or I wouldn't be receiving notes like this one."

She drew the envelope from her purse, hesitating as to whether it would serve any purpose to show it to him; then sliding it over the table cloth like a card player at a game of bridge. He read it twice, stroking his goatee beard, fondling his moustache, emotionless, expressionless, except for the eyes which scanned the lines and then scanned them again. It read:

YOUR ASSOCIATION WITH DR SAMUELSON IS AT AN END OR SOON WILL BE STAY WITH YOUR OWN KIND. YOU HAVE BEEN WARNED SLAGTER

There was no return address on the envelope. Joshua could hardly have expected it. It was postmarked in Welwyn Garden City, July 13—the day most likely Saul had died.

Joshua signalled Lysa for the bill. Indicating they would be leaving. Laura was aloof as they smiled at each other, exchanging pleasantries.

"Was everything okay, Dr Samuelson?" Lysa asked.

"Perfect! The food was excellent. My compliments to your mother."

"My father, actually. It is he who does the cooking early in the morning."

"Well then, to him too. You have an exquisite kichen! And the service, as usual, was incomparable!"

She curtsied to him, blushing at the compliment, bending over to wipe a spot on the table cloth before him.

"Fine girl that," Joshua said.

They went out into the street. For reasons he did not understand, Laura left him momentarily to peek into the Indian restaurant next door and the bakery next to that, leaving his arm each time as she dashed in and out.

"Who is Slagter?" Laura asked. "Do you know who he is?"

"No! Who the hell is he? He has bloody cheek! Sending you such notes. Perhaps I oughtn't to move in with you if it endangers you?"

"Nonsense, Joshua! We'll be safe together. You said you would. You promised! I'm not spending tonight alone."

"All right, I'll come. If you really want me to. Just to show our friend Slagter how little we care about his silly notes. Sort of tell him to get lost."

"Tonight? Will you come tonight?"

"Yes. But I have to go home first for the evening. Put a few things together. I will be sleeping in Saul's bed and sleeping with Saul's wife but I can't bring myself to sleep in his pyjamas. There I draw the line. But I will come, I promise you. Say around midnight. Around closing time."

"I'll wait up for you," she said.

They were now weaving their way through the late afternoon shoppers, towards Oxford Circus tube station. She took his arm. He did not seem to feel the occasional pressure of his arm on her breast, as she bumped into him. He felt the softness without the intimacy. It was like bumping into soft rubber. There was an impersonal coldness to it. Almost an act of courtesy. Neither wore a coat, and the thin dress she wore appropriate to a hot summer's day provided no great thickness from his short-sleeved arm; yet he seemed cocooned from her. Almost respectfully so. She looked around nervously, as if expecting the man in the felt hat to be somewhere behind them, but it would have been impossible to spot him in the jostling crowd. Even walking together was inconvenient sometimes; turning around over her shoulder almost dangerous. An old, military gentleman with a flaming red moustache and bowler, bumped into her, separating her from him. He apologised profusely. She reached for Joshua's arm again, clutching at it in fear, as the word on the note in her purse stood out in front of her. It was not Oxford Street she saw before her—though the crowd was much the same. Jostling people in the fish and meat market in Durban had bumped into her in much the same way. They had attracted a few stares, but in the meat and fish markets no one particularly cared. The signs were all over. In Afrikaans. In a variety of Indian languages too, which she did not understand, and in English too. But it was the one in Afrikaans that was larger than the rest, and she did understand it. She stopped in the middle of the street pulling him back to her. Bringing him to a dead halt. She felt the sharp point in her back, but it was only an errant umbrella. The military man apologised again, and passed on. "Don't you remember, Joshua? The signs in the fish and meat market in Durban?"

"No. I haven't been to South Africa for God knows how long. But now you mention it, I do seem to recall the word in the marketplace. Why?"

"That's right, Joshua! In the marketplace, in Afrikaans, the signs all around us, above the meat shops." He stopped too. This time people bumped into them, and they were oblivious to it. They didn't speak much on the way to the novelty shop in South Kensington. The tube wasn't overcrowded, but it wasn't empty either. They found two places to sit, side by side, the hanging commuters leaning sometimes towards them and sometimes away from them, making conversation difficult. He didn't pay much attention to the people around them. Her eyes darted through the standing figures where a man in a felt hat had his back to them. "There he is, Joshua!" she whispered in panic into his ear, grabbing him by the arm that had strayed past the armrest towards her. "He's following us. And you wouldn't believe me. There! Look! He has his back to us, but he's watching us in the glass opposite. Oh, Joshua!" Her voice had risen.

"Calm down, Laura, will you?" he said firmly. "We don't even know it's the same man. Lots of men wear felts."

"Well, you saw him, didn't you? You'd know. Do you recognise him?" Joshua looked at the doors. Not much he could see, except the broad back and the wrinkles that lined the back of his neck beneath the hat. Once the man did turn sideways but not for long.

"Well?" Laura asked. "Is he or isn't he?"

"I don't know. I'm not good at such things. Remembering faces. Besides how do we know he isn't following me and not you? Or you and not me? He couldn't be following the both of us, because he couldn't know we'd be together. Let's find out who our friend is after. I'll get off at South Kensington. You go on to Gloucester Road. That'll separate us. So we'll know, immediately, who he's after. Switch platforms at Gloucester Road and come right back. I'll wait for you inside the station entrance at South Kensington. And, for heaven's sake, Laura, don't panic. He's only trying to frighten us—and we shouldn't let him. It's all part of his method. Trying to frighten us. Calling himself a butcher in Afrikaans."

Chapter 5

As Julia drove from Welwyn Garden City back to London, passion subsided, and when it did, she decided she didn't like it much at all. Why do I get picked for such assignments, she thought morosely, biting her lower lip gently when engrossed in thought. A wisp of brown curl strayed on to her forehead, and she blew it away.

Not that she minded playing nurse-maid to an Indian. In fact, it was a welcome change to be asked to protect some meek, innocent chap—and one she even knew slightly—from her last assignment. That had been her very first. She was not experienced and so doubly vulnerable. They thought she'd done a good job bringing in Vladimir, foxing him into leaving Mozambique for a rendezvous in South Africa, where he'd been promptly picked up by Farnsworth. She thought she'd botched it completely. But then that was the Intelligence Service for you. They never saw it from an agent's point of view. She shook her head as if to wipe away the memory of it. This was not the time to bring it up. Like placing flowers at a grave. It could be done only in a graveyard. It wasn't much use carrying the flowers around in one's head. No consolation at all. They had to be actually placed for guilt to be redressed.

The memory eased from her mind as she swung through Bromfield, past the old family estate, honking on the horn and waving wildly, slowing down to a crawl to give the old gatekeeper—who had fed her many a muffin from his own high tea—to recognise the car, come to attention and then wave wildly back in return.

It had been a very pleasant childhood.

Adolescence had not been quite that satisfying, beset by fears, ashamed of her feelings, horrified at times by the intensity of fantasy that seemed to occupy her mind as it willed. Being a writer didn't help at all. Only made matters worse, because her imagination produced them in such grotesque shape and form that, sometimes, she was forced to get up in the middle of the night and commit them to paper, in order to rid herself of them. Seeing them on paper always made them seem more harmless. Than actually thinking them. The old Earl and the servants knew about it when they saw the light come on in her bedroom, at odd hours, but other than keeping a watchful eye on her, they let her be.

She had been woefully inexperienced. Even during those years in boarding school in Kent. And being the granddaughter of the eleventh Earl of Bromfield didn't make it any easier. Everyone seemed to want to protect her! Finally, at sixteen, after a great deal of effort and with the help of Cecily, she arranged to meet Cecily's brother, Viscount Edward Andrews also sixteen, in the shrubbery. The Viscount was staying with his widowed mother in the village and they had all come down to see Cecily at school, which made matters very convenient.

She met with him, and they talked desultorily for a while; then picking up courage she opened her lips for a kiss and closed her eyes.

There was a few moments delay. Nothing happened. She opened her eyes and was startled to find both his hands groping for her breasts. She reacted, instinctively, by slapping him hard on the face, at which he, equally inexperienced and unsure of himself, began to cry. She then spent the next half hour in the shrubbery, apologising and consoling him, even taking his hand and passing it over her breasts to show him she was not offended.

The affair had ended there. The last time she'd heard from Cecily, he'd married a widowed Begum—whose husband the Nawab had been killed in a hunting accident in Pakistan—and had six children already. Four grown kids and two little ones. She treated him, Cecily wrote, like her eldest son, and he loved it. And since he seemed to be happy, neither Cecily nor her mother were too upset by it.

The files had been right though.

She was not a virgin. And the affair had been, in its own way, just as unsatisfying. All the way through Oxford and a degree in Classics, men seemed to have little interest in her. Perhaps they admired her from afar. Intelligence had something to do with it. The family name, certainly, didn't help again. It seemed to overawe them. She found herself sometimes almost whispering: I, too, am flesh and feeling.

But if luck plays a part in all of these things, it had no knowledge of her.

She decided to take things into her own hands.

But it wasn't as easy as all that. She found it very difficult to be casually picked up at the pub, though the desire to do so floated in and out of her mind, somehow always being out at closing time. It became stronger each passing year, and sometimes she riled at herself, in chiding tones, at her childish behaviour.

"You're twenty-five years old, Julia! Not a child anymore. A grown, healthy woman. You haven't fallen in love with anyone, and no one has fallen in love with you—and isn't likely to. You're getting to be an old maid. Who are you preserving it all for?"

And at times like this, she would resolve that the next weekend, at the pub, she'd make a one night stand of it—and never did.

He slid into the seat beside her at the Crown and Whistle, smiling casually, waving his beer as he said:

"May I buy you a drink?"

"I'm sorry, I don't accept drinks from strangers."

"Ah! But that's where you are wrong, Julia. I'm not a stranger. I've just come from seeing your grandfather. He told me I might find you here. He insisted I meet you. I couldn't very well leave Bromfield without even saying 'Hello' now could I?"

She looked at him with interest. The tall, bronzed body, handsome and rugged, with the South African accent had a lot going for it. The top buttons of his shirt were open. He did not wear a tie. The fingernails were well kept; the handshake warm and tight.

He covered her hand with both of his own.

"And why did you need to see Grandfather?"

"It's a long story. But we have loads of time. Let me buy you a drink first, and then I'll tell you all. What'll it be?"

"A light ale will be fine."

He slid closer to her on the bench seat. Dropped his voice. "I work for the South African Government. A sort of public relations job, shall we say. In these difficult times we need to keep all the friends we have. So the government made a list of all the private individuals and companies, all over the world, who have put their trust in South Africa. Your grandfather came easily in the top hundred. The South African Government is sending me around to meet with our friends—as a personal ambassador—to thank them for their financial trust and support, to explain our position, which is often misrepresented by the press, answer questions and solicit their continued financial support with fresh investments in South Africa."

"Sounds like a prepared speech to me," Julia said, raising her glass to him.

"I've been entrusted with the very enjoyable task—and it is enjoyable, look at us—of meeting with our friends. I've been all over Europe, and next month, I'm off to the States. Now do you believe me?"

"Yes. I knew Grandfather had a lot of money invested in South Africa. Mainly in mining."

"I'm Saul Prentiss," he said. "Your grandfather was every bit right about you! He insisted I meet you before I left. And I'm so very glad I did."

"Make sure I don't transfer all that money out of South Africa when I inherit it? Good thinking."

She drank that evening a little more than she usually did, and when he offered to walk her home at closing time, she accepted. Dear Grandfather! No one could accuse him of not trying for her. She could see his approval written all over Saul.

The experience was painful. With little pleasure and no feeling to make up for it. In a sense, she was glad it was over. If that was what was meant by it, she was glad it could be lost only once. All her friends had downplayed the pain. Like a little cut there, or a bee sting. It had been more painful than that, perhaps because she had been older than they had been. Even after the pain had subsided there was no arousal. But what bothered her most—it bothered her then and it had bothered her ever since—was there was no emotion. That had been missing. Not that she hadn't tried to be emotionally involved with him. In fact, she'd tried very hard, much harder than most because she was being given a chance so late in life. So she thought. She wanted to make it work. Any way, every way. But it just would not arise, as they had all said it would. The tenderness and the feeling was missing.

The first time he had been relieved.

"Ever thought about joining the Service, Julia?"

"My father was in the Army. Before he died. I never thought about it."

"No, I mean Military Intelligence. The Secret Service. It's the only place you'll find excitement, even in peace time. Especially in peace time."

"Is that why you're here?"

He ignored the question.

"You'd make a fine agent, Julia. Good, solid family. Oxford degree. You have courage. You aren't easily thrown, and as you've just shown, God help me, you're neither emotional nor sentimental. The sort of agent we could easily use. I mean British Intelligence. MI-6. Not South African. Will you?"

She raised herself on one arm.

"Is that why you slept with me? Recruiting procedures? Or Service Regulations? Or something like that? Try out the body first before roping in the mind?"

"Don't be silly, Julia! You're a very beautiful woman. Not very excitable. A little cold and distant. But intelligent. Unlike the multitude of rather dim-witted women one meets these days."

He reached out to her, sliding his hand across her breast to the delicate nipple, twisting it between his fingers like feeling grit.

"Will you? Join the Service?"

"Will that be a double conquest for you? Recruiting me as an agent as you were seducing me?"

"Come on, Julia! Don't look at it that way."

"Will you get promoted?"

"No."

"But you will rack up a few good points with your superiors? Put you in their good books? A commendation, perhaps?"

"No! It's only a job. I enjoy it. I've had a wonderful hour with you. It could have been better if you'd enjoyed it too. But you will! Mark my words. You'll come to me often enough. Most women I've known come back to me again and again. And so will you, Lady Julia!"

Julia brushed his hand away from her breast. She got out of bed and dressed. "There's tea in the kitchen if you want some," she said. "I'm going for a midnight stroll through the grounds. When I come back in half an hour, I don't want to see you here."

"But you will think it over? Can I leave you the address of a man in Welwyn Garden City you might want to call on—if you decide to take up my offer? Just tell him Saul sent you. He'll be expecting you."

"Leave it on the kitchen table," Julia said. "Lock the front door when you leave."

She did a lot of thinking in that half hour, as she walked through her grandfather's estate, at midnight, as she had done so often as a child when she could not sleep, pondering the events of the evening. Things looked so much different by moonlight. You saw things not for what they were but for what you wanted them to be. And who could say you were wrong? When walking alone?

It didn't take her long to decide there might be some excitement in the job offer she'd received in bed. A degree in Classics from Oxford didn't quite prepare you for it, but then no degree would.

The card was sitting on the kitchen table, propped up against the still warm teapot. Dr William Farnsworth, followed by his address in Welwyn Garden City.

She shook her head again as if to wipe out the memory of that evening too.

Leaving Bromfield, Julia decided to take the A1 to London. At that time in the morning—it was nearing lunch time—traffic would be light. The road went south towards Apex Corner, where she branched off onto the A41. But at Hendon, she pulled off the road and bought herself a sandwich and a carton of milk, eating it in the Bentley, with the car door open. This time she knew precisely where she was going to wipe her hands—and it wasn't on her dress. The glove compartment of the Bentley held a sheaf of paper napkins. She touched perfume to her neck and chest. At the junction, she turned towards London on Finchley Road, but before she reached it, she climbed the hill into Hampstead, coming down Fitzjohn's Avenue that ran down from Hampstead Heath to meet Finchley Road at Swiss Cottage. Fitzjohn's Avenue ran on the side of the hill, past the stately homes that had, once, signified gracious living, but which were now converted into flats. Houses that had, at one time, housed well-to-do families. With servants waiting for the tinkle of service bells in the basement. Exclusive because it bordered the Heath. Close enough to London for easy commuting. Now content with being broken up into expensive flats for those who could afford them. Freud had lived around the corner. The telephone was ringing as she entered her apartment. It was Donaldson.

She heard the heavily accented sing-song voice come softly over the telephone.

"Dr Farnsworth asked me to keep you informed, Miss Spencer," he said. "Thought I'd call and introduce myself."

"Very thoughtful of you, Donaldson. What's your first name?"

"Thomas, Miss Spencer. Tom."

"You can call me Julia. Have we met before?"

"I don't think so, Miss Julia. I'm only part time. Sort of a free-lancer. Not many people know me in the Service. Just Dr Farnsworth and one or two others, such like. I don't work for them regular. They call me in when they want to put a tail on someone. Like this here Indian doctor."

"Where are you now, Tom?"

"In South Kensington Station. Our man had lunch with his lady friend in Romano's. It's a little Italian place near Oxford Circus."

"I know," Julia said. "Dr Farnsworth told me that. I was with him when you called."

"He dashed out of the restaurant in the middle of his lunch and started to wave his hands at me. Stamped his foot too!" Donaldson sounded hurt. It just wasn't the done thing. Not in his books.

"Never mind, Tom," she said, soothing him over the telephone. "Keep with him."

"Threatened to call the police if I didn't stop harassing his lady friend. He was most upset! I told him I was enjoying the sunshine, leaning against the window of the shoe store, across the road. I didn't want to make a scene, so I told him, if he didn't like it, I'd go elsewhere to enjoy the sunshine. I'm not a violent man, Miss Julia, but he was asking for a punch on the nose. He hasn't realised it's him I'm tailing. Not his lady friend."

"Where is he now, Tom?"

"Don't rush me, Miss. I like talking to you."

"Thank you, Tom. But where is he now? And are you with him or not?"

"I'm with him. Don't ever worry about that, Miss Julia. Well, as I was saying, before I was interrupted, they had a leisurely lunch. Took almost an hour over it, I reckon. When they got out, I'd taken the precaution of hiding myself, which was just as well because his lady friend was most suspicious. She dashed into the Indian restaurant next door and then into the bakery next door to that too, trying to spot me. That's the problem with tailing amateurs. They don't behave like professionals. Are you there, Miss?"

"I am," Julia said, "and I'm listening. Not much else I can do." She heard him chuckle over the line.

"Well, they started to walk towards Oxford Circus tube station, clutching each other for the most unknown of reasons, stopping in the middle of the pavement and causing minor pedestrian problems, finally reaching the tube station. And on the train to South Kensington. And there I ran into a problem."

"What problem?"

"They split up. I think his lady friend spotted me. Most suspicious woman! I kept my back to them as much as I could, but I got pushed sideways when someone was getting out at one of the intermediate stations, and she saw me. I had to choose between them, Miss, and since I was hired to tail him, I stuck with him—instead of her. Did I do right, Miss?"

"Absolutely! Stay with him! She's in no danger; he is! Where are you now?"

"In a telephone booth, Miss. Where else?"

She gave up. "Well, Miss Julia, can I continue?"

He took her silence as a long-suffering assent.

"That's where I am now. In the tube station with him. Waiting for him to move. He's waiting for his lady friend. She'll go to the next station, turn around and come right back. I'm sure of it. They're just trying to make my life difficult. The novelty shop is just across from the tube station. There's a flat above it that belongs to the lady. I don't know how long they're going to be there, Miss. There's an alley at the back with a rear entrance into the flat. It's going to be difficult for me to keep an eye on him, Miss, if he chooses to go out the rear."

"I'll be down there as soon as I can," Julia said. "Half an hour, if the traffic is kind to me."

"Anything else you'd like me to do, Miss?" Donaldson asked. "Dr Farnsworth said to follow your instructions."

"Just hang around there. When you see me go into the novelty shop, go around the rear into the alley and watch the rear entrance. Don't lose him!" She was about to give him stern words on how important it was to keep him in sight, when he interrupted her. Almost in a panic.

"Here she comes, Miss! Coming up the escalator now. Got to go!" The line went dead.

Julia drove carefully—and fast. No point in being picked up for a traffic violation or being involved in an accident. That would really blow it. But she wasn't cruising either. The late afternoon traffic was now starting to build up. Still a little early for officegoers heading home; more like shoppers trying to beat the rush by leaving early after a day's shopping in Central London. But fortunately most of it was the other way. She made good progress through St. John's Wood. At Baker Street, the traffic stranded her. One lane was closed; the other lane barely crawled. She switched lanes, closing her ears to the mouthed foul language from an annoyed cabbie, changed her mind about her route, and swung westwards, skirting Hyde Park into South Kensington.

There was no sign of Donaldson. He might have seen her but he did not identify himself.

The shop was empty, except for the sales girl behind the counter who came forward, with a smile, to serve her.

"May I be of help?"

She spoke with a heavy foreign accent. The files had said she was Israeli; her exotic looks identified her as being from the Middle East. The dark, long black hair reached to her waist, hanging loose. Julia marveled at the way it stayed in place, brushed back behind the small ears, then plunging like a black waterfall to the curve of the hip. The pretty, white skin, without moles or freckles, was lightly tanned. The sensitive black eyes searched Julia's face as if to discern her tastes.

She was not tall—Julia towered a full four inches above her—but she had a body that was delicately proportioned to her height.

The artistic fingers expressed her speech with feeling.

"May I help?" she repeated.

"Just looking, thank you," Julia said. "For a gift."

"For a friend?"

"You could say so. May I look around?"

"Please! If you need help, call me. My name is Shari."

Julia went through the shop quickly, touching stray items as if with interest. An African mask on one shelf; a German beer mug with a music box in the base that played when the lid was opened. It was going to be impossible to find anything at all in the shop. Not that she knew what she was looking for. The place was stacked high with gift items from every country in the world. Saul had made good use of the travel allowance from two governments, she thought, as she looked around her. Carved wooden tables and trays and sweetly smelling cigarette cases of sandal wood from India, silver jewellery from Morocco, six-foot Eiffel towers from France, Navajo masks from America, and assegais from South Africa.

On the wall she saw a collection of knives from every country in the world that had ever made them.

She drifted back to the girl behind the counter, who had been discreetly watching her every move, while appearing to be immersed in the evening paper.

"You have so many beautiful things," Julia said. "It's very difficult to choose."

"I thought you might need some help," Shari said with a smile. "Is it a man?"

"I beg your pardon?"

"The friend? For whom you are choosing the gift. Is it a man?"

"Yes."

"Do you have a budget? A ceiling on the amount you would like to spend?"

"Yes. Say two hundred pounds."

Shari whistled.

"He must be a very close friend! For that sort of money you could have items of real ivory, from India. We keep them locked up behind the counter, but I'll bring them out for you. A real ivory cigarette case? Or an ivory chess set? With Indian style rooks and pawns?"

"He doesn't smoke and he doesn't play chess. Do you own the shop?"

"Me? Oh, dear, no! I just work here. I like working here. I always wanted to be around exotic things. The owner of the shop felt the same way too."

"Doesn't he feel that way now?"

"He's dead. Died three days ago."

"I'm sorry to hear that. Was it a long illness?"

"He died an accidental death."

"Ah! Those are always the most difficult to take. One has no warning. Expecting it makes it a little easier, perhaps. It must be hard on the family. Did he have a family?"

"A wife. If you can call her that!" Shari dropped her voice. "She's in there now. In the flat above us. That door there leads up to it. Came in an hour ago with her Indian boy friend. No shame! If you ask me. Mr. Prentiss hasn't even been dead three days, and she's having it off with him already. I know I shouldn't be discussing her in this way, but I feel so angry within me."

"Perhaps it isn't as it looks," Julia said. "At a time like this a woman needs a friend."

"Don't you believe it!" Shari said, dropping her voice even lower. "She's not shedding any tears for him. You can bet on that. She's happy he's gone. The bitch! And he was such a nice man. Always so considerate."

Shari was on the verge of tears.

They heard voices behind the closed door leading to the flat. Shari fell silent, and moved away. Joshua came through first. His eyes met Julia's briefly.

There was no recognition. He held the door open for Laura. They came into the shop behind the counters.

Julia stepped behind the stack of Italian vases, some four feet tall, working her way rapidly to the far corner, hidden from their view. She unbuttoned the top three buttons of her blouse, reached her hand into her bra and slipped the shoulder strap, gripping it firmly between her arm and her breast. She buttoned up her blouse; just as quickly made her way back to them.

"Why, Dr Samuelson!" she said. "It is Dr Samuelson, isn't it? Yes, of course it is."

She held out her hand to him. He shook it.

Joshua looked at her, puzzled.

"Do I know you?" he asked.

"I'm Julia. Julia Rayburn-Spencer. I'm on Dr Clayborne's list. Have been for years."

"Ah, yes! Julia! I do remember. I've seen you in the surgery sometimes. Waiting for Clayborne. How are you keeping?"

"Very well, thank you, though I have been meaning to come in and see Dr Clayborne. But he's on vacation, isn't he?"

"He was back this morning. You must forgive me not recognising you, Julia. I have so many patients."

"I quite understand. Nice shop this."

"It belongs to Mrs Prentiss here," Joshua said, pointing to Laura, who was watching them disinterestedly. "I can recommend the shop to you. Did you find something you liked? Look at the collection they have. And the prices are very reasonable too."

He waved his hand across the room as if displaying its contents for her. Julia pointed to the ivory set lying on the counter. She reached her hand into her purse, to draw out the notes, jerking her hand sharply away from her breast; then gave a little cry of embarrassment, clutching her hand across her breast.

The shoulder strap dangled through the short sleeve of her left hand, trailing down her arm.

"I'm so sorry," she said in panic. "I've snapped a shoulder strap, it seems. Oh, dear!"

"Nothing to worry about," Laura said. "These things will happen. They always snap at the wrong time!"

Joshua pretended not to hear. Looked away.

"Would you like to use the bathroom in the flat?" Laura said. "It's upstairs. Past that door. You're very welcome to use it. The strap most likely has worked itself loose from the cup. You might be able to fix it, and if you can't, just tuck it back in until you reach home. Hold your left hand up, with the purse in it, and no one will notice a thing!"

"May I? Thanks awfully!" Julia said.

Once through the door, she raced up the stairs. In the bathroom, she kicked off her shoes, adjusting the strap at the same time, fixing it rapidly in place.

She didn't have too much time.

The flat was both upstairs and downstairs. The kitchen and the living room were below her, behind the shop; the bedrooms and the bathroom opened into a corridor. The study was directly above the shop.

But first she had a look around the bathroom. Samuelson had been Saul's physician. Or perhaps it had been Clayborne. Either way, had he been prescribed medicines that might tell forensics something about Saul's state of health? The medicine cabinet was in the bathroom. On the wall directly above the sink. The usual medicines—aspirin, cough drops, eye drops, lozenges, deodorants. God! Everyone's medicine cabinet looked like everyone else's. Held all the same stuff. Sickness was a great equaliser.

No child-proof bottles with untwistable caps containing pills with exotic, medical-sounding names. Why should the bottles be child-proof? There weren't any children in the house. Julia, she told herself sternly, you don't have a moment to lose, and you're wondering why there aren't any children in the house? Or child-proof bottles?

There were no vials with suspicious names that might portend a serious illness. Not in Saul's name; not in Laura's. Nothing that had a medical ancestry. Drugs over the counter didn't have a medical ancestry that was worth pursuing.

She took her shoes in one hand and slipped down the corridor, letting herself into the study. The floor was not carpeted, and though her feet were bare, would the sounds carry into the shop below?

She searched swiftly through the papers on the table, and in the drawers. Nothing of interest. Mainly small bills from suppliers—unpaid bills. Some angry letters from debtors, threatening to sue. There was no filing cabinet in the room; no safe either. In any case, even if there had been one, she would have had no time to crack it. The filing cabinets were in the shop below; presumably they held the store accounts.

That was so frustrating about a hurried search! She didn't know what she was looking for? And if Saul had chosen to hide some of his papers—really tried to hide them in the mass of books that lined one wall of the study—she could never hope to unearth them. That happened only in books. Not the type she wrote, heaven forbid! Such luck never came by her way.

The only papers she could hope to find on the table were the ones that were supposed to be there. Some correspondence; a sheet in the typewriter, as if he'd started to type something and then changed his mind—and his desk diary.

It was the last thing she could look at. They must begin to wonder down there, what she was doing up above. But the diary! She couldn't leave without a quick look.

The last day's entry—the day he'd died—was very brief.

At eleven-thirty that morning, he'd had a meeting. At least an appointment had been made in Welwyn Garden City. Who with, it didn't say. Just the time and the name of the town.

But before that he'd seen two people. At least, if his diary was to be believed, he'd had appointments with them. And she knew them both.

At nine that morning, he had an appointment with Joshua. Where wasn't written. Just the time.

And at ten-thirty that morning, he had an appointment in Bromfield.

With her grandfather.

Chapter 6

Reason? There was no time to reason it out now. She closed the diary and fled towards the stairs. At the top of the stairs, she slipped on her shoes, noisily clicking her heels down the steps as if to assure them she was coming.

At the bottom of the stairs, and on the side away from the house, she saw the back door of the flat leading into the alley. She was tempted to open it and have a quick look, but decided against it. They would almost certainly hear her and wonder. Donaldson was out there keeping it under observation. She could trust Donaldson. Farnsworth had said so. He'd sounded trustworthy over the telephone too. If she could trust her instincts, that is.

She was relieved to see that Joshua hadn't left.

"Fixed it?" Laura asked in kindly tones.

"Yes. I'm so sorry. Most embarrassing."

"Nonsense, my dear! Can happen to anyone."

Laura looked her over.

"Maybe you ought to try a larger cup," she said in a motherly sort of way.

Julia blushed, the pink in her cheeks a close red to the wet colour on her lips. "Dr Samuelson," she said, "I've been meaning to see you."

"Dr Clayborne was in this morning."

"It isn't a medical problem. Oh, no! I'm dreadfully healthy."

"The best type of patient," Joshua said, turning to kiss the cheek Laura offered him. "The type I love."

"You will remember," Laura said.

"I will come, my dear. I will, I promise. But I have to go back to Hampstead for my things. After Shari leaves, keep the door locked and don't worry about a thing. You worry too much."

"I'm going to the real estate agent on the High Street. Shari will lock up and leave as usual."

"I couldn't help overhearing what you said, Dr Samuelson," Julia said, collecting her chess set, now all wrapped, by Shari, in gift-wrapping paper adorned with African masks and Indian tribal headgear staring back at her. He paused inquiringly.

"I'm going back to Hampstead myself. May I come with you? Then, perhaps, I could discuss my problem?"

"With pleasure," Joshua said.

They stepped out of the shop together, the three of them. Joshua and Julia turned towards South Kensington tube station; Laura went up the High Street.

They walked side by side. Their arms brushed in the traffic on the sidewalk. With the high heels she was wearing, she was taller than he was. He touched her on the bare arm to warn her of a passing taxi as they crossed the road; held on to it as they weaved between cars to reach the other side.

"Surest way to get killed," Joshua said. "Crossing the road in this way. I ought to know better!"

She didn't tell him about the Bentley parked around the corner. She had to talk to him, and the longest possible way home was distinctly called for.

She suggested the tube.

"Won't it be crowded?" he said mildly.

She pretended not to hear; was slightly ahead of him as they descended the escalator. She bought his ticket, waving away payment when he offered it.

By now it was the rush hour. The offices were closed or were doing so, the crowds of London-weary officegoers pouring down the escalators and the stairs as if being fed by some unseen hand into a gigantic mashing machine. Ending up on already overcrowded platforms, in both directions.

They could not talk much in the crowd on the platform. But at least she had established contact. Now she would just tag along and play it as it came. She'd told him she wanted to see him about a problem.

What if he asked?

Could she say as a writer of short stories and novels, she needed some medical advice? Something that sounded dreadfully medical to explain the victim's sudden death? Yet something simple enough for her female investigator, Shirley, to come up with—without having to be a doctor or a nurse. The problem with that was the story she'd written about was about a body in a fire! And that was too close to the truth. He'd see through her, and it would only make him suspicious. And then she'd get nothing out of him.

She could say she wanted some personal advice. The columnist, who advised the lonely and the confused in 'Woman's Heart'—which she read regularly—was forever telling them to go and talk it over with a clergyman, or rabbi, or doctor. It might work. But what if he didn't have much sympathy for the weak and the troubled? He'd, then, think of her as a dim-witted female and a scatter-brained fool! Surely a doctor wouldn't feel that way?

The simplest way really would be to allow him to pick her up.

The files had said he was a lecherous bachelor who picked up au pair girls in his pub. She wasn't bad looking was she? But what if he didn't care for English girls—the dirty old man!

I must be fair to him, she thought. He may be lecherous, but he isn't old. The full head of black hair, the small black beard and black moustache, and the turtle shell glasses all gave him a young, doctorly look. He ought to change his glasses though. The frame seemed much too big for his face. Well, maybe not. A smaller frame might make him look like a stockbroker. Heaven forbid!

The crowds massed in around them, effectively cutting off any real conversation.

"The train's going to be awfully crowded," he said, looking anxiously the length of the platform towards the tunnel from which it would appear. "We'll be lucky to get in. Maybe we should have taken the bus? Or a taxi? I would have paid for it."

"Use your elbows, Dr Samuelson," she counseled. "Don't be backward about pushing. Everything's fair on the London tube."

The trains came at less than one minute intervals—and even that was woefully insufficient for the crowds that kept pouring in through the gates and down the stairs. The trains came in full and went out even fuller.

They missed the first one. The doors opened. No one emerged. The rushing crowds bypassed them, surging around the open doors which would not close on the bodies that blocked them. So some got off, ruefully, standing close to the edge, first in line for the next one. Not quite sure where the doors would actually end up when the train came. The pushing and shoving was polite. Even when forceful.

She got on to the second train; he was lost in the surge and couldn't even reach the door. She got off the train. There was no point in going without him.

"We'll just have to fight our way in, Dr Samuelson!" she said with a touch of asperity. "Or we're just never going to get in."

"I'm trying! I'm trying! I should have brought the car. Or we should have taken a taxi. I knew it would be this way."

She felt sorry for him. He was a busy doctor. He wasn't used to this sort of travel. She could understand his reticence at elbowing past sturdy, London secretaries and white collar men with bowler hats.

"Just stay behind me," she said soothingly, patting him on the arm, a little ashamed of herself for her impatience. "Push hard! Hold me by the waist and don't let go. That way you'll be close behind. I'll clear the way."

"Charge, my dear," he said. "I'll be right behind."

And charge she did, using her elbows and her handbag to squeeze out the tiniest of footholds in the open door of the next train. He would have been left behind again, on the platform, but this time she reached forward for his arm, tugging at his coat sleeve, while he clutched at her.

The doors closed. Tried to close. Catching Joshua in the side and the back as they came to a stop. The train jerked, but would not start. The station man called out. The doors opened, tried to close again, and failed.

"You'll have to get off, sir," the station man said. "Or this here train isn't going anywhere. There now, sir, be a good sort and step off."

"Oh, no! He doesn't," Julia said, putting an arm around his back and pulling him up to her as the doors slid shut.

The train started jerkily, throwing her up against him, flattening him into the now mercifully shut doors. God! What a bloody way to travel, she thought. Even sardines had it better than this, protected as they were by the fishery laws!

They were on the Circle Line which would take them into Baker Street, seven stations away.

No one got off at Gloucester Road. The door was on the other side. More people squeezed in, and she felt the pressure on her back. She tried to protect him, but the intense pressure of bodies jammed against her threw her into his arms—and onto his toes. He winced. Her handbag, digging into his chest, popped open, and the clasp lodged itself somewhere under his chin. She snapped it shut, lowering her hand to her side.

"I'm dreadfully sorry," she whispered in his ear, which was now alongside her.

"Think no more of it," he said.

"I'll step off your toes as soon as I can make a tiny bit of room for myself. Do you think you could move one leg ever so slightly to one side so I can slip in?"

He tried by shuffling his foot, allowing her leg to slide between his; his between hers. She breathed easier. At least she could keep her feet down without stamping all over his feet.

If his toes hurt, he didn't feel it, because Joshua had problems of his own. The burly labourer standing next to him, turned sharply to make room for himself, nudging Joshua hard in the ribs below the armpit. Joshua winced in pain, bringing his hand up to protect himself. He had intended to place his hand between the burly man's elbow and his chest, but the train took a sharp bend throwing Julia forward into him. He put out the palm of his hand and the open fingers to steady her—into the fullness of her breast.

No one could move anymore. Except the train, and it swayed them back and forth at its will, sometimes drawing her away from him, never breaking contact, teasingly releasing some of the pressure on his hand and on her breast, only to slam her body back into his. She found her thigh was between his; his between hers.

"I'm so sorry," he whispered. "I really am!"

"It's not your fault," she said. "Not much we can do about it, except be as comfortable as we can in this sardine tin!"

At High Street Kensington, the compartment could not have held and additional diminutive pygmy. Six people got on. Movement was impossible. So was talk. Only awareness; both of them erupting into an awareness of each other. At first it was sexual. His hand had meant to steady her body at the waist; instead it was wedged underneath her breast and cupping it. And each time the train rocked, he pummeled it. He felt her body tremble. Was it against her wishes? Would she despise him for it? The engorged nipple rested firmly in the palm of his hand, unwilling to pierce it when the train rammed her up against him, retreating crushed into the breast that bore it, unwilling to break contact when the train relieved the pressure on it, reasserting itself into his palm when she was drawn away.

Her thigh pressed into him in the groin, sending waves of pleasure surging through him. Surging into her too. Common waves that lashed them both. And no relief. Not at Notting Hill Gate, nor at Bayswater.

She was glad he couldn't look into her eyes. They would have given away the excitement within her. The rocking of the train, like a regular heartbeat, timed the surges of pleasure that throbbed and pulsated within her without her consent. She knew when to expect his hand to pummel her, and first she found herself anticipating it;

then, surprised at herself, even breathing hard so that she met it halfway.

Paddington provided no relief from the tension. Not Edgware Road either. Both had fallen silent, abandoning themselves to their closeness.

That is when awareness arose. It came simultaneously, like a joyous act, to the both of them. She realised, for the first time, that she was almost in his arms. Her hand encircled him, not around his slender waist, but around his back, the fingers spread out to protect him from the door behind him. His cheek was barely a hair's width away from hers. At times her hair brushed past his lips; she could feel the warm, sharply drawn breath on it. She had her moment of annoyance too, not against the silent, coldly withdrawn people that pressed into her from all sides except the front—she felt a warm gratitude to them for sharing the compartment with her and Joshua—but against the chess set and the handbag which constrained her other hand to her side. There was a moment of panic too, when she smelt the touch of an after-shave fragrance emanating from his cheeks, above the beard, and the back of his neck. Had she dabbed perfume that morning on her throat and behind her ears? It subsided with memory that reassured her. Not only had she used it that morning, as she always did, but she'd retouched her face with it after having her sandwich and carton of milk on the way to Hampstead.

His awareness was more muted, because it was tinged with uncertainty and guilt. He, too, was aware she was in his arms; he could feel her heartbeat on his chest, but when, accidentally, their cheeks had touched as the train had swerved round a particularly vicious bend, had she drawn away? The brown hair, stray wisps of it, had glued themselves to his wet lips.

And the awareness had arisen—Julia could not explain it—at least in her, not in the privacy of her own bedroom or sunbathing on the French Riviera—and she'd tried so hard there—but standing in a crowded Circle Line train, fully dressed, and surrounded by friendly strangers.

At Baker Street, the doors opened, ejecting them both onto the platform. Julia buttoned up her blouse, that had unbuttoned itself in the crush three buttons more than would be appropriate even for a warm day. Joshua straightened his tie.

She smiled to put him at his ease, for he dared not look into her eyes. Her smile was reassuring. She helped to brush the dust off his jacket; he held her handbag and the chess set while she straightened her skirt.

At Baker Street they changed to the Jubilee Line, for Finchley Road. It wasn't crowded leaving Central London, and they found two seats side by side. Neither said anything. His shoulder touched hers, and he half expected her to draw away; instead she relaxed towards him.

Julia smiled at him, silently. And he smiled back.

At Finchley Road tube station, reason returned to her.

If he'd got a little pleasure with his hand on her breast and his thigh between hers, good luck to him. She wasn't entirely blameless, she decided. But there wasn't any point in becoming involved with him. She had a job to do; that is why she was with him. To find out what it was he knew that was so important, Saul had sent a RED ALERT and then been murdered. Implicating him. She had to protect him too. But only because agents from other sides were equally interested in what he knew and might reach him first. He posed a risk to himself. They would not hesitate to harm him, and that would never do. At least not until he told her what she wanted to know.

But when she had what she wanted from him, she wasn't concerned with him. Farnsworth had made that quite clear. She could just walk away from him.

"Would you care to have a drink?" he said.

"I'd love that," she replied.

Leaving the tube station, he offered her his arm and she took it. An act of courtesy. It was a fine evening for a walk.

Neither spoke for some time. The pub was on the other side of the street from the tube station, lying between Finchley Road and Swiss Cottage. They crossed the road without haste, walking leisurely—almost slowly—towards the pub, her heels clicking on the cobbled pavement, speech between them non-existent. Their sounding footsteps, sometimes in unison sometimes in discord, made up for it; his quieter footfall allaying the anxiety in her disquieting ones.

In the distance they saw the signboard with the familiar sign of the evening star, after which the pub had been named. Her hand had crept forward so that her fingers lay lightly on the back of his hand. Sometimes their shoulders bumped in a friendly sort of way.

"May I ask you a question?" Joshua said.

"Of course."

"Why do you carry a gun in your handbag?"

Chapter 7

Julia knew the Evening Star well. She had been in it before often enough, though not on the regular basis that made it Joshua's home in the evening and on the weekends.

It was a fine pub. With good beer. A friendly place, filled mainly with Indians and Pakistanis and Irishmen, who were the regulars. Some English too, who found they enjoyed their drinking in the frenzied babel of foreign tongues emanating from pockets in the room. Some had been to the Far East; others had not. Some had even lived there. Most of the regulars knew each other, at least by sight. Some drank in groups, fierce arguments erupting on volatile matters—such as the idiocy of the government, Indian, Pakistani, Irish or English, depending on which pocket you were in. Some drank together. Others drank alone, filled with their own sadness, until they'd had a few and then even they'd been known to sing.

All of them very English in their love of strong English beer.

There were quarrels sometimes, but nobody seemed to get hurt. Threatening gestures and a few swear words in a language that meant nothing to anyone except the one who swore, seemed sufficient to resolve most disputes. An Irishman, once, had been ejected from the Evening Star, because when he'd had a few, he insisted on climbing over the counter to kiss the barmaids. All of them. Since the Guv'nor of the pub was Irish, and all the barmaids were Irish too, he didn't scream 'discrimination'!

The curving L-shaped counter hemmed the girls in, and John—the Guv'nor—kept them in line. There was a flat above the pub, they slept in after closing time, and he made sure they had valid reasons for being away. Dating drinking regulars, at that late hour, was not a valid reason. But he did turn a blind eye to the soft touch of fingers as the beer changed hands. Joshua had decided a long time ago that they, not he, were all lonely people trying very hard to be happy. Even succeeding sometimes as he heard the deep-throated Irish laughter mingle with the higher pitched Asian sounds. Not too many Africans drank at the Evening Star. Except Jomo Mbangeli.

There weren't too many au pair girls either at that time of the day. They would come later in the evening.

Joshua guided Julia to the corner bench that ran alongside the wall. They could sit together; yet talk facing one another. He bought two light ales; then settled back for a long draw on it, licking the froth off his lips with his tongue.

He seemed in no hurry for a reply.

Joshua's brother, Joe, came up to greet them. It gave her a little more time.

"How does my brother always end up with the pretty ones?" Joe said. "Don't tell me! I know. Because he's the doctor in the family. The intelligent one!"

Joshua introduced them. Julia thought she saw a resemblance. The moustache and beard were patterned after Joshua's; even their builds were close. But they were not twins. Joe was three years younger than Joshua, and his hair was wavier and better groomed.

Joe left them, and without as much as a 'by your leave' returned with two cherry brandies.

"Is that for me?" Julia said. "Thanks."

"My brother's friends are always my friends," Joe said. Then he disappeared.

"Is he always so generous?" Julia asked. "Or is he repaying favours?"

"Both. I help him out when he has a date. It eases the financial strain of the evening, for him. But I think, today, maybe one of his horses came in. That's why he can afford to do likewise. He's not very lucky with the horses. Of late you'd think he'd been playing all the lame ones! But he's generous—when he can afford it."

"It pays to be generous, does it?"

"At this time of the evening, yes," Joshua said, raising his glass to her. "Girls like generosity in a man. It makes them generous too."

"I see."

"Don't be critical, Julia. It's one way to be alive."

"Did I sound critical? I didn't mean to be. Perhaps a little sad." Julia sipped Joe's cherry brandy, thinking furiously. It wouldn't be long before he came back with his question again. He seemed in no hurry. Almost as if he was enjoying through his beer, the indecisions that criss-crossed through her eyes.

"Aren't you going to ask me again?" she said finally, when she couldn't stand his avoidance of it.

"Yes. But you don't have to answer. There are no conditions to the evening. But I would like to know though. Is it loaded?"

"Yes. But the safety catch is on. I'm a sort of policewoman. Special Service, sort of. I do have a license for it."

"A copper! A female copper! Is that what you are? A copperina!" He pretended to choke on his beer.

"Must you use such a horrible word for me?"

"It's the very first time I've had a drink with a female policewoman. Of sorts. I shall just have to watch myself all evening. Now look, what happened in the train wasn't my fault. There was this burly chap next to me, and he had his elbow in my ribs. I only brought my hand up because it hurt and before I knew it your—you were up against me. Honest!"

"Dr Samuelson," she said, stopping him. "May we be serious? May I talk about my problem? The one I told you about in the shop?"

"But of course, my dear. I'm sorry to have forgotten all about it. That's why we're here? Why you're having this drink with me? What is the problem?"

"You."

"I beg your pardon."

"You. You're my problem."

"I don't understand," Joshua said, holding the cherry brandy up to the light. "It must be the cherry brandy. It has to be. I hope Joe has not been spiking it. I'm supposed to be intelligent."

"I told you I was a policewoman—of sorts. I've been assigned to protect you."

"From what? Who from?"

"I don't really know," Julia said, sounding both appealing and confused at the same time. "But you can help me find out."

"And how do I do that?"

"Just tell me everything you know."

"Everything? About what? Do you want to know my life history from the time I was born in Durban? That will take an awful long time. And there are parts of it I'm ashamed of and would rather forget. Do I tell you all of them too?"

Julia sighed and returned to her beer. This is going to be very difficult, she thought, with a tinge of exasperation. How did one get a man to talk? They didn't cover that too well in the Service Handbook. And what little it said had to do with making enemy agents talk—not some one whose body had so pleasurably crushed yours in a crowded tube train and who was now having a drink with you. But she had thought about it. And she'd worked it out for herself. There were three ways.

A man might talk when he was drunk. Spill it all out without even knowing it—or wanting to. But success could not be guaranteed. His capacity for liquor might be a darned sight more than hers. Probably was, with the sort of hours he kept in the Evening Star. Besides, deep down, he must want to talk.

He might tell her what she wanted to know out of gratitude. It was the way Vladimir had wanted to try in Johannesburg. She had been responsible for bringing him in—enticing him across the border from Mozambique. British and South African Intelligence, working together, interrogated him. He was a balding, middle-aged man. A quiet, peaceful sort of fellow, looking more like a rotund greengrocer than a spy. It was hardly the image she'd projected for a top Russian agent working with ANC forces in Mozambique. He was tough in his own quiet sort of way. He answered all their questions with civility—and gave nothing away.

They had to know—and he wouldn't talk.

That was why, she decided, with considerable admiration, he was one of their best. He took everything Farnsworth dished out to him—all of Farnsworth's well-tried, psychological inducements and punishments, alternately administered—and no signs of cracking.

Farnsworth tried everything; the South Africans were getting impatient—and Vladimir would not talk.

They held him captive in a small house outside of Johannesburg. It was her first assignment. She learned a lot from it.

"So my friends, this is the end, is it?" Vladimir said with a smile, passing his hand over his bald head, a gesture, she later found Farnsworth to have imbibed from him.

"I'm afraid so, Vladimir," Farnsworth said.

"Don't feel so bad about it, Farnsworth. I slipped up and this dear girl got me. I can only admire her for it—and I do. Your treatment of me has been excellent. I have no complaints. I would have treated you in much the same way had I picked you up in Budapest or Warsaw. With one little difference. Here you have no control. So now you turn me over to them?"

"Yes. And I have to tell you, it will not be pleasant. They will use methods, we abhor. Perhaps because what you know is so much more important to them than to us. After all, we are in their part of the world. And you will talk—eventually. Take my advice, Vladimir. Get out of this mess alive. We'll take care of everything. Safe passage to England. Political asylum. A house in Kent, perhaps. The usual amenities. I promise you. Just a few simple answers to a few simple questions. Yes?"

"It is a very tempting offer," Vladimir said. "And I might even accept. But only because of the very charming Miss Julia here. I have been watching you these past few days—as I have over the whole of this past year. What a pleasure and a joy it has been! I don't even know whether I almost wished to be caught by her. No!

No! That is not fair to her. I withdraw the remark. Strike it from your records."

"I don't understand," Farnsworth said, feeling his way slowly. "Are you trying to tell me something?"

"Then let me come right out and say it. I first saw Miss Julia in Beira. I could have had her picked up straightaway—and I didn't. Why?"

Vladimir threw up his hands as if he, too, was uncertain of the answer.

"We saw through your cover almost immediately. Your credentials were impeccable. That is what set us thinking. A reporter for the London Times? Reporting on the Russian presence in Mozambique? I ask you! No agent could possibly get away with so sensitive a cover. But then I have an advantage. Look at the way Miss Julia looks. I look like a greengrocer. Put an apron round this big waist of mine, and you would soon find yourself buying green beans from me. But Miss Julia? And with her breeding? We could never be quite sure, you understand, and you might even have got away with it, Miss Julia, but we, too, have moles in MI-6—the less said the better."

Vladimir paused. He was the only one who was at ease in the room.

"I could have had her picked up—and I didn't. Because, Farnsworth, I enjoyed being with her. Each day I said:

Tomorrow there will be plenty of time to reel her in; let me have a quiet lunch with her today."

He covered her hand with both of his own. She did not withdraw it.

"This past year has been the most pleasurable, the most exciting, the most memorable year of my life. Can you believe that? I want you to believe it. For the first time I have felt emotions, I never knew existed. I woke up each morning plotting how I would thrust myself into your company. All those meetings we had, you can't believe they were accidental?"

Julia was silent.

"Whatever happens, I would like you to know, I have no regrets. None whatever. And were we to start this past year all over again in Beira, I would play it just the way I did. No matter now if I die, I will at least have known what it is to be in love. I should be ashamed to say it—a balding, middle-aged man of almost fifty—but I am not."

Farnsworth fidgeted uneasily in his chair. He signalled Julia to leave the room, but she ignored him. She patted the hands that held hers.

"Why don't you tell me what you want to know?" she said gently. "I would like you to live."

He withdrew his hands and sat upright in his chair.

"I have all the information you want, Julia," he said, tapping his forehead above his right eye. "Dates, times, places. Not only of the thrust through Mozambique, but through Namibia and Zimbabwe as well. The names of Russian military advisers, military strengths, number of field divisions. Supporting artillery. Everything."

He stopped talking. No one moved. Farnsworth looked like he was hewn from white marble. Julia was frozen too.

Only Vladimir seemed comfortable and relaxed. In control. Not overly anxious to proceed. Settling himself back into the hard-backed chair they had provided for him, smiling at them.

"But this is not the place to tell. Let us have a quiet dinner somewhere. You know Johannesburg better than I do. All I have seen are satellite photographs of it—and this room. You pick the restaurant. A bottle of champagne. I will pay for it all, of course! Then, perhaps, we can go to your apartment here in Johannesburg—and I will tell you all. I promise. I will not try to run away. I could have done that a long time ago, if I had wanted to. They can follow us around, if they want to. Put a guard outside the apartment too."

The silence was heart-stopping.

"While you and I, Julia, are in it."

"I don't know," Julia said. "This is all so sudden. I had no idea it would turn out this way."

"Out of the question," Farnsworth shouted, bouncing out of his rigidity. "Quite impossible! The British Government would never agree to such a preposterous arrangement!"

"The British Government isn't involved," Julia said.

"You had better leave the room, my dear," Farnsworth said, holding the door open for her. "I think your part in this assignment has come to an end."

She had left the room without argument or protest. And now that hurt. She had seen the sentence almost framed in Farnsworth's eyes:

"If I, an Englishman and a gentleman, can't have you, why should this Russian bastard have you?"

Farnsworth turned him over to South African Intelligence and washed British involvement of the whole affair. That evening they took the flight out of Johannesburg to London.

Three days later, Vladimir's broken, hacked up body was handed over to the Russians on the border with Mozambique.

And unfortunate accident was the only official comment.

Then there was silence until Saul sent to Johannesburg to report, confirmed what they could only have guessed.

He had been closeted with Slagter for two days—and he had talked. Freely.

He had been a nice man. She might not have been ecstatic that night—she had never been ecstatic with Saul either—but it would have saved his life. If only he had asked her privately? With Farnsworth out of the room. Would she have asked Farnsworth's advice? And what would she have decided in the matter—given free choice? Even now she could not honestly answer the question, had it been posed then.

There had been no choice then. But if it ever happened again, she knew what the answer would be. The British Government or MI-6 or Farnsworth would have nothing to do with it. It was her body. She would do with it as she pleased.

And then there was the third way a man might talk. Out of fear. If only she could convince Joshua his life was in danger. He was a doctor. Death, probably, held no fears for him. But if it was going to be a slow and painful one, would he be more cooperative?

In all cases though, deep down, he must want to talk.

"You seem to have lost interest in your problem," Joshua said. "That's not very flattering. Just when I was beginning to feel important. Are you really protecting me?"

"Yes, Joshua," she said, and if either noticed she'd called him differently, neither showed it. "And unless you tell me all you know, I won't know how to help you."

"Well, then, ask whatever it is you wish to ask, my dear. I'll tell you everything you want to know. About anything you want to know. I won't hide a thing. Or tell a single untruth, I promise. Fire away."

"You will?"

"Yes. Isn't that what you want from me?"

"No conditions?"

"Conditions? No. Why should there be?"

"Aren't you going to make some outrageous demands for telling us what we want to know?"

"No, I'm not. Who's us?"

She ignored the question. This was going to be easy. Much easier than she'd expected. Maybe it was the liquor! He was just begging to loosen up and spill it all out. Brushing aside his protestations, that it was his evening and he'd pay for it all, she went to the bar and bought another round for them.

"Why did Saul die?"

"I don't know," Joshua said. "He wasn't meant to, I don't think."

"You don't think it was accidental, then?"

"No. Someone burnt him after he was dead. I won't know for sure until I have the results of the autopsy. They are expected soon. May even have come in today. I can't be sure. Clayborne was his doctor and they may be with him. He's in today looking after all of our patients. He's had his vacation—and I'm on mine. I feel like a kid who's been let out of school for the hols! Do you ever have that feeling?"

"Very often. Why? Why should someone kill him and then burn him up so badly afterwards. It had nothing to do with identification—or they'd have smashed his jaws in too!"

"Good thinking, Julia. And an interesting question. But I, honestly, don't know. Neither as his doctor, nor as his friend."

"Did he have any medical problems?" Julia persisted. "Incurable cancer? A painful end in sight? That sort of thing."

"Saul? Medical problems? He was healthy as a horse. A darned sight healthier than some of the ones Joe's been putting his money on! You're way off target, dear girl, if you think it was a medical problem. Besides, if I knew about it, so did Clayborne. Go and see him. He'll be in, even though there's no surgery this evening. He's always in the surgery. Here are the keys to it. Let yourself in. You know Clayborne well enough to take him into your confidence about whatever it is that's bothering you and about which you haven't told me a darned thing."

"Well then, I will," she said. "What if he's not in. Can I see Saul's file? Do you have the key to the filing cabinets? I know where they are, behind Amelia's desk. Give me the both of them."

"Conditions! Conditions!" he said, his eyes dancing with amusement, as he handed over his keys. There were several keys to the ring. The key to his apartment and the keys to his car as well. She hesitated to take them all. He held up the key to the surgery and the smaller one to the filing cabinet, for visual inspection; then dropped the bunch into her handbag, not bothering to look into it as she clicked it shut.

They heard the metallic sound as the keys hit the gun.

"How are you going to get home?" she said. "And what about your car? How can you drive?"

"Joe will take me home. He has a key to my apartment. And I certainly don't intend to drive anywhere after all this."

He waved his hands at the empty glasses that littered the table between them. "And besides," he said, leaning forward mischievously, "this will give us an opportunity to get together again. After all you will want to return my keys to me, won't you?"

"Oh, Joshua, you're impossible! All right, I'll take them all. But don't hold me responsible if you spend the night on the street because you can't get into your flat. Or find yourself taking the London tube more often than you want to."

"Only with you, my dear," he said piously, bringing another suffusing glow back to her face.

"Well, if it isn't anything medical, then it must be something else you know," Julia said.

"Why do you keep coming back to me? What do I know about what is troubling you?"

"Because, my love, you were one of the few people he saw on that last day—the day he died. Did he say anything that was significant? Think back, Joshua! Why did he see you that morning?"

"He didn't."

"What do you mean by 'he didn't'?" Julia said with some heat. "He saw you at nine that morning. Before going on to Bromfield and then onto Welwyn Garden City. It's in his diary."

"How did you see his diary? Ah! I understand. The broken bra strap. In order to see his diary? Julia ! Julia!"

"I'm sorry, Joshua," Julia said, searching his eyes for understanding. "But I am a policewoman—of sorts. I did tell you that."

"Never mind. The man's dead. What difference does it make to him who sees his diary! But he didn't see me that morning. For sure."

"You're lying, Joshua," she said quietly.

"I'm lying? Well, that's a nice, healthy way to start a warm and trusting relationship. Why would I lie? If the man came to see me, I'd say so. I was in the surgery that morning, well before nine. I was doing Clayborne's share of the work load, seeing he was on vacation. Amelia will bear me out. Go ask her."

"I withdraw the remark," she said. "It must be the liquor. I'm saying things I wouldn't normally say. Will you forgive me?"

"Come on, Julia. That isn't necessary either. But you have to believe me. I want you to believe me! I didn't see him at nine that morning. But the odd thing is that Laura thought so too. He told her he was going to see me—and he didn't. Why?"

"Laura?"

"Saul's widow. I had lunch with her today. She's a very old friend. She was on at me in the same way. What had he seen me about that morning? Now at least she has some excuse to keep on at me. Some chap called Slagter has been writing her notes about me. But why you keep on at me, I'll never know."

"Slagter! He sent her a note? What did it say?"

"Nothing important. Some sort of stupid warning. To keep away from me. He obviously doesn't know Laura at all, because it had just the opposite effect on her. She threw me a fast one about being scared for her life—and asked me to move in with her for a few days."

"Will you? Are you going to?"

"What? Move in with her? I don't know. Would you advise me to?"

Julia drained her light ale. Threw back her hair and knocked off the remainder of the cherry brandy, tipping the glass and her neck back to do it, swiftly weighing her own emotions, demanding answers from herself—and receiving only one. "No, Joshua. I would not advise you to move in with her. Donaldson and I are going to find it very difficult to protect you, with customers moving in and out of the shop."

"Is that the only reason? Because you, and who, will find it difficult to protect me?"

She ignored the question.

"And who's Donaldson?"

She ignored that too.

"I thought this was all some sort of joke. Made me feel important. But you're deadly serious. That I'm in danger?"

"I'm deadly serious, Joshua. Do you know why I'm sure you're involved in Saul's death in some way?"

He nodded miserably.

"I shouldn't really be telling you, but I will. Saul sent a message before he died."

"Who to?"

"South African National Intelligence"

"Really? What did it say?"

"It was in code. A RED ALERT! Insisting they make you talk. You're the only one who will know!"

"Is that what he sent? You're sure? I was the only one who would know? Interesting. Know what?"

"That's what we're trying to find out, Joshua."

"Who's we?"

"I can't tell you. I've told you too much already. More than I should have!"

"Why?"

"Why, what?" Julia said, feeling the conversation slip away from beneath her. He had that way of talking. Skipping away into matters that weren't relevant.

"Why have you told me more than you should have?" Joshua demanded. "Is it because you've had too much to drink, or because you were standing on my toes pressed up against me in the London tube?"

"Could be a bit of both," Julia said, the flush coming back into her cheeks. "I'm sorry about standing on your toes."

"Think no more of it, dear girl. I haven't felt so close to a woman in years. My hand could feel your heart beat—and a lot more besides. I even took your pulse, by timing the throb in your vein at the base of the neck. Almost a hundred, but that was only to be expected in the circumstances, so you don't need a prescription. Just keep on doing what you're doing, would be the doctor's advice."

"Joshua, my love," she said, and she realised it was the second time that evening she'd used the phrase. Perhaps, after so many drinks, he hadn't noticed. "Will you please concentrate on what's important. Why would Saul have sent such a message?"

"I haven't the faintest idea. Maybe he was wrong? Or maybe he went insane before he died? And now he has all of you on me for no damn reason at all! I don't even know what it is I'm supposed to know. Anyone knows you can't get blood from a turnip!"

"Slagter can," Julia said, feeling the desperation in her voice and unable to control it. "Empty a person of it too. A CIA agent in Miami was one of his victims. She was a trained agent. Not someone like you. She was cut up so badly, you wouldn't believe it. The post mortem showed she'd been drained of all her blood before she died."

"Now you're only trying to frighten me," Joshua said. "And damm it, you're succeeding. I'm a coward. I'll admit it freely. But how, in God's name, can I tell you what I don't know—if I don't know it?"

She felt sorry for him. His voice had risen. He put the beer mug back on the table with a trembling hand. Why did one always think it was women who were afraid, she thought. Men could be afraid too. She steadied his trembling hand with her own. He clutched at her fingers, clasping them unashamedly on the table between them.

"All right, Joshua," she said. "I believe you. Let's say you don't know. So then we look around to find out what it is they think you know."

"Great! Except that I don't know that either."

"Joshua, my dear, I'm only trying to help."

"Why? Why are you trying to help?"

"Let's just say, it's for all the drinks you've bought me this evening. I like to pay my debts. This cherry brandy is expensive."

"Joe bought that."

"Well then, for the beer."

"You bought one round. Of the two we've had."

"Must you be so picky?" She withdrew her hand from his, gently, sliding along the bench as she got up from the table. She opened her handbag, checked it, snapped it shut; then slung it around her shoulder.

"Where are you going? Leaving already?"

"To talk to Dr Clayborne. I'll ask for Saul's medical records. I'll borrow them and let our experts in forensics have a look at them. Maybe they'll stumble on to something."

"So now you're saying I'm a lousy doctor too."

"Only taking a second opinion, Dr Samuelson. Isn't that what you would advise all your patients?"

"You're absolutely right, Julia," Joshua said, tickled by her reply. "And what happens to me in the meantime? Who's going to protect me while you're raiding my surgery? You can't go off the job just like that, you know? It isn't a nine to five thing. Or is it?"

"You'll be all right."

"I could be murdered."

"Here? In a pub?"

"Well, it's possible. Isn't it?"

"Don't worry. I've taken care of that too." She was about to reassure him, when she saw the difficulty he was having in controlling his laughter. The black eyes flashed wickedly as he allowed his hand to tremble reaching for his beer mug.

"Aren't you going to steady the tremble in my hand?" he said. "Or is it all over?"

"Oh, Joshua! You're terrible! I'll steady many a tremble in your hand, if you'll only be serious for a moment! I do have a person watching you constantly. His name is Donaldson. He works for me. So don't be nervous, if you find someone tailing you. As you found out this afternoon. The man leaning against the window of the shoe store? That was Donaldson. He called me and told me how upset you were at him. Quite hurt him you did."

"I had a patient once," Joshua said, returning to his now empty glass and deliberating whether he ought to get one himself or signal Joe for another round. "His name was Donaldson too. Thomas Donaldson. Poor chap! He was such a nice fellow. He would keep chatting away, non-stop, even when I was examining him. He loved to talk. He was Welsh, but he'd spent his childhood in India. Made him a delight. I think that is why he chose to come on my list. Gave him a chance to be nostalgic about the places he knew in Bombay—the Marine Drive where he'd lived, and the Elphinstone College where he'd been educated, and the Crawford Market where he'd bought his fish and fruit. Why don't you introduce me to him? If your Mr Donaldson is as nice as mine was, we'll get on famously."

Julia leaned down across the table. Almost over him. For the first time that evening, she felt lost. A dreadful feeling of being used came over her. The lights had gone out, leaving her groping towards him.

He had signalled to Joe she was leaving, inviting his brother to come over and join him, waving his empty beer mug in the air, suggesting that a refill might be in order.

"Joshua, why did you say 'poor chap'? And why do you keep talking of him in the past? What happened to your Mr Donaldson? Joshua! You're not listening to me!"

"Sorry, my dear. I thought you were leaving. Have you changed your mind? Shall I ask Joe to buy you another? He has actually gone to the bar to get me another round! Did you see that? One of his horses must have come in. Today, I shall make him pay. Nice rhyme. I like it. It gives me a chance to get back all the times I've seen him through."

"Tell me about Donaldson, Joshua. Please!" The urgency in her voice seemed to sober him a little. His attention moved back to her. After craning to make sure Joe had actually gone to the bar and not just disappeared.

"Ah, yes, Donaldson. The poor chap was murdered a few years ago. I don't remember the exact date or anything, but I hadn't been long with Clayborne when it happened. It all came out at the inquest. The poor chap was on drugs. That surprised me because I didn't know anything about it—and I should have. So I took a little more interest in the case, than otherwise. Besides I liked the chap."

"What happened?"

"The inquest was held up in Welwyn Garden City. I remember that well, because Clayborne and I had to drive up there for it, and that made Clayborne very angry. Half a day lost. Patients screaming blue murder. Fortunately Amelia always holds the fort. That woman's a gem! Where was I?"

"You went to Welwyn Garden City for the inquest."

"Oh, yes. Well the evidence was murky. To say the least. Even to suggest it!"

"Joshua, will you tell me what happened?"

"I thought I was, my dear," Joshua said mildly. "Apparently he broke into a surgery in Welwyn Garden City to steal controlled drugs. The doctor wasn't in, but his woman was. She thought she was going to be attacked, so she said, and shot him with a hunting rifle. Jane was her name. I remember. Jane Timmons. Self defense, they said. Poor Donaldson. He wouldn't have hurt anyone."

Julia could hardly bring herself to ask. "And the doctor? Whose surgery it was? What was his name?"

"I think it was Farnsworth. Yes, that's right, William Farnsworth. He has a general practice up there. He was born in South Africa, but was educated here in England. It all came out at the inquest. His live-in also doubles as his nurse. She was born there too. In Port Elizabeth, I think. They got off, if you ask me! Murder it was. But what he was doing in their surgery is beyond me? Why are you asking me all this, Julia? Have I helped? Will I see you again?"

Julia did not see anything or anybody, as she made for the door. She did not answer Joshua either. Elbowing her way past the standing drinkers in the now crowded pub, flattening herself to get through between men of all sizes. An overcrowded pub. Filled with slightly merry people, hardly paying any attention to her. Making themselves heard to each other, and sometimes to themselves, over the din of frenzied speech, foreign tongues and sloshing beer. A piano player was belting out some old favourites in the far corner, away from the door, and beer drinkers in the public bar—they had been in the private one—where the beer was pennies cheaper, were drifting in to join in the singing. It was that time of night when the action would liven up without the end of the evening in sight. Towards the end more sobering reflections would descend on those not completely inebriated, while those that were would be past caring.

But at this time, all were in the mood for more.

They paid no attention to the swift glances she threw around her. She was looking for a Welsh voice to stop her and say: What shall I do now, Miss Julia? But none stopped her.

And she had no eyes for much else. Except Donaldson.

So she did not see the tall, well-built, handsome African who brushed past her on his way to the bar.

Chapter 8

Jomo Mbangeli seemed to fit naturally into every surrounding. When he was in the Ciskei, he wore a red blanket, and lived in a kraal, and consulted the medicine man and Tikoloshe, the water sprite, about making sacrifices to his dead ancestors. And when he was in London, he wore a three-piece suit, with a tie, and drank beer at the Evening Star with Joshua. His English was perfect, with a well modulated Oxford accent which occasionally broke when he was excited. Or drunk. The sensitive black face, with large lips and short curly hair, had a scar down each cheek. His students at King's could easily visualize him, with a red doek and a red blanket, carrying an assegai, and the image lent authenticity to his lectures in African studies.

Like Joshua, he felt genuinely comfortable in his adopted England. Unlike his brother Boko, who being elder to him was still the head of the family.

Jomo placed the drinks on the table before Joshua, slipping easily into the seat that Julia had occupied, with a grace that came easily to the African hunter. He leaned forward confidentially. "Pretty girl. Who's she?"

"Someone I picked up. Someone on Clayborne's list; not mine. Very English. Very young too. Well, maybe not that young."

"You're not very good at lying, Joshua. At least not to me. Who's the girl?"

"I don't really know her. She says she's a policewoman—of sorts."

"What did she want?"

"I couldn't quite gather. A few questions about Saul's death. Nothing that really concerns us."

"Anything that concerns Saul concerns me," Jomo said, jabbing Joshua with his finger. Not too lightly.

"I'm sorry, Jomo," Joshua said, touching him lightly on the hand. "I really am."

Jomo's eyes filled. Joshua pretended not to notice; glared into his beer, and looked around for Joe. Where was Joe when he needed him? But Joe had spotted a couple of au pair girls coming in, and couldn't be bothered. He and Joshua both knew the game pretty well. Nothing would come of it, if eye contact wasn't established quickly enough. For that you had to be close. If not, others would soon horn in, and the field would narrow rapidly as the losers trailed off. They had an honour among them. If one or two—preferably two—could strike up a conversation and buy the girls a round, the others accepted failure with envious resignation and retreated to a safe distance. The winners paid for the evening, and at closing time, would more likely be left at the bar, while the girls said firm goodbyes—leaving behind telephone numbers which, if dialed, gave the correct time and little else; one girl with a grotesque sense of humor had left Joe the number of the local mortuary—disappearing towards the tube station.

Yet once in a while.

Jomo saw Joshua's eyes wander; inspite of the pain he could not resist a smile. It was a game he did not play.

Joshua returned to Jomo, guiltily, sternly reminding himself he was in no mood for such distractions.

"I could have saved him that day, Joshua. I will never forgive myself."

"He came to see you before he died?"

"Of course. As always on Tuesday. Tuesday was our night. He never failed to come unless he was out of town or Laura was unwell. Even at the sound of the doorbell, I sensed that something was wrong—it pealed long and hard—and when he put his arms around me and we went to bed, I was sure of it. He was so excited as if he was on to something important. He wanted to tell me—and he couldn't. He told me everything in bed, Joshua. It was the one weakness he had; the feeling of absolute power in sharing top secret information with a lover! To him, it was like no feeling on Earth. It was impossible to restrain him after that."

"What sort of things?"

"Everything that made for exciting telling. Anything that made the evening emotional and memorable! Sometimes it was the thrill in him and sometimes it was the hurt."

Joshua did not speak.

"You don't believe me, do you?"

"Why should I not believe you? I have no reason to doubt you. Why would you lie to me about a thing like this?"

"But you still don't believe, Saul shared his innermost thoughts with me? Let me see. What shall I tell you that only you think you know?"

Joshua sat up slowly.

"Shall I tell you, for instance, where you were on that last evening before we left Durban? Before you drove down to the Ciskei to fetch Ewa for us?"

Joshua glanced around him. The Welsh accent on the seat along the bench that skirted the wall had been unmistakable. Joshua had not bothered when he talked but when he felt the silence he turned to look. The man had his back towards him, gripping the mug in front. He couldn't see the felt hat, but it could have been safely tucked away underneath the seat. As long as he was talking, he could not overhear; they were safe. But when they fell silent, Jomo had to be cut off in conversation.

"I'll tell you anyway," Jomo said. "You and Laura were on the beach, twenty miles south of Durban. A deserted beach. And there she stripped naked for you. And you made love to her on the sand. Do you know how much that hurt him? He told it me in bed that night. And I consoled him. He should never have married Laura. He should have given her to you—if she was willing. A man like Saul was meant to be free."

"She wasn't willing. And we didn't make love—as you say. She came to say goodbye."

"That's not how it seemed to him up there on the shoulder of the cliff, crouched in the undergrowth, watching you two on the sands below. You fondled her. She didn't object. She encouraged it. And then she swam, nude, in the water, while you tended her clothes. You helped her to dress, hooking together the cups of her bra which opened in front; you zipped up the back of the cotton dress she was wearing—the colour was light-green—and you still say you didn't make love to her?"

"Stop it! I don't want to hear any more. Or you will be drinking alone."

"Poor Joshua! You do believe me, don't you? He told me everything in bed, including what happened to your Mr Thomas Donaldson. Yet he didn't tell me that day, what he was craving to tell. Why?"

"Don't blame yourself, Jomo. Even if he had, you might not have been able to save him. It could have been unrelated to his dying."

"No! It was something important. I know it! I begged him to tell me, but he wouldn't, because he said, he wanted to protect me. From what? What is that endangered me, if I knew it? And then his beautiful body so captivated me—as mine did his—it didn't seem important anymore. But he told you when he came to see you the next morning. Why?"

"He came to see me? He didn't see me the next morning. Here we go again. You're the third person who's convinced I saw Saul that morning—when I didn't. What makes you think I saw him?"

"Because he told me he intended to see you the next morning at nine. What about, he wouldn't say. I had no reason to disbelieve him. He didn't come?"

"No. And this is not even funny anymore. If he couldn't tell you anything, why would he tell me?"

"Because he wanted to protect me."

"And I wasn't that important? Is that it?"

"I didn't mean it that way, Josh."

"Not to worry, Jomo. It doesn't hurt. Neither does his death. Not in the way it hurts you. He may have told the whole goddam world he was seeing me at nine that morning, but he didn't."

"Is that what you told the girl?"

"Yes. I don't know what it is I'm supposed to know."

"Boko doesn't think so. He wants to see you. Now."

"Tell him, I'm busy. Dammit, I'm a doctor. We're supposed to be busy people. Tell him to go to hell."

"He knows you're on vacation. Clayborne came back today. From Nice. He's the head of the family. I can't tell him to go to hell—and neither can you. He wants to see you. Will you go?"

"No. I will have nothing to do with Boko or his methods or his dreams of a free South Africa. I associated with him once, and for that I nearly got thrown out of the country. Saul saved me—as he did you. I don't agree with what Boko wants to do out there. If he wants to start a war, let him do it on his own. I want no part of it."

Joshua found himself fiercely thumping Jomo. Who did not flinch from his blows. Joshua restrained himself. He pushed his half-drained pint of beer towards Jomo. No more for him, it signaled. Jomo drained it without a murmur. They had an unwritten understanding that no one wasted good beer. Joshua had come in one night, late, sober, and had obliged Jomo in the same way.

"Don't forget you're South African too," Jomo said.

"I won't ever forget. Not ever! But not Boko's way. That's the surest way for me to stop being me. And who else can I be?"

They glared at each other. In a friendly way. They had known each other so long, they had no inhibitions. Each pummeled the other when the need arose—and gave as fiercely as he got. Jomo drained his own pint; then angrily, in frustration, pushed the empty mug towards Joshua, indicating it was his turn for a refill. Joshua, unsteady on his feet, spotted a crestfallen Joe, who had lost out in the eye contact game being played at the other end of the bar, and signalled him for a refill.

Joe obliged.

"Too lazy to get one yourself?" Jomo growled.

"Too drunk, you mean. Who the hell cares any longer? What does Boko want to see me about anyway?"

Jomo leaned forward eagerly, not anticipating the sudden change in mood.

"Will you go and see him? Please! For old times' sake?"

"Maybe if you'll give me honest answers to a few questions."

"Fire away," Jomo said.

"Saul came to London. From where? Nice or Paris?"

"Paris. He went there from Nice."

"Why did he go to Paris? Who was he seeing there?"

"I can't tell you. I don't think it is right of me to reveal the love life of a dead friend."

"As you wish. The deal's off. Tell Boko he can come and get me anyway he wants."

"All right! All right! I'll tell you. Saul was sleeping with a French stripper at the Coq D'Or. It's a nightclub on the Rue de la Bruyere in Montmartre. He adored her! She was very well stacked. She was the very first woman he'd had while on a visit to Paris, and he could never forget her. I honestly believe she was the only woman he really loved. Oh, sure, he possessed many more—he loved to possess them—but this was something else."

"How long was he in Paris?"

"Just the night. She called him in Nice. She had to see him right away, she said. It must have been important, because he left whoever he was with in Nice and went to Paris."

"Why? What did she tell him?"

"I don't know, Joshua. I really, really don't. That is what killed him. And if he'd told me that day, I could have saved him. That is what hurts so much."

"Who is Slagter?"

Jomo had not been expecting the question. The beer mug slipped from his long fingers, hitting the tabletop with a light thud, rocking over as it sloshed beer, saved from emptying itself in Joshua's direction by Joshua's quick response.

Not bad reflexes, Joshua thought, for a man who is past caring. Jomo reflected it helped to drain beer mugs as soon as they were set in front of you. Just as soon as you got them. It reduced the danger of spillage under these circumstances.

"Who is Slagter?"

"Strange you should have heard of Slagter," Jomo said, ruefully surveying the spilt beer, deliberating whether this wasn't an opportune time for a refill, or whether he'd had enough. A refill perhaps. He indicated that to Joshua, without response.

"Laura got a note from him about me. And Julia, the girl who was here, mentioned him too. Who is Slagter?"

"He's a freelance killer often used by South African Intelligence to extract information from enemy agents. Brutal chap, you'd do well to keep away from. Strange she should know about Slagter. I thought you said she was a policewoman?"

"That's what she told me. Of sorts."

"Julia?" Jomo repeated the name, as if hearing it spoken aloud might evoke a response within him. It did. "Julia? Julia Rayburn-Spencer?" Jomo asked. "Hyphenated? Granddaughter of the eleventh Earl of Bromfield? Has a flat in Hampstead?"

"Yes. I told you she was on Clayborne's list."

Jomo leaned back into the bench. The black eyes filled with mirth. He broke into a broad Xhosa smile that lit up his face before he burst into outright laughter. Joshua watched him, feeling the load lift a little. He'd been worried about Jomo.

"She's MI-6, Joshua. So British Intelligence already got to you. Boy! They sure do work fast! What did you tell her? I bet you spilled it all out. Knowing your weakness for women."

He leaned his head on the padded rest and closed his eyes to stop the tears of mirth that threatened to break loose.

Joshua smiled.

"And you thought you were picking her up?" Jomo went into another round of his laughter, unable to drink his beer—or what was left of it—because of it. He slapped Joshua on the shoulder.

"I enjoyed it," Joshua said, defensively. "She's a very nice person. It was a pleasure to be picked up by her—if that's what you're implying?"

"I'm no implying it, Joshua. I'm stating it as a fact. Don't be fooled by her. She'll kill you if she has to."

"Would you? Kill me if you had to?"

"No, I couldn't. Not even if I had to."

"And Saul? And Boko? Would they kill me, if they had to?"

"I don't know, Joshua. I prefer not to think about it."

They sat side by side in the now merry pub, drinking beer—Joshua had one last round, for the road, against his better judgment—slapping each other without raising an eyebrow. Sometimes they laughed loudly, almost at nothing. At times, their voices rose in anger, locked in futile debate. Joe would have bought them another round, but Joshua signalled it was near the end of the evening for him. That was the last Joshua saw of Joe that night. Another pair of au pair girls, probably from another pub, had drifted in and Joe disappeared.

"Who is Slagter?" Joshua repeated for the third time.

"I just told you," Jomo said. "You've been drinking too much. Why you bloody well don't know your own capacity for liquor is beyond me. Your short term memory is starting to go."

"No, Jomo! You'd better lay off the booze too. You can't even understand simple English anymore. Who is he? Do you know who he is?"

"That's a very closely guarded piece of information. I can tell you the names of a dozen agents in this country, but I don't know who Slagter is. Saul was on his trail. Every time British Intelligence heard Slagter had been assigned to make someone talk, Saul would be sent to cover it—and came away empty. At least six documented cases. Saul told me about them all. All over the world. Boko wanted the same information. He suggested I find out from Saul, but I would never agree to a thing like that! I think, though, Saul was close to knowing—if he didn't already know."

Joshua clutched Jomo's shoulder, shaking off the lethargic look that was creeping into his eyes.

"That's it! That is why Saul was killed. Because he came too close to Slagter. There we have a reason for his death. And who did it."

"You'll never make an agent," Jomo said. "That will never wash. Saul wasn't killed in Slagter's style—if I may say so. And if he had known that night in bed with me, he would have told me. What he didn't tell me had to be much more important! He couldn't tell me."

They shook hands warmly.

"Will you go and see Boko?"

"Yes."

"Tonight?"

"Yes."

"Now?"

"Yes. For heaven's sake, Jomo, don't keep pushing, will you? Do me a favour. Go and sit with Joe. He looks a little down to me. He doesn't seem to have had much luck at the au pair game. And thanks for telling me about Julia. MI-6? Fascinating! The first time it's ever happened to me. And all the time I thought I was in control. I even let her have the keys to my surgery. Smooth operator that, Jomo. Why must they use women who are so young—and so pretty?"

Joshua, unlike Julia, paid no attention to anyone as he made for the door. He did not search out a Welsh voice. He did not throw a quick glance under the seat, as he arose, looking for a felt hat.

He did not even turn to look at the man sitting beside them, and who had not yet left the pub.

Whether he was still there, or had left, didn't seem important any more.

And he could not have cared less about it.

Chapter 9

Julia walked away rapidly from the Evening Star.

Joshua's almost casual mention of Donaldson had shaken her more than she cared to admit. Who was Donaldson? Had he really died some years ago? Had he been shot and killed by Jane Timmons? Deliberately? And if so why hadn't Farnsworth come out and told her so? And if he wasn't Donaldson—the real Donaldson—then who was he?

About the only fact she was sure about—and it lent some credibility to Joshua's remarks—was about Jane Timmons being Farnsworth's live-in! She'd suspected that for a long time. Not that it was any of her business, but why didn't they get married?

There was one point in her favour. Donaldson couldn't possibly know that she'd accidentally stumbled on to what had happened to the real Donaldson. Had he seen her leave the Evening Star? She hoped not. Far better for her if he still thought she was somewhere in the pub. The public bar was on the other side, and the exit had let past it, though she decided, ruefully, he couldn't possibly think she'd gone in there. There was a distinct disadvantage in this business to being the granddaughter of the eleventh Earl.

He had almost certainly seen her leave. If he was in the pub keeping a careful eye on Joshua, and if he was half as good as Farnsworth had said he was, he must know she'd left. She found herself trying to sort out the voices in the pub. That was impossible! There were too many nationalities and so many different tongues being spoken at the same time; she could never have identified the Welsh ones.

The streets were silent as she cut across the alley from the back of the Evening Star to Fitzjohn's Avenue, the street lamps barely lighting up the sidewalk in shadowy circles that made ghosts out of tree stumps. Far better to be in complete darkness, she reflected. Then, at least, you saw nothing at all. Instead of seeing familiar objects made strange by your own fears. Seeing things as others wanted her to see them, rather than for what they actually were—tree stumps in the dark.

It could, of course, be the real Donaldson after all. Farnsworth and MI-6 could easily have staged the whole incident for reasons which weren't clear at all, hoodwinking a pair of London doctors into believing he was dead. The Service was quite capable of doing that with the help of Scotland Yard.

In which case what had happened so many years ago was just as relevant as the events of last week—and maybe more so.

There was one big flaw in the argument, and it hit her immediately. He could not be the Donaldson Joshua knew, or Joshua would have known him right away. And Farnsworth would never have assigned him to cover Joshua. Even Farnsworth wasn't as big a fool as that!

She felt the silence as she neared the surgery. It was set back from the street, in a house that made every attempt to abase itself, hiding behind vines that overhung the entrance. A garden path of random paving led up to it through a wrought iron gate.

The gate was open.

She slid her body through it without touching it, opening the handbag to draw out the keys, her heels clicking on the paving stones as they had done in her walk with Joshua from the tube station to the Evening Star.

This time alone.

That was what was wrong with her, she decided. As an agent, she was too naïve. Was this the footwear to wear for this sort of work? She didn't take every possible circumstance into account. Who could have known that a social evening in the pub would end up with her breaking into the surgery of a pair of respectable London doctors? Steady on, Julia, she thought. No need to go overboard on this thing. She wasn't breaking in. One of the doctors had given her the keys. And the other was her own physician.

The door was open.

She stopped at the door. Uncertain. The surgery was in darkness. No sounds. No sign of Amelia or Dr Clayborne. Just the silence.

She put the keys back into the handbag, slowly, and drew out the gun.

There was no one in the waiting room. She hadn't expected it at that time of night. Yet there was a glow in the room without the lights being on. She could see the outlines of furniture in it. The desk behind which Amelia sat, keeping an eye on patients. A friendly face that could be trusted to maintain order while being genuinely sympathetic to their problems. Efficiency. That is what symbolised Amelia. Whether you were the granddaughter of an Earl or the charwoman, you took your turn at seeing the doctor. Julia could respect her for it.

Beside the desk were the filing cabinets with the medical records. Not unlike the ones in Farnsworth's study.

They were both open.

The curtains were drawn. There should have been no light in the room at that hour; yet she could plainly see objects around her. She drew back into the shadow of the door through which she had just entered.

The band of light came from below the door leading to Dr Clayborne's consulting room. The two consulting rooms were side by side.

Joshua's was in darkness.

That could explain the open door. Dr Clayborne had come back from Nice that morning, and had attended surgery. Then, in the evening, he'd stayed on after Amelia left, perhaps, to catch up on the writing of reports. Maybe study difficult cases?

She replaced the gun in her handbag—she'd frighten the daylights out of him if she walked in with it in her hand—and knocked lightly on the door. As lightly as could be heard. She didn't want to startle him.

No answer. An eerie silence crept out from under the door at her feet, wrapping around her a feeling of desolation as it rose up to engulf her.

Waiting for an answer to a knock on a door, which did not come. She knocked again. Perhaps he had a patient with him? Some emergency that had brought him down there so late? But then, might she not have heard the muffled sound of their voices or the rustle of paper?

She knocked a third time, this time calling out to him softly. Then she tried the door.

It was unlocked.

He was lying, naked, on the floor beside his chair, and he was dead. Soaking in blood that flowed through the open slashes made with almost surgical precision. And much more pain.

The eyes were open, the eyeballs fixed in horror. Pleading for mercy and a quick end? It had come very slowly. She could see that. He had a bullet wound in the knee. That is when he had tried to rise or run or call. It had brought him to the floor.

The rest she could only surmise. He had put down the gun; drawn out the machete. Made Clayborne strip himself, perhaps helping to rip off his clothes with the point of the machete. Why could he not have been killed with his clothes on? They lay, blood stained, in the corner, as if deposited there one by one. On top of each other.

She turned her eyes back to him, forcing herself to look at him.

There was no sexual mutilation. An absence of slash marks around the region though blood from elsewhere had dripped into it. She considered covering up his groin with a piece of his clothing—his vest, perhaps—but it was against service regulations. They were specific on procedures to be followed in such circumstances. Don't touch anything! Don't remove any evidence, unless it is directly related to service activity! Such evidence would be discreetly brought to the attention of Scotland Yard at the highest levels, when relevant aspects would be allowed, after declassification, to filter down to the police.

And, for heaven's sake, always, always, wear gloves!

She reached into her handbag and put them on. It didn't matter if she'd left dozens of prints all over. She was a patient there. That would explain it.

There was no doubt about it. This was a killing in the style of Slagter. So he was there with them. The victims in the photographs, in Saul's reports, had looked just the same way. Different bodies, that was all. The same sharp stabs to the chest and across the stomach, almost as if it was the only way he'd been taught to kill. A series of programmed cuts in a set pattern, delivered as if he knew no other and was unprepared to learn.

Or because he enjoyed this insanely cruel way of killing?

It filled her with revulsion.

She went into the waiting room, sat on a straight-backed chair and put her head in her hands.

She had known him now for almost ten years—since she was sixteen. He had been a fine doctor, always so compassionate. He had time for his patients, and unlike many, he, too, loved to talk.

She blew her nose. She didn't care who heard her. I'm a lousy agent, she thought. Slagter could be in the bathroom, or in Joshua's consulting room next to Dr Clayborne's office, and all I can do is sit here and cry. I don't even know, she continued, rambling on to herself, whether I could shoot to kill, if I saw him come through that door with a blood-stained knife and a gun in his hands!

She shook off her doubts. There wasn't time to indulge in them. Not now. Not in this place. She indulged in such thoughts far more than was healthy for a good agent. She had either to get rid of them—or get out of the business.

It wasn't even fair to someone like Joshua to have someone like her to protect him. That thought brought her to her feet.

She crossed over quickly to the filing cabinet, using the light from the now open door to Clayborne's office, to help her find what she was looking for. Saul's medical file.

It was missing.

Laura's was there. Just ahead of his. But not Saul's.

Perhaps it was on Dr Clayborne's desk? As Saul's doctor he would have interest in it.

She went back in to the room. He had not moved. The eyes still looked up at her in glazed horror, the body still nakedly grotesque in the out flung arms and feet. She reached out to close his eyelids. They refused to close, the eyelashes snapping into her gloved hands. She touched the face. It was stone hard. So he'd been dead for several hours. But of course! That was the afternoon the surgery was closed. Joshua had said Clayborne was in that morning. And Amelia must have left around the noon hour, or just before it.

There were papers on his desk, but Saul's file was not among them.

Then she did what she should not have done.

She took the vest, crumpled, blood-stained, and placed it lightly on his groin.

Chapter 10

Joshua walked to Boko's flat in Belsize Park. He deliberated about taking a taxi—there were several cruising Finchley Road at that time of night, waiting for customers from the pubs and the tube stations—but he decided against it. The walk would do him good; help to clear his mind.

He needed that if he was to make any sense with Boko.

He went up the hill from the Evening Star, cut past the local cinemas and the neon lights of Belsize Square to a row of townhouses that stretched in interminable lines that weren't quite straight. Shallow curves like flocks of starlings changing direction for no identifiable reason except a leader's dictation.

The house was the last in a line of houses. First from the other side. Joshua checked the number on the wall.

He had never been in it before.

Jomo had moved out of it long ago and taken a flat in Greencroft Gardens, on the other side of Finchley Road. He had wanted Ewa to move in with him, but Boko said no. And Boko was the elder of the two; the head of the family. In their household his word was law.

In the fifteen years since they had all left South Africa, Joshua had met Ewa and Boko several times—Ewa much more often than Boko. It was always a pleasure for him to meet Ewa. She worked in a pharmacy in Baker Street, and he often broke a journey into Central London so that he might drop in and see her. At all such times, without hesitation and regardless of who was around, she came forward with open arms to embrace him tightly, while the owner of the pharmacy—an Indian who'd been displaced from Uganda—

beamed his welcome to the 'Doctor Saheb'. She looked very fetching in her white uniform, the white cap pinned precariously to the top of her curly hair.

She still called him 'Uncle Josh' when she felt the need of an uncle, and 'Joshua' when she felt the need of a friend. And he responded likewise.

As her adopted uncle, it was his one regret she was not married. At the age of twenty-six, back in the Ciskei, she would have been married a long time ago, with many fine children! It wasn't quite that simple in England. At such times, she told him not to worry; she was happy as she was—and held him even tighter. He offered to marry her once, but she took the offer with considerable amusement, inquiring mildly as to whether he'd been drinking, and chastising Jomo for leading him astray.

He had met Boko too on several occasions, none of them quite so pleasurable. They ranged from indifferent, casual affairs at Jomo's parties to full-blown quarrels on Hampstead Heath, with each thoroughly detesting the other. Boko's hatred came through every time, and after the first few meetings, Joshua couldn't sympathise with him any longer. That didn't help any. He brushed off, as best he could, the slurs Boko was apt to sling at him. Such as 'white man's mat' and 'white man's pet doggie'. That he could understand. Boko felt that Joshua had abandoned the cause by allowing himself to be assimilated in London. Joshua emphatically denied the charge, resenting the hurtful phrases, but feeling more intensely the frustration of unacceptable solutions. Violence of any sort, by any people, was, to him at least, an unacceptable solution. But then were there any other meaningful solutions?

This was the first time he was actually entering Boko's flat. The curtains were drawn. As they always were, day or night. Joshua had passed by the house, once in a while, and could never understand why Boko would choose to keep the curtains drawn. Always.

Boko opened the door to him and Joshua saw why.

He was in a kraal in the Ciskei. The African masks on the walls hung onto grass thatching woven into mats that lined every square inch of wall. Beside them, and looking down at him fiercely, were the spears and the assegais that would have adorned a hunter's home, their blades pointing to the ground. The furniture in the room was sparse, rough cut and made from tree trunks and logs of wood as might have been his in a poor, tribal home. The door was curtained with beads; the floor was carpeted. It seemed to Joshua it was his only concession to a home in England—until he felt the colour of it. The dark-brown colour of burnt mud.

He smelt the mealies of their evening meal that came from the kitchen, an appetizing fragrance of corn. The meal Ewa had cooked had been eaten many hours before he came, yet the fragrance lingered.

He heard the rattles on Boko's legs made from the cocoons of the great caterpillars that fed on the flowering mimosa tree. Round Boko's shoulders was thrown a red blanket; on his head was a doek of scarlet.

He was a Xhosa at home in the Ciskei.

Boko invited him in; motioned him to sit.

"I'm so glad you could come," Boko said, throwing off his red blanket.

Joshua saw the artistry in the exquisite beadwork of red, gold, white and blue beads adorning his torso, trailing down to the red kilt girding his loins. He towered above Joshua, the rippling muscles barely discernable in the lean, hard body that moved with so much grace.

"Did I really have a choice? Why don't you come down to the pub if you want to see me? Why must you insist I come here? I'm glad I did though! I would have missed all this."

Joshua waved his hands around him, sweeping the walls with them.

"When I step outside, I am an African in London; when I come through that door, I am a Xhosa. Is that so very wrong?"

"On the contrary. I think it is admirable! Did I sound critical? I didn't mean to be. I'm amazed you can live this way in the heart of London."

"I'm so glad you approve," Boko said. "Would you like some tea? Ewa will bring us in a pot of very English tea."

He disappeared into the kitchen, moving the curtain of beadwork that lashed him as it swung back into the doorway. He heard his orders conveyed in English; Ewa's voice raised in angry protest, quelled with harshness in a language he had long since forgotten.

Boko came back into the living room. "We will have tea presently," he said. "You must forgive Ewa. She was not agreeable to making tea at this time of night. Or bringing it in. But she will do as I ask. Let me come to the point. Do you know why I wish to see you? Did Jomo tell you?"

"Not really. I presume it is about Saul."

"It is."

"I have told him and I will be pleased to repeat it to you, I don't know what you want from me?"

"The African is a very simple person, Joshua. Very honest. Very direct. The subtle deceptions of the Western mind escape him."

"Don't give me all that garbage about the Western mind, Boko! I'm, bloody, as South African as you are. Cut out the rot and tell me what you want from me."

"It is easy to see you are a little drunk. Aggression will get you nowhere. We are a very gentle people—except when it comes to making animal sacrifices. You did watch me make the ritual sacrifice, did you not, when we feasted Jomo's return to the Ciskei?"

"Yes. When you bloody well chose the wrong animal. According to your medicine man."

"Ah! An oversight. But you noticed I had to make the animal bellow before slaughtering it. Otherwise it would have been unacceptable. Wasted! So I carried out the ritual sacrifice of the ox—the wrong animal as you so aptly put it—with an assegai. Not unlike those on the wall. Sharp bladed, with a short handle. There are two ways, Joshua, in which the animal can be sacrificed—after it has been made to bellow, of course. Would you like me to tell you about them?"

"Not particularly."

"I will anyway. The one is by a jab of the sharpened assegai in the back of the neck at the base of the skull. It was the method I used on the goat, when we'd decided on the right animal. Unfortunately, you didn't witness it, because Ewa had drawn you away. A relatively painless way. The other method calls for the head of the family—or the medicine man—to insert his hand through a cut made in the living animal's belly, below the ribs, and rip off the aorta from the heart."

"Fascinating."

"Death comes to us all, Joshua, but the way in which the Great Spirit chooses to sacrifice us is important—at least to us. Wouldn't you agree?"

"If you're trying to frighten me," Joshua said, "you should at least have waited until I was fully sober."

They heard the teacups being placed on the tray in the kitchen. The soft footfall of bare feet moving towards the door. Boko stopped talking. Joshua looked up at the door. The curtain of beads hid her from his view.

Ewa pushed the strings of beads aside with one shoulder as she came into the room. The smile of greeting, warm and endearing, he had for her congealed on his lips. He erupted out of the chair; a low, painful cry of strangled surprise choked within him.

She was naked above the waist, the firm, beautifully curved African breasts framing the teapot between them. Around her waist was a short skirt, reaching only a third of the way to her knees, showing the powerfully built thighs disappearing into it. The hair was cropped close; round her forehead was a headband of beads. A necklace of the same beadwork around her neck swayed past the cups and pulled away from her as she placed the tray on the table before him. Her head was lowered; her eyes too.

"When my sister comes through that door, and enters this house, Joshua, she too is a Xhosa. She is unmarried so she bares her breasts. She does not keep company with a boy who has been through the abakwetha ceremony, so her skirt is short. You seem surprised?"

Joshua was speechless.

"Perhaps she feels ashamed of herself before you, Joshua. Notice she does not look you in the eyes. Shall I ask her to leave the room? Ewa, my dear. Joshua and I are going to talk important matters. Since you seem to be so ashamed of yourself before him—he is not Xhosa—you have my permission to leave the room. I will pour out the tea for our guest."

She raised her head, planting herself firmly before Joshua, her feet spread slightly apart for stance, her hands on her hips. Without a word of warning, she ripped the necklace from her neck, flinging it at Boko, hitting him in the chest. It dropped to his feet.

"I have felt ashamed of myself this way, serving your uncouth friends who have come through that door," she said. "Yet I have served them. Do you think I am ashamed of myself this way, standing before Joshua who is so very, very dear to me? And do you think I will refuse to serve him a cup of tea?"

She held out her hands to Joshua, coming towards him as she would in the pharmacy, folding him in a tight embrace, her arms clasping the sides of his back, her fingers at the back of his neck. He felt her breasts crush into him. He rubbed her back, passing his hands lightly down the sides, reassuring her as he kissed her on the hair.

"The last time you held me this way," she said, ignoring Boko, "you offered me your vest. Do you remember?"

"Yes," Joshua said, feeling his body relax with the memory she invoked; feeling her body relax too. "Would you like my vest now? You are very welcome to it."

She laughed as if she was eleven, digging her head into his chest.

"No, I don't think so, Joshua. I didn't have much in that department then, and your vest fitted me beautifully. You told me so yourself! It isn't likely to fit me now, is it?"

She pulled herself away from him, still holding his hand, unwilling to lose the comfort in his touch.

"No," he said. "It would not fit very well. Ewa, if you don't wish to pour out the tea for me, I won't be hurt."

She released him, seating herself on the ground directly opposite to him, her back to Boko.

"I want to," she said.

She poured out his cup first. Boko, tight lipped and annoyed, refused tea. She poured herself a cup, sipping it slowly, politely inquiring if he might need more milk or sugar, sitting up on her knees to pass him a teaspoon to stir his cup.

Joshua stirred it silently. She carried on the conversation with great ease. When his eyes strayed over her—and try as hard as he could, he could not prevent them—she smiled to reassure him that she was not offended by it.

"Why should I feel ashamed before Joshua," she said to Boko. "Do you know I spent a night with him on a sofa in his living room? While you were hiding out in Durban and Jomo had appropriated the use of his bedroom upstairs? I spent it much more comfortably than he did. When I awoke in the morning, we were both on the very edge of it. He was practically falling of it, and I was cuddling him like I did my teddy bear."

Boko put the red blanket back on his shoulders.

He lit a short stem pipe, picking up a hot coal from a metal dish on the ground, passing it to and fro between his fingers as he lit the pipe with it. He leaned back and put the dish with the glowing coal back into the unlit fireplace.

"Would you like some more tea, Joshua?" Ewa said, lifting the lid and peering into the pot. "There is plenty more in there. All of Boko's friends, some of whom are total strangers to me, always accept a second cup. Why should you not have one too?"

Joshua declined, staying her hand as she reached for his cup, caressing the fingers away from it, handing her the cup to replace on the tray.

"I love you, Ewa," he said. "And I always will. But, please, no more tea today."

She cleared away the tea things, stacking the empty cups on the tray, closing the sugar bowl, and left the room.

It was the last he saw of her that evening.

"Just a child, Joshua," Boko said, puffing at his pipe. He offered it to Joshua, in keeping with Xhosa custom, but Joshua declined politely.

"May we return to the business for which you are here?" Boko said.

Joshua nodded.

"May I make a deal with you? I will tell you how Saul died. In exchange you will tell me what it is you know. Is that a fair deal?"

"I can only tell you what I know. Not what I am supposed to know."

"Naturally. No man can tell what he does not know—even if others may think it."

"Sounds fair to me," Joshua said.

"A deal? A promise? On your honour? Your word on it?"

"Yes. But you must have a very high opinion of me, Boko, merely to trust in my honour."

"Oh, I do! I do! I admire a great deal in you, Joshua. I always have. Your quiet courage and clear thinking, for instance. What I despise in you is your inability to see it hasn't worked all these years—and it never will! You are dealing with people who have crossed over the borders of sanity. Or civilised behaviour. Wouldn't you agree?"

"Yes."

"And yet, fully knowing this, when I see both acceptance and resignation in your eyes—merely because you have this abhorrence of violence—I positively loathe you. If you will forgive me saying so."

"You'd make a fine ambassador for the gentle Xhosas," Joshua said, the sarcasm cutting abrasively into Boko, who ignored it. "There have to be other ways, Boko; otherwise victory, when it comes, at least for me, will be a hollow one."

"That is what the losers say. Are you afraid of being a loser?"

"No. You could say I've always been one. The mantle fits me naturally. At least I am at peace with myself."

"Well, you won't be for long, Joshua. Not when I tell you how Saul died. We are talking about the day he died."

Boko reached for another coal from the metal dish in the fireplace, in no hurry to proceed.

"He called here. I wasn't in. Ewa took the message. It was for me not Jomo. This was about six in the evening. It was an odd message. He wanted me to meet him at an address in Clapham. At ten-thirty that evening. Not earlier. He was quite specific about it to Ewa."

Joshua shook off the tiredness that was settling over him.

"And I had to bring a five-gallon can filled with petrol when I came."

"That was an odd request."

"I thought so too. And had I been there, I would have questioned it. Ewa did not. She merely took the message.

She assumed, she says, his car had run out of petrol somewhere in Clapham, and he needed help. A natural assumption. I thought so too. Would you have thought otherwise?"

"And you complied?"

"Yes. I had no qualms. We all owed Saul something. It seemed like a harmless request.

I went by car. Carrying a five-gallon can filled with petrol does attract attention.

I reached the street in Clapham, and I knew something wasn't quite right. The area had been marked for demolition. A whole line of old, condemned, abandoned buildings. On both sides of the street. Not a soul moved up and down it either. At ten-thirty in the night, it was like being in some cattle town in South Africa—whose water hole had run dry. Some of the houses had been vandalized; windows were broken, doors were off their hinges.

There were no lights anywhere, not even in the street."

He paused to puff on his pipe.

"I found it difficult to tell myself I was in London.

He was dead when I found him, Joshua. He'd been dead a half hour or so. I'm not a doctor, but the body was still warm.

He was sitting in a house exactly halfway up the street. Sitting on a step halfway up the stairs that led to the bedrooms above.

Leaning against the banister."

"Did you go up the stairs?"

"The first thing I did. Before I even touched him! The thought struck me too. There was no one up there. And there never had been.

On the step beside him there was a syringe and a letter. The syringe is on the shelf."

Joshua got up to look at it.

"Don't touch it, Joshua. I wouldn't advise you to touch it," Boko said, making no physical effort to stop him from doing so. "I think it has Saul's fingerprints all over it. I will need that little piece of evidence, untampered, if I am ever implicated in this mess."

"You seem to be very sure they are Saul's fingerprints."

"I am sure. Can you imagine Saul, built, if I may say, a trifle more huskily than we are, permitting some rather aggressive gentleman to inject him with a syringeful of whatever it was that killed him? Unless it was his doctor. The fingerprints on that syringe, Joshua, are either Saul's or yours."

"Then they must be Saul's."

"Ah! That is what I thought. That is what I have preferred to think all along."

Joshua did not touch the syringe lying across an ash tray on the shelf of the mantelpiece. The needle was towards the edge, and overhanging it. He bent over, and putting his nose close to it, he sniffed it. There was no odour. No last few drops of liquid within the bottom of it either. No traces of dried solution. The cylinder looked clean and dry.

"You're quite sure he was dead? Could he have been revived?"

"He was dead, Joshua! How many times must I repeat it? There was no way I could have revived him! If he wanted revival he would have asked for you or Clayborne—not me! That is why he said ten-thirty to Ewa. He wanted to be sure I didn't come too early. For revival!"

It was unusual for Joshua to see Boko in that way. Joshua had seen him angry before, but never in doubt. It showed in the raised tones of his voice.

"I can't agree," Joshua said quietly. "There is nothing in this syringe—except air. I haven't seen the results of the autopsy yet, but if I take a guess on the strength of this syringe, he died of a massive air embolus in the blood vessels of the lung. Self-administered. A doctor could have revived him. You said there was a letter?"

"Ah! The letter."

Boko leaned back. Almost as if he was contemplating whether he ought to show it to Joshua. Swaying one way and then the other. Unable to make up his mind.

"May I read the letter?"

"Yes. All right. You may. It is also on the mantelpiece. At the other end. I would suggest you use a pair of surgeon's gloves, if you are going to handle it."

The letter was face open towards him. He did not touch it.

He read it twice; then once more. It was terse; maddeningly brief. But then a man about to kill himself, and with a deadline to meet, wasn't likely to be long-winded about it, Joshua thought.

But then that was Saul. Deep. Very few words, even to the point of being incomprehensible. Hiding himself behind the muscle and the power—and still constantly looking over his shoulders at the looming shadows. Until they closed in around him, edging him, forcing him into the only way out. There had been other ways, but Saul had been incapable of seeing them clearly enough to think of them as viable options. Incomprehensible, except to Laura. She knew him well enough to understand him. And Jomo. He understood too—in a different way.

There was no bitterness in the letter, but it hurt. There was so much that could be learnt about one's friends in the final page. When the end was in sight, then what did they really want for you?

It read:

Dear Boko,

When you arrive here shortly, at ten-thirty I trust, you will find me leaning up against the banister. I will need it for support. The petrol you have brought with you will make a nice bonfire of me. I thought of asking Jomo to do this, but, Boko, you are the stronger of the two, and Jomo might so something foolish—like lighting himself up with me.

So it has to be you.

You will be left with one final problem. Joshua. He is the only one who will know! What you want to do about it is up to you, but I would suggest you kill him. Thanks,

Saul

The handwriting was unmistakably Saul's. The signature, in the flowing hand, had graced many a note passed from Saul to Joshua and Jomo, generally commands for nocturnal activities to relieve the boredom of classwork. Boko's eyes followed Joshua back to the chair. They had been watching intently for the flicker of eyelids that might show pauses in the reading of the letter. There had been none.

"I have told you all I know about Saul's death, Joshua. And if we have answered some questions, we have posed new ones. Now it is your turn. To settle a few doubts in my mind. Yes?"

"Very well. What can I tell you—that you don't already know?"

"What does Saul mean when he says you are my final problem?"

"I've been agonizing over that myself."

"Why are you the only one who will know? Know what?"

"That puzzles me more than it does you. You aren't planning to take all this seriously, are you?"

"I don't know what to make of it. That is why I called you here. To talk it over with you. I don't want to be hasty. On one hand you are a man of honour. On the other hand, Saul is quite specific about it. What should I make of it? Who should I believe? Can you come up with some reasonable explanation of what Saul meant?"

"No. I appreciate your concern. And I would help if I could. I gave you my word on it. As a gentleman. But I just don't know what Saul meant."

"Then you have nothing to say? No way you can enlighten me?"

"I wish I could. Even you must know I'm not a fool. I'd tell you if I knew—just to save myself. Wouldn't I?"

"Possibly. And then again, Saul knew and could not save himself. Perhaps you know and are unwilling to save yourself. You have at least as much courage as he had."

Boko cut off Joshua's protestations with a wave of his hand, silencing him firmly.

"I believe you, Joshua. You do not know—or know that you know. If I were to follow Saul's advice, I would have you killed. It will not be particularly difficult, even in London. But I owe you one small favour too. You did bring Ewa back to Durban from the Ciskei when I wanted it. Regardless of what you might think, I am very fond of her; I could never have left without her. I, too, like to pay my debts."

Boko got up. The visit had come to an end. He walked to the door and held it wide open for Joshua. Outside the street lamp on the pavement lit up the entry foyer and the living room beyond, bouncing off the spears and assegais on the walls in blades of light.

"It is not necessary to say goodbye to Ewa. She has probably gone to bed. I will give you two days, Joshua. Two days! No more. To find out what it is you are supposed to know. To tell me what Saul meant in his letter. One does not write a death note lightly. Strong men, like Saul, do not die easily. And when they kill themselves, the reasons must be overriding ones. Wouldn't you agree?"

"Yes."

"Two days, Joshua."

"And after two days?"

"You will come here, of your own free will, to this house, and tell me all you know. If you don't, you leave me no alternatives. With or without your consent, I will make you bellow. And then I will kill you."

Chapter 11

The telephone was ringing when Julia entered the flat. The key was stuck in the lock, the lights weren't on. She left the keys in the door, threading her way, in the dark, past the furniture she knew so well, brushing the rocking chair that squeaked as it rocked, reaching for the telephone before the last ring gave out on her.

It was Donaldson.

"Hang on a minute, will you?" she said. "While I get the lights. I've just come in through the door."

"You'd better make it quick, Miss! I'm in a telephone booth across a house in Belsize Park and our man's just coming out of it."

"Keep talking, Donaldson. The lights can wait. So can the door."

"He left the pub about twenty minutes after you did."

"Did you see me leave, Donaldson?"

"Call me 'Tom', Miss. I feel so much better. Yes, I saw you leave."

"Where were you when I left?"

"In the pub, Miss. Having one or two myself. You don't mind that, Miss, do you? Drinking on the job, I mean."

"No, of course not, Tom. But where were you? In the public bar or the private bar?"

"The private bar, Miss, though God knows I can't always afford it with what the Service pays! Across from you. I waved to you once or twice, unobtrusive like, but you didn't notice. You were so wrapped up in the gentleman."

"Tom, will you cut out the asides and tell me what happened?"

"Sorry, Miss. I do get carried away sometimes. Well, to continue, I thought I'd be there for the whole evening. I was looking forward to it. Not often that I end up tailing someone sitting quietly in a pub. But no such luck, Miss. The African bloke came in just as you left. He brushed right past you, but I don't think you saw him either. He sat with our man for a while. I thought I'd try to get some of the conversation too—they weren't speaking any too softly either—so I moved on to the bench seat, placing my felt underneath it, in case he caught on. And it worked. I can report a good bit of what they said, Miss, when we have the time for it."

"Did you get anything useful? In the conversation, I mean. Heaven help me, I don't hold with eavesdropping on people, but in this case, I'd like to think we're doing it to protect him."

"Don't worry, Miss. I don't have any qualms about listening in to him. Any time. I'm being paid for it. Actually I did get something that might interest you, Miss.

Apparently our man that got killed—what's his name, the white South African bloke?"

"Saul."

"Yes, him. He went round telling everyone he was going to see our here Indian doctor that morning at nine. Because the black African bloke asked him about it too. I couldn't get much after that because he looked around once or twice to check on me, but I had my back turned to him. He lowered his voice, but I think the African bloke was asking our doctor to do something or go and see someone, because soon after our man left the pub. And seeing he came to this house in Belsize Park, I think I'm right."

"Alone? Was he alone?"

"Yes. He walked past the cinemas to this flat here. It seems to be the home of another black African bloke—who lives like a real African too, right here in the heart of London! Will I never cease to be surprised in this business? He was wearing a red blanket when he opened the door to our man. With a red turban on his head, and beads all over his chest, and things strapped to his legs that looked like caterpillar homes. Fair shook me, Miss, I can tell you. And the walls have spears on them, hung on what looks like grass thatching. Not that I think there's anything wrong with that—don't get me wrong, Miss—but I wasn't expecting it." She interrupted him over the telephone.

"Tom, can I meet you somewhere?"

There was a silence over the line. It seemed endless until, finally, he spoke: "I don't think that would be wise, Miss," he said softly. "I'd love to meet you, but I have to keep my cover in this job. In any case, I'd have to check it out with Dr Farnsworth first. You aren't offended, Miss, are you?"

He sounded genuinely sorry over the telephone.

"No, Tom. But you do that. Check with Dr Farnsworth, and then I want to see you!"

"In the meantime, Miss, what shall I do about our man? He's driving me off my feet. He keeps such weird hours. Shall I stay with him?"

"As close as you can, Tom. I think he's in great danger. Clayborne's dead."

"What!"

"Don't shout, Donaldson!" she said in stern reproach. "You nearly had my eardrum off!"

"Sorry, Miss. So he copped it? Geez!"

"I'm afraid so."

"Badly?"

"You wouldn't believe the way it was done. Bloody horrible! He was shot in the knee so he couldn't run. And then Slagter let him have it with some sort of carving knife. In the region of the chest and the stomach. Just like the others. God! I'm not going to sleep tonight, thinking about it. Maybe I'm not cut out for this sort of work, Tom."

"Take it easy, Miss. You're doing just fine. And don't you tell yourself otherwise. And don't let anyone else tell you otherwise. This sort of thing can upset most anyone! I've seen the most hard-boiled of agents weep like little children—and that includes me, Miss."

"Thank you, Tom."

"Quite all right, Miss. You're very welcome. May I ask a question or two? Seeing we're working together on protecting this here Indian bloke."

"Fire away, Tom. If I can't answer, I'll tell you so."

"Sounds fair, Miss. I'll start by telling you I've seen most of the files you've seen in Dr Farnsworth's office.

And one or two more. So you don't need to explain anything about this here doctor. We don't have too much time anyway. Though fortunately our man, who's just left the house, is standing under the street light, trying to make up his mind what he ought to do. Maybe shaking off his liquor. He had an awful lot to drink in the Evening Star. Which is just as well, because I can't get out of this booth without him spotting me. Makes tailing a lot easier when they'd had too much to drink. I think we have a minute or so more. But I do have a question."

"Yes?"

"You're sure it was Slagter, Miss?"

"Positive! Stripped naked. No sign of sexual mutilation. Not a doubt about it, Tom. I covered him up, though, before I left. Was that right of me?"

"Quite right, Miss. Let the bloody London police figure it out for themselves. Anything missing?"

"Saul's medical file. Slagter took it."

"I don't think so, Miss."

"How do you know?"

"Because I was assigned to obtain it, shall we say, after Saul died. I did that just before lunch. While you were with Dr Farnsworth. I have it with me. There's nothing in those files of any interest, Miss Julia. Save you barking up the wrong tree, you might say? Our Indian doctor sure was right when he kept insisting Saul was healthy as a horse!"

"You heard that part did you?" Julia said, her ear wide open for any clues that might give his identity away. There were none forthcoming. Whoever he was, he was a first class agent. She had to give him credit for that. A man might speak in many languages, but he could laugh in only one. And she hadn't heard Donaldson laugh. One low chuckle once. Not enough to give him away. Always polite and deadly effective.

"Did you hear a lot of my talk with Dr Samuelson?"

"Why yes, Miss. It was impossible not to hear the doctor then. He got really riled up, if I recall. Spoke so loud, he could be heard across the other side of the room. Even over the bloody din in there. And I wasn't too far away from you, Miss. You don't mind, do you? My listening in a little bit? I had to,"

"You're impossible, Tom! And even if I did mind, I'd hardly have been able to stop you, could I?"

She heard him chuckle again. Softly. As if he was fighting himself. Had she heard the chuckle before?

"I think our man's making up his mind to move, Miss! I may have to move in a hurry, so don't be offended if I hang up on you."

"What!" she said in mock surprise. "No more questions, Donaldson?"

"Actually, Miss, I do have one last one. May I ask it? It's kind of personal."

"You may."

"You seemed to be quite taken up with this here Indian doctor, Miss. If I may be permitted to say so. Are you?"

Julia did not reply. She didn't know how to reply. The seconds ticked by. She heard him breathe heavily.

"I'll take that as 'yes', Miss. If the answer was 'no', you'd have said so in no uncertain terms. A word of warning, Miss. From someone much older than you are. Don't fall for someone you don't know the least bit about. And on the job too! Surest way to come to grief, because he might not have much time going for him, and you'd only end up being hurt. And I hate to see someone as young and pretty as you are throw yourself away on a potential corpse! Besides you don't know the least thing about him. You owe that to yourself, Miss, to know him a bit longer before you do anything hasty—like falling for him."

"Thank you for the advice, Donaldson," Julia said. "I'll keep it in mind."

She meant it too.

"In the meantime, keep with him, Donaldson. I'll hold you personally responsible if anything happens to him."

She heard him sigh with weariness over the telephone.

"All right, Miss. I'll keep with him. But if he stays awake much longer, I'll just hit him on the head in a quiet park, and put him to sleep for a while. So I can get some shuteye myself."

She couldn't help smiling as she hung up. The thought of Donaldson creeping up behind Joshua and hitting him on the head with just the right amount of force to put him to sleep—without killing him—seemed incongruous and funny.

Good chap, Donaldson. Very good agent. One of the best, so she'd been told. But what did best mean in this business? Who did he work for? Like Saul, had he several masters, Farnsworth being only one of them? And who would he obey when faced with difficult choices? What if he hovered over the borderline between protector and assassin? He was in an admirable position to carry out both.

Very good agent, Donaldson. He hadn't slipped up, but Farnsworth had already slipped him up by his talk of the 'agency'! Over the telephone, when Donaldson had called while Julia was being briefed. It had registered. That had to mean he worked for the CIA too. That didn't surprise her. The woman in Miami, Stella, who'd been murdered by Slagter, had been American. And she'd worked for the CIA. And as the files showed, she'd been treated no differently than anyone else. They, too, must have an interest in Slagter. But why was Donaldson's identity being kept secret from her? And even before she asked the question, she knew the reason why. Because he wasn't just a freelancer. An ordinary tail. He was so high up in MI-6, probably as high as Farnsworth, that revealing his identity put him in jeopardy. Farnsworth sat behind a desk; Donaldson operated in the field.

But it was the last question she posed herself that bothered her the most. Why assign Donaldson to her in the first place? And the answer told her what the Service thought of her. They didn't trust her to finish off Slagter when she'd uncovered him. That was the real reason. Then he'd show himself by stepping up behind her, and doing the job himself. She had to sniff him out; Donaldson would do the rest. She would not be able to kill when the time came. But the Welshman could. They were sure of that. She went to the wall and put on the lights in the room. Then she retrieved her keys from the lock to the outside door. She went into the kitchen and poured herself a long drink. A glass of orange juice.

She sat on the rocking chair and rocked, nursing the drink in her lap. It had been her mother's rocking chair—her grandfather had sent if off to her London flat, saying he had no use for it. But she knew better. The photographs of her mother had made her out to be a kindly woman. Had she been rocked in that chair before? The old Earl didn't speak very much of his daughter, but even after so many years, Julia knew his hurt. She really ought to go up to Bromfield and see the old dear more often. He was forever begging her to come and visit the old family estate. Even the servants needed to see her once in a while, he said, so shouldn't she come down sometimes for their sake?

The rocking chair should have soothed her. She thought it might. Instead her anger worked its way to the surface as she clutched the empty glass. He had been a fine doctor to her. His sexual preference had been his own affair. It hadn't bothered her at all. If anything, she had felt a compassion for him. Having to live in a closet, unable to profess his true nature. It had not affected his competency as a doctor, or his concern for her as a patient.

The last time she had seen him, she had been in Nice. The week she was there. Sometimes he had been with Saul, but he had waved to her whenever he had seen her. Sensing her compassion for him had made him bold and unashamed. He was grateful for the opportunity she gave him to be himself.

Now there were two people crying out to her. For an account to be settled with Slagter. First Vladimir, and now Dr Clayborne.

"Slagter!" she said aloud to herself, surprised at the passion with which she heard the words being said, unable to believe there could be so much rage within her, "I'm going to find out who you are, and when I do, God help me, whoever you are, I'm going to kill you."

She would do it herself. She didn't need Donaldson to come out of the shadows and do it for her.

Chapter 12

Joshua was fast becoming a bundle of nerves on two feet, when, just before midnight, he reached South Kensington for the second time that day. He took Boko's threats very seriously. He had no doubt that Boko was responsible for the bombing in Johannesburg, killing seven people. That had led to a parting of their ways. Boko had denied it—though he insisted he approved of it. And there the matter had rested unsatisfactorily for the past fifteen years. Now, for no good reason it seemed to Joshua, they were being brought together again, and it didn't please him at all.

He felt uncomfortable. Boko made him feel that way.

Not that Boko would carry out the threat himself. He was too close to Joshua for that, and Jomo's friendship with Joshua made him a prime suspect for interrogation, but there were others—faceless urban guerrillas—who would carry out the sentence.

Julia had better be good at her job of protecting him! The thought of Julia brought some cheer back into his tired eyes. The liquor had begun to tell; he found himself wiping his eyes as if to skim away the blur. Only to have it replaced when his eyelids closed on him.

"I'm a doctor," he moaned to himself, "and I don't even know what's good for me."

The novelty shop, on the High Street, was in darkness, the neon lights of the advertisements above the shop fronts opposite throwing a pulsating blur on the barred and shuttered windows of the store. Force of habit took him to the front entrance. It was locked.

The policeman on the beat frowned at seeing him rattle the front grille of the shop, but there were a few drunks around at that time of the night, after closing time, and he uttered a friendly warning to pass on, mentally noting in his diary of events that he'd seen a drunken Indian at the front door of the shop, just before midnight.

Joshua went around to the back. There were no street lights in the alley; no shadows either. Just total darkness, of the sort Julia would have preferred in her walk to the surgery.

He rang the bell; heard it peal disdainfully within the flat. No answer. No signs of movement to suggest she was in the flat. He tried the bell again, the jangling sounds reverberating within the flat and out into the alley, without producing Laura.

He stood on the mat that said 'Welcome', wondering what he wanted to do. Not what he ought to do, which was go on home to bed, but what his instincts urged him to do. She was not in, even at this late hour.

That could not be right.

He had assured her he was going to spend the night with her; she had pleaded with him for it. And she was not there? Perhaps she had tired of waiting up for him and had gone to bed. Most wives did. She wasn't his wife, but could anyone sleep through the nerve shattering sounds of the infernal bell?

Maybe she had changed her mind about his spending the night with her? In which case it would not be right of him to enter her flat.

The doubt lingered, as it had for the past fifteen years; yet he looked under the mat and found the key, as he knew it would be. He replaced the key under the mat and entered the kitchen.

The door leading to the novelty shop was closed and bolted. From the inside. He thought about entering it and choosing a small gift for Julia. Something small and nice. Preferably expensive. As a doctor he did very well. Wasted most of it too. The prices would be marked and he'd leave the money on the counter with a note for Shari.

No! The note would be to Laura. It was she who owned the shop. But that could come later. First he had to settle a long affair with Laura—in his mind.

He went up the stairs to her bedroom, the carpeted silence preceding him into it, announcing his presence.

It was empty. The bed had not been slept in.

He undressed beside it, throwing his clothes on the floor—as any husband might. Would Laura have picked up after him?

Then he slipped in between the sheets. He had thought about this moment for so long. Slipping into Laura's bed, feeling the touch of Laura's satin sheets against his naked body. Even though she was not in the bed with him, it stirred him.

He lay flat on his back, his hands above him, cradling the back of his neck, his feet apart, replaying the vision of her on the beach that day. Replaying it again—as he had done so many thousand times before in the fifteen years since.

He heard the key in the lock below. The back door. He heard her climb the stairs and come up to the room, not entering it, surveying him in her bed, from the entrance to it. She didn't seem surprised to see him in her bed. As if she was sure he would be there, faithful as ever after all these years.

She didn't speak. She kicked off her shoes first, balancing alternately on the other foot, steady as ever with the skill of practice. He sat up in bed, the bedcover falling to his waist, and watched.

She reached back to unzip her dress, letting it slide to her feet, stepping out of it and gathering it up to fold it neatly for putting away, not throwing it at him as she had done on the beach. She freed her breasts from her bra, lifting the cups above them to ease the killing tightness in the clasp at the back, reaching behind her with both hands to unclasp it. She walked across to the chair, straddling the undergarment across the back of it, within easy reach of the bed.

Then she dropped her panties, stepping out of them, not bothering to pick them up off the floor, to stand naked before him.

Strange, he thought, how accurate memory could be. She was as he had always pictured her to be. Only the setting was different. He could not hear the rollers break on the sand or feel the breezes that ruffled the tips of the waves coming off the Indian Ocean.

But Laura was still the same. As beautiful to him as she had always been. The breasts were a little lower; a little more weight in the thighs; the same ash blonde hair.

She stood motionless with her legs apart, her hands on her hips. Then she threw back her shoulders for him.

"I stood before you this way once," she said softly. "Do you remember?"

"How can I ever forget? I have lived with it for fifteen years. It has haunted me every night and every single day."

"Poor Joshua! My poor Joshua! Don't think I haven't known it. So often when we sat together—Saul, you and I, drinking in the Evening Star—I have felt it. Your eyes would wander all over me as you undressed me, one piece at a time. It was often quite obvious, especially when you'd had too much to drink. Even to Saul. Did you know he saw us that day on the beach?"

"Yes," he said, looking into her eyes and away from her body for the first time, "I found out today. This evening. How it must have hurt him?"

"Hurt him? Is that all you can think of? His hurt? What about me? Do you know how much it has hurt me all these years? He never let me forget it—the bastard! Not that he spoke to me about it—except on the night he married me—but I could see the accusations framed in his eyes. What good did that do me? He and his sordid little affairs. I had to forgive them all, Joshua, because it was I who had sinned first."

"Sinned?"

"Yes! Sinned! As if you didn't know. And then I thought of you. And your bloody eyes drinking me in like I was some white goddess to you. And your fifteen wasted years. Who the hell told you not to get married to some obedient little Indian woman in Durban? At least you could have let me off. But no! You had to carry the damn torch and watch me burn."

"I didn't fall in love with some obedient little Indian woman in Durban," Joshua said. "I would have married her if I had. I don't know if there are any obedient little Indian women left in Durban."

He leaned forward and touched her on the bare shoulder, sliding his hand down her arm, drawing her towards him. She stood beside the bed. Sat down on it. He put his hand around her neck, caressing her short hair, sliding his hand down her bare back, feeling the softness of the hair in her armpits, before moving on to her breast.

"Let's not talk this way, Laura," he pleaded. "Please. Let's just make love."

"No, Joshua! I don't want to just make love. That's all you've ever wanted from me. I want to talk. I wanted to talk that day on the beach too. There were so many things you could have said, and you didn't. And I want to hear them now. All the things you've been meaning to say because I couldn't follow you out of South Africa. Don't think I haven't seen all those accusations framed in your eyes. As bad as Saul's! You have both tortured me—both saying you loved me. Well, I want to hear them now. Aloud! Not just thought so you can lash me with them. Maybe if I hear them they will go away."

"There is really nothing to say," Joshua said, dropping his hand from her breast. "You have said them already. You found the courage to leave South Africa and follow Saul to England. When they moved him out of there."

"That was different," she said, lying back on the bed, her arms above her head, stretching herself in tiredness. "I was married to him by then. I had to go where my husband went. Wouldn't you have wanted me to? It brought me near to you. Didn't that make you happier? At least you could see me sometimes. Very often, if I recall."

"Yes," Joshua said. "You don't know how often I've been grateful to them for forcing Saul out of South Africa into England. Laura, my love, why are we going on at each other in this way? Like married folk. I dreamed of this day, when I could make love to you, as the most memorable of my life."

"And yet, look at you," she said, almost in mockery, as she stripped the bedclothes off him, her laugh hurting more than he thought it would. "You're not even aroused! I'm lying here on the bed, fully naked, and willing—and you're not even capable of it."

He slipped in back beneath the sheets, alongside her. She lay on top of them; he lay underneath.

"I've been drinking too much," he said. "It always reduces my potency. Does so in most men. I'm sorry."

"Why have you been drinking too much?" she demanded, reaching under the bedclothes, with one hand, to help him. "You knew you were to spend the night here. I would have thought you could have abstained from your lecherous little games at the Evening Star—at least for tonight."

He did not tell her about Julia.

Instead he put his arms around her, caressing her breasts in passionless emotion, letting them flow through his fingers, molding them softly to the shape of his palm, twisting her nipple between his fingers like feeling silk. She sighed in contentment, her thigh thrown over his, responding to his endearments and kisses with placid resignation. There was a deference to his touch that precluded intimacy, and she sensed it too.

"I almost knew it would be like this, Joshua. You are so—so respectful. How can you love anyone that way?"

She leaned over him to light a cigarette, allowing him, like some child playing with a new and breakable toy, to fondle her wherever he wished, finding comfort in the pleasure it gave him, tinged with the sadness that it had taken so little and she had waited so long.

"Don't blame yourself, Joshua," Laura said, when they lay back on the bed, still touching, but only occasionally. "Even magic has a way of growing old. Darling, I've decided to go back to South Africa."

"Oh? And when did you decide that?"

"After Saul died. I'm not young anymore. None of us are. And I can't really take this climate. So cold all the time. I could do with more sunshine and warmth and beaches with golden sands. Home. Will you miss me?"

"Yes. Is that what Saul wanted you to do after he died?"

"I don't know what he wanted for me! Why should I care? All he wanted for himself were other men and women. You wouldn't believe the affairs he's had, Joshua. Do you want to know?"

"No."

"I'll tell you anyway. Your friend Jomo was Saul's lover. The very first, actually. Even before me. And Clayborne too. And four other men in South Africa you know nothing about. And the women he's had! Do you want to know about them?"

"No! I don't want to know. Must we talk about Saul? Even when we are in bed together?"

"He poisoned every woman he touched. And none of them loved him the way I could have loved him—if only he'd have let me."

The anger within her caused her to tremble. She seemed to have forgotten all about him or that he was lying in bed beside her. Speaking almost to herself. No longer feeling the touch of his body beside her or the caressing fingers on her breast.

"He was a beast! A monster! Couldn't even forgive an act of charity. And you were a friend. No stranger. I'm glad he's dead. I should have left him years ago. Instead of letting him lead me round on a leash for fifteen years. They're my wasted years too. And I have paid for them."

Just when he thought she might start to cry, she recovered herself.

"Do you know who his latest love was?"

Joshua pretended he had not heard.

"The woman who came in here the other day wanting to buy something from the store. The one who broke her bra strap to gain entry into the flat. I let her go in. Did you notice how long she was in there? Probably hunting for some momento of Saul to take away with her. Something to remember him by? I don't care. She can have all she wants. I only want to forget."

Joshua sat upright in bed. Laura laughed with delight.

"Her name is Julia. But you know that already. You left the store with her. Did you pick her up? Didn't you try—as you usually do?"

"You aren't serious? About her and Saul? Are you?"

"Why does that shock you, my darling? Because she's so young and pretty? That's the way Saul liked them. Young and pretty. No matter who you pick, Joshua, you'll always play second fiddle to Saul. Do you want to know more about her and Saul? He had her for a full year! Not just one night. All that will be left for you are his leftovers."

"You're only trying to be cruel," Joshua said. But even as he said it he saw the truth of it. It burned into him, drawing his eyebrows together, flushing his face and body with the surge of anger that distended his blood vessels, causing his temples to throb and his pulse to race.

"Am I being cruel, Joshua? Hasn't it always been that way between you and Saul? All that will be left for you are his dinner scraps. And even when he's dead and gone, you can't seem to make a meal out of his leftovers."

"Stop it!" he screamed, slapping her across the thighs, raining slaps on her face and back and shoulders, sitting astride her and hitting hard at any part of pink flesh she turned towards him, leaving his finger marks in red strokes across her body; then ashamed of himself he covered her body with his own, kissing her in muted apology on the mouth and cheeks and neck.

While she, smiling softly to herself, put her arms around him, drew up her legs and drew him into her.

They lay that way for a long time, her arms around him, comforting him, his face buried in her hair that covered the pillow beside her.

"You will take care, Joshua?" she said, kissing him near his ear to make sure he'd heard. "While I'm gone? You're safer here with me. Stay with me, my love, for the time I'm in England. It's you they're after; not me. I don't want you to get killed, Joshua. Please, Joshua!"

He rolled off her, and they lay beside each other as they talked.

"It's kind of you to tell me that. But I knew it already. In Romano's. You did a fine job with the fear bit. Don't worry about me, Laura. I may not look it, but I can take care of myself."

It was the end and they both knew it. Sleep lay ahead of them for the night. Then separate lives. An occasional letter. Warm memories. Each had freed the other; freedom was very hard to take.

It was a little before five in the morning that Joshua got out of bed. Laura did not stir. He did not touch her. He collected his clothes from the floor and dressed in the bathroom. He washed his bloodshot eyes, peering at them in the mirror, concluding he wasn't much of a catch for any woman. As a doctor, he knew, well, why events had occurred as they did; as a patient he was overwhelmed by the guilt of it. Love, anger, and revenge had all been a part of it. Stirred with a lot of liquor. That was hardly a way to make love. Out of revenge? He hoped Laura hadn't seen it that way. Unless, of course, she was taking her revenge too. On Saul.

He did not usually drink that much, but last night had been unusual—with Julia and Jomo, not to mention Joe, plying him with drinks.

"Don't you think you ought to know, you fool, when enough is enough?" he said into the mirror.

The thought of Julia sent mixed emotions fluttering through him. Julia and Saul. They would have made a fine pair. He had to admit they were well matched. Is that why she'd been showing so much interest in him? Because she was obsessed with tracking down Saul's killer? He hadn't thought that way the night before, so why was he thinking that way now? It had been wonderful while it had lasted. The one evening. And like all his good things, it hadn't lasted.

But if it was all over, he'd feel better if he gave her something. A parting gift. The way Laura had parted with him, but nothing quite so personal. Perhaps a little souvenir? Or a novelty item?

He unbolted the door leading from the kitchen into the shop. It squeaked as it swung open. It was still dark; no light filtered in through the barred and shuttered windows. The curtains were drawn.

He groped for the light switch inside the door.

She had put up a fierce fight; the chaos in the room bore testimony to it. Broken glass and porcelain littered the aisles. The Egyptian case had toppled over, breaking its back across the counter as it fell, strewing pieces of Egyptian pottery and jade all over it. Blood stains reached in spattered drops across the wall behind the cash register.

He thought the body had been removed from the shop—almost hoped it had—until he saw it lying in the narrow cross aisle, just inside the front door.

She was lying on her back, her arms out flung over her head, the long, black hair spread like a fan beneath the naked body.

There was no sexual mutilation; he could see that. The killing was brutal, but no signs of the elaborate tortured ritual that was the mark of Slagter. Sharp stabs to the chest and stomach were the cause of death, which had come quickly. Once she had been incapacitated. It was a killing in the style of Slagter, but almost as if Slagter had not had the time to complete it his way. Had he been disturbed at it and finished the job fast? Or was this just an imitation killing? Someone choosing to kill like Slagter and unable to copy him exactly?

Her head was turned away from him, one out flung arm shielding her eyes. He could not look into her eyes.

Joshua went back into the kitchen; closed and locked the shop door leading to it.

He sat on a chair, as Julia had done, but he did not cry. He put his head into his hands, to still the painful throbbing in his temples.

This had gone too far.

It had to stop.

He made himself a cup of tea, cradling the hot cup between his fingers, juggling the pieces in his mind.

There was no point in waking Laura up. She had suffered already, like all of them, more than he had, and he could spare her this. When he had left with Julia, earlier that evening, she had left for the real estate agent's office in Gloucester Road. Shari had watched them leave; then she'd closed up.

It had to have been someone who came in before she'd locked up, perhaps asking to be allowed to buy a gift, apologizing for delaying her. Someone who had been watching the shop and waiting for all of them to leave it.

Joshua drained the cup; washed it in the sink.

He hadn't treated it all very seriously. All those warnings, so many people had given him, should have alerted him. Laura, Jomo, Julia, Saul, and even Slagter in his letter to Laura, had all, one way or another, warned him of danger around him—and he had chosen to ignore it.

And if Slagter—whoever he was—didn't kill him to make him talk, Boko would do it in two days. God! What a mess to be in. Not nice at all. He was just asking to be hit.

He had to do something about it. And the answer was obvious. It wasn't entirely to his liking, especially after last night, but he had no choice.

He had to find out for himself what it was he was supposed to know. What it was others were convinced he already knew.

When he did not.

He left the flat from the back door, locking it behind him. He hailed a taxi from across the street, waving wildly as it nearly shot past him. It swung around and came by to pick him up. There was very little traffic about at that time of morning. The cabbie was pleased to have found him.

"Heathrow," he said.

In the bedroom above the shop, Laura stirred in her sleep.

Chapter 13

Julia was preparing breakfast when Donaldson phoned. The eggs were soft-boiling, the toast had popped; Darjeeling tea was brewing in a pot with the tea cozy snuggling it like an all-embracing lover.

Dying breed, the tea cozy. People didn't have much time these days for hot, second cups.

Certainly not Donaldson. He seemed panicked.

"He's leaving, Miss!" Donaldson said, panting for breath as if he'd been rushing around furiously. "He's decided to get out of England, while he's still alive."

"Calm down, Tom," she said, the firmness in her voice helping to allay his agitation. "Where are you now?"

"Heathrow, Miss. In a telephone booth in the European Terminal. He's bought his ticket but hasn't gone through Immigration yet. Keeps looking at his watch as if he doesn't have much time. Or he's waiting for someone or something. What shall I do, Miss?"

"Where is he headed for?"

"Paris. I had to pretend I was a friend, and I'd missed him. Oh! The lies I've had to tell in this business, Miss, is something awful."

"Never mind, Tom. You're doing it for a good cause."

"I hope so, Miss. Anyway it worked. The girl at the counter told me he'd gone through on an Air France ticket. The nine o'clock to Paris. It leaves in thirty minutes. What shall I do?"

"Can you stay with him?"

"Yes. If you want me to. If you ask me, I think we're protecting the wrong man. He doesn't need all this protection at the British taxpayer's expense. No one's been near to him all of yesterday. You'd think if it was that important, they'd have shown their hand by now? Wouldn't you? Instead of which nice Dr Clayborne gets hit. And God knows who else!"

"Where did he spend the night, Tom?"

"With the widow. Went in real late. And she came in even later. But they spent the night together."

"I see."

"Got to go, Miss. What's the word? Shall I dump him?"

"Stay with him, Tom! As close as you can. And don't lose him."

Julia looked out of the open window onto the overgrown backyard. Paris would be nice at this time of the year, with all the flowers blooming in set rows in the parks and gardens of the city. In the Jardin du Tuileres, behind the Louvre, or the Parc du Champ de Mars at the base of the Eiffel tower. The French knew how to grow their flowers. She'd try her hand out at a little gardening, she decided. He had been one of her favourite retainers, the old gardener in the family estate at Bromfield. The lines creased his face like water courses, and the arthritic hands could hardly hold the flowers he picked for her, but he sure knew how to grow them. And what would not grow in the outdoors of the English summer, he'd grow indoors in the greenhouse. That was his special pride. He'd taken her through it once—begged her to take his tour—pointing out the difficult ones that pleased him most. Like the Oleander-leaved Protea with bluish pink bracts, tipped with soft black fur, the flowers nestling deep within the stems and the branches.

"I grow that one specially for his Lordship," he said. "Your family tree, Lady Julia, has a few connections in South Africa through some of its more rugged branches. And this is their national flower. There are a hundred and fifty varieties of the Protea, but his Lordship likes this one best of all."

Paris would be nice at this time of the year. Nice had been nice too. Lying nude on a private, deserted beach that belonged to an old family friend of her grandfather and who was himself vacationing in the Bahamas.

Soaking in the sunshine that never seemed to penetrate English clouds, she closed her eyes and pretended she was quite alone.

She would have preferred to be alone.

"What are you thinking about?" he asked.

"A tan! I try so hard, but I never seem to get a real tan. Or one that lasts any length of time."

"You look just fine to me Julia—the way you are now."

"I don't know why I come to the South of France? This English skin of mine just can't seem to change its miserably healthy complexion."

He turned over onto his side, and raised himself on one elbow to look at her. He took a handful of dry sand and let it trickle through a fine hole in his fist, on to her nipples; then he brushed them clean. And did it again.

"Does your wife know you are here?"

"Let's not talk about her, shall we? And if she does, she doesn't care. So don't let it bother you."

"Most wives care. Even if they don't show it. I know I would if my husband was playing around with some other woman on a deserted beach in the South of France—or her bedroom for that matter."

"You're not capable of caring for anyone, Julia!" he said, the biting scorn in his voice as vicious as the hand he passed over her and through her brown hair. She did not resist him, raising her hands above her head, not in submission but to shield her eyes from the hot sun. And as on all previous occasions, and there had been several in the past year, there would be no arousal and no emotion. Sometimes not even a pleasant experience; even painful when he became angry at her resistance to him. Not physically; she did not resist, but there wasn't the surrender he sought in her; the abandonment he craved in her never surfaced—and it maddened him.

"Why do you always seem so far away? I don't ever seem to be able to reach you. God! Damn it! It isn't as if I haven't tried. I've aroused every woman I've had—but not you. What is so goddam special about you? Do you keep thinking of yourself as Lady Julia, granddaughter of the eleventh Earl of Bromfield, lying with some poor servant you've picked, to have it off with you?"

He slapped her on the face, hard, and it hurt.

"You're a very cruel man," Julia said. "Maybe that's why I can't seem to feel the way you want. Is that how you see yourself? As one of the servants on my estate?"

He slapped her again.

"If you try to hit me once more, I shall have to ask you to leave."

"I'm sorry, Julia. It's so frustrating. Not being able to reach you. And I want to so much."

He lay back on his towel on the dry sand, clenching his fists in the open air.

"I'm very glad you're married," Julia said. "I feel guilty as it is, leading you on. I'd feel much more, if you weren't."

He rolled over onto his side again, facing her.

"Perhaps that's it! It's because I'm married. And those inhibitions of yours deep down arise out of it. But I can easily change that, darling! I'll divorce Laura and then you won't feel as you do. Will you marry me if I divorce her?"

He brushed the hair back from her forehead in apology for the slap that had left finger marks on her cheeks. She shook her head free, reaching for her robe, sitting up on the sand to pull it around her, drawing it over her knees.

"I wouldn't marry you, Saul, if you were the King of England. I think I'll go in. This is over. Finished! I'll never see you again—this way. I don't ever want to see you again."

He laughed, still lying on the sand, looking up at her standing above him.

"You said that once, dear girl. Remember? You couldn't keep away from me then. As long as we both work for MI-6, you're going to find it difficult keeping away from me. I'm a fool! I could find a dozen other girls on this beach, further up—with bodies better than yours—who'd show me a lot more appreciation."

She had to admit he was right. The powerfully built, superbly physical body, with the hairy torso and the small hips, was animal in its lure.

"You're welcome to them all," she said, tying the cord around her waist, brushing back her hair, as she prepared to leave him for the house. "I don't want to see you anymore. And you're wrong. I won't be working with you anymore. I'm leaving MI-6."

He raced after her, catching her by the arm, bringing her to a sudden halt.

"You're not serious? About MI-6? Have you discussed this with Farnsworth? This is all very sudden."

"It isn't. I've been meaning to leave for some time now. Ever since Vladimir got killed. I'm not very good at it, I confess."

"Nonsense, Julia! What you need is a lucky break. Every agent could do with that."

"You seem to have more than your fair share."

"I work at it, Julia. I'm working on one now. That's why I wanted to talk to you in private this afternoon. I'm going away this evening."

"Oh! Where?"

"Paris. I have a contact there. A woman. I had a phone call from her. All hush, hush! But I'll be back tomorrow and I'll share it with you. There's your break."

"I thought agents were supposed to keep all these things secret. Do you often give them away?"

"Only to a lover in bed! I feel so good about sharing titbits of information—then. With you. In bed! Maybe if I were to share some top secret stuff with you, why, you might care more for me?"

"No."

"Please, Julia! It feels so good with a lover."

"No! I don't want to know. I'm not your lover. If being a lover means giving you my love, I have never been your lover."

"God! Damn it! Can't you at least give it a try? Once more! Does it hurt so much to at least try? Your grandfather approves of me. We could be very happy together. I'd make a worthy husband. We'd have a fine twelfth Earl—and heir to Bromfield. God! You're a lousy agent. Most others would sell their souls for the piece of information I'll have by tomorrow morning."

Julia shook herself free from his restraining hand; continued walking towards the house. He followed her, overtook her, and brought her to a halt once more, this time by standing in front of her. He put his hands on her shoulders and shook her hard.

"You have to give me one more chance, Julia. I want you, Julia!"

"I decided a long time ago, Saul," Julia said, trying to be as kind as possible, "that I could give away my body—it was mine to give—but I would have no control on who would have my love. And if it's only my body you're after, you've had that already. Several times over. I don't want to know the information you're being passed by the French stripper at the Coq D'Or."

"How do you know about her?"

"I'm not as lousy an agent as you think. I've known about her for a long time now. So don't give me all that rot about how important I am to you. We're through, Saul, and you might as well know it. I'm glad to be free."

He did not reply. He walked on for a few yards on the beach towards the house, and found her missing from his side. She had stopped some yards back, gazing at his sand-encrusted back. He came back to her.

"Is something the matter?" he asked.

"Do you really share top secret information with your lovers in bed? For kicks!"

"Yes."

"What sort of secrets?"

"Anything that will make for an exciting and memorable night."

"Such as?"

"Depends on the person I'm with. Why do you ask?"

"But if the person you're with asks for a specific piece of information, would you let her have it?"

"Depends."

"Depends on what?" Julia persisted.

"Who I'm with."

"Me?"

"You, Julia? You're willing to hop into bed and make a real go at it? A full night—not just an hour or two? An emotion-filled night? With me?"

"Yes."

"Give yourself to me completely? Do everything I ask? Be everything I want?"

"Yes."

"What a delight. Do you mean that, Julia? This is all so sudden! You will?"

"Yes, I promise. I can't promise my love, but barring that I will try, really try for—as you say—a memorable night."

'That's wonderful, Julia! Why it may lead us in the right direction? You never know how these things work out. For the first time, you actually want something from me. Fire away, old girl! Tell me what you're after so I can make sure I know the answer when I come back from Paris. If I don't know it already. Ask now—and I'll give it you in bed tomorrow night. Here, in Nice."

"Who is Slagter?"

His face changed. There was a silence as if he had not understood her, or if he had, the words had stunned him into immobility. A dazed look spread into his eyes; their horror changed the pallor of his face into a frightened glassiness. She thought he had not heard her, or had not understood; so she repeated it. He started to walk away abruptly from her with quick strides. She ran alongside him, her thighs breaking through the robe knotted at her waist.

"Who is Slagter?" she shouted at him.

"I can't tell you."

"Then you know who he is?"

"Do I? Maybe."

"Then why can't you tell me?"

"I don't want to discuss him anymore. This conversation is closed."

"I thought you enjoyed power plays," she taunted. "Don't you want to tell me? In bed! You reveal such things to your lovers, don't you? For the thrill of it! Well, reveal his name to me in bed. I'll make it worth your while."

"That's impossible."

"You know who he is, Saul. You've been after him a long time."

"How do you know that?"

"It's pretty obvious. Abdul in Tangiers, and you were actually there. And the girl Stella in Miami—and they sent you there. Gangoly in Bombay and Sharon in Haifa and Pierre in Paris—and you covered them all. And Vladimir in Johannesburg, and Farnsworth sent you down there to report back. You had to be stalking him, Saul. Who is he?"

"You're out of your depth, little girl. Don't swim in shark-infested waters. You might lose a breast."

"He doesn't sexually mutilate his victims. He never has."

"You know that too? Very good. What else do you know about him?"

By now they had almost reached the road, where his car was parked. His eyes avoided looking at her, as if he was afraid they might give something away. She looked into his, but saw only the anxious look of a man wanting to flee from her.

And all she had done was to shout at him.

He started the car; reached for the safety belt. Almost by habit. The window had been lowered to vent the car in the heat. She put her hand into the car and gripped his shoulder as if to restrain him.

"Unless you're Slagter!" she screamed at him.

The spell was broken. He leaned back into the driver's seat; reached forward and shut off the engine. Laughter had replaced the anxious look in his eyes.

He was laughing at her.

"Is that what you believe, Julia? That I'm Slagter?"

"I can! I do! You're the cruelest man I have ever known."

"You haven't known many men, Julia. Don't let's talk about him anymore."

"Then you know who he is?"

"Yes."

"And you won't tell me?"

"Not at any price."

"Will you tell Farnsworth when you get back? Fill in a report to MI-6?"

"Certainly not."

"Will you at least make sure he never operates again? God! What sort of person are you? What kind of fiend is he?"

"He's only a very good agent, Julia. And so am I."

That was the last time she had seen him. The faintly mocking look in his eyes, that had followed one brief moment of real tension, lingered in her mind. And his words too.

"He's only a very good agent."

Julia made herself the second cup of tea. The tea cozy had kept the pot warm. She sat in the rocking chair and rocked. Hardly hearing the squeaks as she thought about Paris. It would be really nice at this time of the year. Maybe she'd go back there instead of Nice, when this was all over. There was nothing left for her in Nice, except unpleasant memories. Paris held no memories for her. Farnsworth had promised MI-6 would fly her out again—he'd promised to send in the requisition slip that very day to his Chief—and Paris would be cheaper than Nice. They ought to be pleased. She'd saved them a few pounds.

But before she could think about going back there, she had two very important matters to attend to in England. At once, while she had a little time. While Joshua was still in Paris with Donaldson looking after him. Taking some of the strain off her. Good man, Donaldson. He was out there keeping a sharp eye on Joshua. Making sure he didn't get into trouble. Or that no one got near him.

One matter was an important piece of female shopping. She had to get rid of her high-heel shoes and buy a few pairs of flat-heeled ones.

The other was a quick trip to Bromfield to meet her grandfather.

Chapter 14

Julia decided to attend the second of the two matters first. She went up that morning to Bromfield to see her grandfather. She went unannounced. She did try to reach him on the telephone, but the line was busy, and rather than waste time, she slung an overnight bag into the boot of the Bentley—together with a case of white wine—and headed north.

The eleventh Earl was always on at her to come down and see him, and she went as often as she could, but the past year had been on assignment in Mozambique, followed by the brief vacation in Nice, and so their meetings had been infrequent. She had gone up to Bromfield twice, and each time he had been in London on business. Still it was good to be back in the family estate, wandering through the rooms of her childhood, touching loving pieces of furniture, all of which were carefully dusted and waxed for her return.

"You'll come back here one day, my Lady," Emma—her governess from those days and now the housekeeper—had said. "Mark my words! And when you do, you'll find everything exactly as it was."

Julia had never doubted she would—until yesterday. A chance ride in a crowded London tube with an almost total stranger left her in considerable doubt and confused.

She stopped the car at the entrance lodge to chat with the old gatekeeper. He was still on active duty, even though he had some difficulty with the heavy gates that swung open. She pulled up, stepped out of the car and preceded him into the lodge, where he put on the kettle, while she stood at the window and looked out onto the grounds in front and the house in the distance.

There was another reason for this intentional delay in reaching the house.

She had not informed them she was coming, particularly the time she was expected to arrive. And if she'd just driven up to the front door, Emma would have been in a panic. The servants would have to be rounded up from their duties, quickly, to form a reception committee for her ladyship. That could take a long time.

But it was a bit more complex than that.

Most ladies greeting their servants on the estate, including some of her grandfather's friends visiting Bromfield, left their gloves on. It was expected of them. There was no statement of class or rank in the act; merely convenience. Servants might be out working in the garden or the kitchen, and even though hastily wiped, their hands might not be as clean as one would wish.

But not Lady Julia.

Climbing up the flight of stone steps that led to the front door, from the car, saw her strip off her right glove.

Invariably.

Then she offered her bare hand to each servant in line, with a gentle inquiry, perhaps, as to the state of his health or that of his bedridden wife, or if neither was appropriate, perhaps, about a favourite dog or horse.

Emma had remonstrated.

"It isn't the done thing, my Lady!"

Julia respected Emma in most things. She had virtually doubled as her mother in the years when she needed one; there was a special relationship between them which could not be expressed. By them. But in this matter Julia refused to budge. They struck a compromise.

"If only you could give us more time, Lady Julia. Perhaps by informing us in advance, of your visit?"

"I wish I could, Emma. But I can't always be certain of that. What would you have me do if I decided to come home, sudden like?"

"Why don't you pull up at the lodge for a cup of tea, and some of your favourite muffins, with old Crabtree. He'd love that. And at his age he deserves it too. It'd give us more time. Ten minutes! That is all Tomkins and I need to prepare for your visit."

"Yes. I suppose I could do that," Julia said. "But how would that help?"

"It'd just give us more time," the old lady said stubbornly.

And that was all she'd say.

It was not until several years later that Julia found out what actually took place in those ten minutes.

The servants were rounded up hastily. All of them washed their hands with carbolic soap and water. Two inspection lines were formed with Tomkins and Emma inspecting the hands, both front and back and particularly the fingernails for the slightest speck of dirt. After which Tomkins inspected Emma's hands, and she his.

There had been a minor incident some years ago with a new servant—a young lad of sixteen, and employed to run errands.

"Who's to say," he said cheekily, "that 'er ladyship's 'ands are all that clean?"

That had nearly had him fired. The Earl had listened gravely to both sides—Emma and the lad—and then passed judgment.

The boy could stay on—it was hardly a crime that warranted as severe a punishment as being fired—but he could not stand in the reception line for Lady Julia. Unless he followed the housekeeper's rules.

"And serve him right!" Emma fumed. "His Lordship was much too lenient with you, my lad. Firing was too good for you!"

It ended a little differently though.

The lad, whose name was James, was barred from the reception line. So in order to see the Lady Julia, the first time she came to Bromfield, he crept away to the lodge, hiding himself in the shrubbery inside the estate fence.

He saw her step out of the car, tall, lady-like, elegant, wearing a printed blouse of Indian silk and a loose skirt with flares that hung below her knees, her hair drifting over her shoulders—exquisitely beautiful, so it seemed to him. Overcome with puppy love and admiration, he raced back to the house, fell on his knees and begged Emma to be allowed to comply.

And when she offered him her bare hand, at the very end of the line—Emma had made him wash his hands twice and inspected them rigorously before permitting him to stand in line—he bowed low over it and kissed it.

So Julia, as usual and in keeping with custom, pulled into the gatekeeper's lodge, and had her cup of tea with old Crabtree. James, the boy, was now twenty. He greeted her at the car with Emma; Tomkins trailing behind her. Emma frowned, but Julia stepped back and whispered instructions to him about the luggage in the boot of the car. He nodded sharply and disappeared.

She stripped off her right glove, passed down the reception line, shaking hands with all of them, with a smile for James that melted him.

Then came the customary speech of welcome by Emma or Tomkins—they alternated in this duty. Tomkins was more long-winded than Emma, but Emma was more likely to break down—and then a few words of reply by Julia.

Only this time she informed them that in sincere apology for having been away so long, she had a case of wine for them in the kitchen, which she hoped they would enjoy—with her compliments.

Her grandfather was not in.

She did the customary rounds of the gardens, the grounds and the estate, met with the housekeeper to discuss the menu for the day's meals, gave instructions to Tomkins on the schedule of event for the next two days—that was all she could stay—and then drew Emma into the study for the information she wanted.

"Where's Grandfather?" she asked. "When will he be back?"

"I don't know, Lady Julia," Emma said. "He had an important call from London, while you were in Nice, and he took off. Without a word to anyone. It was at night, so I couldn't even ask him when he might be back. You know how busy his lordship is. Sometimes he could be gone for days, and then he could be back tomorrow. He left a brief note for Tomkins, telling him he had to leave that night, and asking us all to carry on as usual. His Lordship did tell us to call you in Nice if there was an emergency."

While she was in Nice! That was almost three days ago. That was how long she'd been gone from Nice.

So her grandfather could not have met with Saul either.

Had Saul come to Bromfield?

And why? He had an appointment in Bromfield at ten-thirty. His diary said so. But why?

Julia sat at her grandfather's study table, cleared of all papers on it, the drawers locked when he was away. Always locked, even when he was in. Matters of State dealing with the House of Lords. She could understand that.

"Tell me, Emma," Julia said, without looking up at her, "did Mr Prentiss come to see Grandfather while I was away?"

She tried to make it sound casual. And, perhaps, she did it rather too well, because Emma's face took on a glow.

"Why, yes! Oh, Lady Julia! He was most disappointed he could not meet with his Lordship. I thought he might ask for you, but I can see now why he wouldn't. Such a handsome man, Lady Julia! You two would make such a fine couple! So well bred too! Is that why he called? If you will forgive me asking you?"

"No, Emma. That is not why he called."

Saul would not have asked for her. The reason was obvious. He had just left her behind in Nice. He could hardly expect to find her at Bromfield.

"Did you show him in? Personally, I mean?"

"Yes. Tomkins was unwell, and since the Master was away, I told Tomkins to take the day off. In bed he was."

"Sit down, Emma, and tell me all about it."

"What would you like me to tell you?" Emma said, sitting straight up in the straight-backed chair, confused by the questioning.

Not quite knowing what was required of her, or if she'd done wrong. Willing to obey as best she could.

"Tell me everything that happened that morning," Julia said gently. "As best you remember."

"Well, let me see. He rang the doorbell, and I heard it peal—loudly, impatiently. So I doffed the apron, washed my hands in the sink—I was helping cook with pastry, and my hands were covered with flour—and heard it peal again. And by the time I reached the front door, it went a third time. I was quite prepared to give anyone of no consequence a piece of my mind—but of course not Mr Prentiss! He was very special. I showed him into the living room; I was all flustered I can tell you, because he was the very last person I expected to see outside the front door. He asked for the Master, and I said I was sorry he wasn't in and would he care to leave a message."

"Did he ask when his Lordship would be back?"

"Come to think about it, actually no. He asked for a glass of water—it was so hot outside or he'd been rushing, I could see the beads of sweat all over his face—and whether he could write a note while I fetched it. I showed him into the study, and Tomkins not being well, I brought him a glass of water."

"What was he wearing?"

"A light raincoat. Not one of those cheap transparent ones. One of those regular, brown ones with large pockets and a turned-up collar. And he had a felt hat. Yes, I remember that. He kept it on the hall stand when we went into the study."

"Was he carrying anything else? Like a package, or a parcel, or an envelope? Anything at all?"

"No, Lady Julia."

"Give me the note. The one he left for Grandfather."

"He didn't write one."

"Oh? I thought that was why you showed him into the study?"

"Yes. But when I brought him his glass of water on a tray—the silver one we use for guests that stay overnight—he said he'd changed his mind about the note. He said to tell his Lordship he'd called. Nothing special, he said, but I knew better. Said he'd call again. Only this time he'd telephone first, so he wouldn't have a wasted trip. And then he gave me one of those smiles of his that fair dissolved me! But, then, you know all about those smiles of his, Lady Julia."

"Yes, Emma, I do. Go on."

"I showed him out. He picked up his hat from the hat stand. I stood on the steps and watched him drive down to the entrance lodge. Crabtree let him out."

"Thank you, Emma," Julia said. "You've been very helpful."

Emma curtsied, and left.

Julia looked around the study. This was an entirely different set of circumstances. A glass of water—or a broken bra strap—served to gain illegal entry. Why? She had sought illegal entry in the hope of finding something. With no time to do it in.

Why had he sought illegal entry into the study? Had he hoped to find something? Then why take an appointment?

Unless he hadn't come there to find something, but to hide it.

She had to find it. It wasn't quite the same thing as being in Saul's study trying to find it, with all of them in the shop below her awaiting her return; not knowing what she was looking for. Here, too, she did not know what she was looking for.

But this was her grandfather's study. And hers when she had been a child. She had done her homework in that room. The suggestion had been made that she ought to have a study of her own, and theoretically she did, it being the room adjoining her bedroom where she might do a spot of writing in the middle of the night. But in the daytime, her grandfather insisted she be with him.

It was the one time she'd seen him really firm with Emma. And her.

"You can just as well do your homework in my study, Julia. You can have your own table. There by the window. Don't touch the papers on my table—and I won't touch the papers on yours. You don't disturb me, and I won't disturb you. What do you say? At least I'll get a chance to see something of you when you're home for the hols."

It had been as much her study as his. She knew every side and corner of it; all the books on the shelves—treatises on International Law side by side with Enid Blyton and Louisa May Alcott; every drawer—even secret ones that opened in antique tables when you pressed the wood at the right spot. And the drawer that opened in the cuckoo clock. The loose panel in the paneled wall, which was merely a loose panel that hid nothing, and the painting of the horse in the field, which hid the safe.

She'd crept inside the coats of armor, watching battles of old through polished visors.

This was a different search. No time constraints, no strangers—though she could hardly call Joshua that now—waiting below, wondering how long it took to fix a broken bra strap.

She had all the time she needed. She could lock the study door, which she did, and search until she found it. If there was anything to find in the room, of course.

There was. And she found it. Discreetly tucked away behind three volumes on International Law. A thick, brown, manila paper envelope, sealed with tape at both ends. No marks on the outside. No writing either.

It was the thickness of it that gave it away to Julia. The eleventh Earl's set of International Law numbered six volumes, and, to her fingers, some had seemed to project further out than others.

Saul had intended it to be found.

She sat on the study table and slit it open.

It contained a list of names and figures, with brief explicit description. Three hundred pages of it. Single spaced. Front and back. At the left was the name of a company or individual. In the centre was a description of the precise holding in the type of activity, such as mining or munitions. And on the right was the investment in millions of rands.

She stared at it in disbelief. She had not really believed Saul that day when he'd slid into the seat beside her at the Crown and Whistle. The list had been made in happier times. Two copies of it. The one was in the secure files of the finance ministry in Pretoria. So Saul had said. The other in the hands of their roving ambassador, meeting with those who'd placed their money in South Africa.

And now in her hands.

She stared at it mesmerized. So this was how it had been planned. Her throat went dry at the thought of it. Except that Saul had started to play his own game. And when it became necessary, on the day he came back from Paris, he planned to plant the list on Joshua. Except that he hadn't planned to leave the list actually in Joshua's flat. Merely spread the word that he'd seen Joshua that morning. Leaving everyone believing that Joshua had a list he knew nothing about. It was a damaging document. Both the South African Government and the ANC would dearly love to have it.

No! That couldn't be quite right. Because he'd made an appointment to come to Bromfield too that morning. He'd told everyone he was meeting with Joshua; no one knew about his meeting with the eleventh Earl.

He had never intended to give the list to Joshua—that part of her reasoning was correct, she thought—but he had intended to leave it with her grandfather. Even resorting to the simple ruse of asking for a glass of water to gain entry into the study.

Why?

Why would he want to leave such a sensitive document with her grandfather? Was it for protection? Or safekeeping? Or transmittal? And when the suspicion formed in her mind, the excitement within her caused her hands to tremble. As she took down the painting of the horse in the field, to expose the family safe behind it. At eye level. The deep set frame had a recess in it where the dial projected from the wall. She felt the drops on her neck, underneath her curls, trickle down the front into her blouse and then, guided by the cleavage, soak into the fine lace fabric of her bra. She wiped her lips with the back of her hand. Childhood habits died hard. Especially now.

She swung open the door of the safe and reached for the key. To her grandfather's study table. The one key to the flat drawer unlocked all the drawers. The deep ones held files. Hung on rails that allowed the drawer to slide open. The flat drawer underneath the tabletop would hold his papers. Present correspondence, perhaps. The one key she held would open them all. She sat at the desk and toyed with the key for along time.

"Forgive me, Grandfather," she murmured to herself, "for invading your privacy in this way. But a man's life is at stake and hanging by a thread, and though he may not know it, he means a great deal to me."

The tabletop was clear of all papers. He'd been called away unexpectedly. Emma had said he'd left in a hurry at night. What would his natural reaction have been? He'd sweep all the papers lying on the tabletop into the flat drawer immediately below it. She had seen him do this once before. When she had, just the one time, come unexpectedly into his study—as an adult while on a surprise visit from London. Then he had come forward to greet her with open arms.

It had not seemed of much significance then.

She opened the drawer. The very first paper, on the very top, told her what she wanted to know.

It was not a piece of paper. It was an airline ticket. On British Airways. Made out by a travel agent in Soho. She knew the agency well. Spifford and Block. It was the only one she was allowed to use for official travel. With the ticket, attached to the back, was the requisition request made out to the eleventh Earl asking for authorisation. Citing unusual circumstances. Signed by Farnsworth and addressed to the Head of the African Bureau.

The ticket was from London to Nice. Open dated. The name on the ticket was hers.

Not just the South African desk! That was headed by Farnsworth. She knew that. The whole of Africa—the entire continent of it—all the way from Egypt and Morocco down to South Africa. Her grandfather was the controlling director of the African Bureau. One of the seven directors of MI-6. One for each of the regions that covered the globe. She knew the general organisation of MI-6, but she'd never known who any of the directors were. If she went through his papers, she'd know the names of the directors of all the other bureaus—Europe, Near East, Far East, North and South America, Pacific, and, of course, the USSR. There had to be correspondence between them and those who worked for them—such as Donaldson.

Why should she be surprised? And when she asked herself the question, the answers became all too clear. What would the eleventh Earl have to say if, suddenly, she confronted him with the knowledge she now had?

The kindly blue eyes would have broken into the familiar twinkle, and the military moustache would have seemed so much less formidable with the parting smile on his lips. And if she was young enough to be taken on his lap, he would have done that too. And he would have said, mildly: "Even an Earl has to earn a living, Julia. And I am doing what I do best. Protecting the security of the British Government and the British people. And a way of life. Is that so very wrong?"

He would be right too. That was what people like her, of royal blood, were best suited to do. Their loyalty was never in doubt—even though there had been some bad eggs. They could be entrusted, without fear, with the safety of the Crown. He came from a hereditary earldom that had been granted to her family in the sixteenth century. And if she had a son, he would be the twelfth Earl—even if she married a commoner.

And she was being groomed to take over the African Bureau from him, when the time came.

Why should it surprise her? She worked for MI-6. What was so wrong if he worked for MI-6 too? And in a position of far greater responsibility, and so far more effective than she was. She closed the flat drawer firmly. She did not want to pry into his papers. It did not matter who the Heads of the other Bureaus were. She had no wish to know. Not by invading his privacy. She had already done some of that and she was ashamed of it.

But the identity of Donaldson? That was different. It had direct bearing on the case in her lap.

She opened the deep drawer on one side. The one that held the personnel files, neatly hung like bodies from the rack. Alphabetically arranged for convenience.

Farnsworth under F.

No file for Donaldson. Or it was missing. But the old Earl had been back—possibly at night, without Emma being aware of it—or her airline ticket would not have been in the drawer! Which told her that old Crabtree was also of MI-6. The old mansion had plenty of side entrances some of which even she was aware of! Had he come back to take away Donaldson's file? And if so, why?

She rang the bell and asked for James to be sent up immediately. When he appeared she said:

"James, I have to return to London immediately. Please fill up the Bentley and bring it round to the front in ten minutes. And if you do it in five, I'll tell Emma to let you have an extra day off next week. I'll even leave twenty quid with Crabtree at the lodge, so you can take your girl into London and live it up with her."

He smiled broadly, blushing a little at the mention of his girl.

"Five minutes, Lady Julia! Time me if you will."

He disappeared at a run down the hallway.

Chapter 15

Joshua checked into his favourite hotel—a small, family owned establishment, almost at the corner of Boulevard St. Martin, just off the Place de la Republique. He had stayed there several times before. He felt comfortable between their clean sheets. He liked the smell of their coffee, and the smiles with which it was served. The old Frenchman, with his old world charm and waxed moustache, ruled his family like a sixteenth century French monarch—and just as liberally.

After lunch, over a bottle of white wine, Joshua invited him to join his table on the sidewalk, underneath a big, red and white umbrella, and share a glass of wine.

"It is always a pleasure to see you here, M'sieu le Docteur," he said, sitting opposite Joshua with relish and unbuttoning his jacket around the waist.

Joshua poured him a glass of wine, and they toasted each other. And when that was over, they toasted passersby in the street.

"I love Paris, Henri," Joshua said. "And there isn't a more hospitable family in the whole of France."

"Hyperbole, M'sieu, but please don't stop. I would like to think that the pleasure of my company, or that of my daughter—who has been madly in love with you these past few years and who will not marry any of the fine young men who flirt with her—has drawn you to us. But, alas, it is not so?"

"I would find any excuse, Henri, to come to Paris. What could be more pleasing than to sit, beside you, in the warm Parisian sunshine, drinking a glass of white wine, watching all the pretty women go by?"

Joshua leaned forward confidentially.

"Tell me. What happened to her last husband?"

"He was a bounder, Joshua. She was a fool to have married him. I warned her he was no better than the first. But did she listen? He took off when it suited him, leaving her with two kids. Which was the only nice thing she ever got from him. And so now, I have four beautiful grandchildren—and no son-in-law!"

Henri drained his glass; signalled the waiter for another bottle, shouting out the name in rapid French, waving aside Joshua's protests. "The stuff I sell you, Joshua, is good. But the stuff I treat you with is excellent."

They toasted each other again, and when that was over they toasted each of his four grandchildren. Separately. Joshua had to admit he was right.

"So it is business that brings you here, mon ami?" Henri said.

"I'm afraid so."

Henri sighed.

"I thought Joshua, you and I might, how you say, go out on the town together?"

"I couldn't possibly avoid that, Henri. Tell me. Where is the Coq D'Or? What sort of place is it?"

"Not our type of club, Joshua. It's been there for some time now. A place for bisexuals. They undress men and women there without discrimination. Cater to all the passing fancies. Not your sort of thing, Joshua. I would avoid it if I were you."

"Business, Henri. Business, not pleasure."

"Ah! That is what they all say. I will not probe, M'sieu. But may I give you a word of advice? Be careful. There have been two unexplained murders there already. It is better to be warned."

"Who was murdered?"

"Tourists. Visitors like yourself. That's what gives it a bad name. Paris lives on the goodwill of visitors. When we start killing them off, it's bad for business. It frightens them away."

"Who was murdered?"

"Both were black Africans, who, reports say, tried to muscle into the dressing room of La Reine—the Queen—their star lady. Not very good, M'sieu."

"What is she like? This La Reine?"

"I would keep away from her, Joshua. She has an appetite for men that makes us look like adolescents. Perhaps she is the only real woman in the whole world. The way a woman was meant to be! Perhaps it is all reputation to attract business to the club. Who can say? Certainly from all accounts, she is a very beautiful woman, gorgeously built, and an exciting entertainer. They say she had an unhappy love affair with a man from South Africa some years ago, but that is only hearsay, of course."

"I'll be careful, Henri," Joshua promised. "And I will look forward to many occasions to drink, with you, sitting out here in the sunshine, a glass of this fabulous wine."

Henri snapped his fingers to his daughter to clear away the empty bottle, he'd already knocked over twice.

As she reached over for the bottle, Joshua held her arm. He drew her towards him, and kissed her on the lips. Henri beamed with pleasure.

"How have you been, Anne-Marie?"

"Very well, M'sieu," she said, giving him a little curtsy. "And very busy. This is the height of the season. May I advise you, M'sieu, not to allow my father to lead you astray? He does little more around the place than to drink with his guests."

"How are the children? I could not possibly let you leave without learning about them."

She placed the tray on the table, reaching for their photographs in the pocket of her dress, underneath the apron. She knelt beside Joshua, Henri drew closer, and between the two of them in a little English and a lot of French, he gleaned their life stories.

Joshua told her they were adorable. Meant it too.

"I don't drink with my guests, Joshua," Henri said, when Anne-Marie had returned to the kitchen, "to fleece them. As many a hotel-keeper will do. I do it because I meet interesting people. Like yourself, educated, well-travelled men of character."

"And women of passion?"

"Them too. But why does the Coq D'Or interest you? Why does La Reine interest you? Other than as a woman?"

He did not really expect a reply, and Joshua gave him none.

Instead they clinked glasses, sitting at the table on the sidewalk, underneath the red and white umbrella, and watched the pretty girls go by.

Joshua booked the late show. The last show.

The Coq D'Or was set back on the Rue de la Bruyere, almost at the corner with Rue Pigalle. He decided not to take a taxi. Instead he walked. It was a fine night for a walk, and the nights of Paris were always exciting to him. He took the Boulevard de Magenta, turning left into Rue La Fayette. Then he wandered through a maze of side streets, stopping to admire the old buildings closing in above him, peering into the shop windows and boutiques, ogling the beautifully slim, lifelike mannequins who held out their arms to him.

The theme for the evening, the Emcee announced to the intimate audience seated around the small stage, was the vulnerability of the human body.

"Messieurs et Mesdames! You will see this evening the total fragility of the human form. Not just the body, but the mind, the spirit, the very soul will be stripped naked before you and laid bare! The human psyche will be dismembered in a way you could not have imagined. And the experience, Messieurs et Mesdames, cannot but enlighten you, arouse you and elevate you. The comedy of it will move you to laughter, and the tragedy of it will move you to tears. But the human body is so beautiful—it can never disgust you."

The star attraction was La Reine. She came in early in the evening, in a star-sequined dress that covered her from her neck to her toes, to be introduced to the audience.

"She will be back," the Emcee promised, "in a tableau titled 'The Rape of a Queen'."

So much for subtleness, Joshua thought, as he settled back for the evening with his glass of free champagne.

The show was not all it was promised to be, but it was not without its moments of eroticism—or human pathos. The largely foreign audience—Parisians didn't go in for this sort of thing—was generous in its applause. Joshua looked at the men with clinical detachment; at the women with lust. If it was not for the business he'd come for—such times were always anxiety-filled—he would have enjoyed it more. As it was, his eyes kept looking for the rear exit behind the curtains. He left his seat at two of the duller, and darker, moments to search out the corridor that led to the dressing rooms and the washroom on the floor above.

La Reine came in only once. For the very last tableau. She was still dressed in her star-sequined dress. But this time she was accompanied by a male, dance partner. They stalked each other in the dance, passing first at a distance, then closer, until he grabbed her in electrifying suddenness, tearing the dress off her in bits and pieces, while she was not bashful in doing the same to him.

The audience loved it.

But business came first. Joshua sighed as he threw a last glance at her. She was reduced to pasties; her male partner was already naked, when Joshua disappeared behind the curtain into the corridor.

It was deserted.

He went up the top of the stairs, the clash of cymbals following him up into the corridor above. As the star of the show, she had her own dressing room at the far end of the corridor. With her name on it.

He made a quick search of the room. There was nothing of interest on the table; just the usual items of feminine make-up, accentuated in this case by an over-abundance of the darker shades of blood red and magenta.

He did not know what he was looking for. A diary of sorts? Letters? There were none.

He looked at the walls. What he saw startled him, simply because he wasn't expecting it.

On the wall, opposite the door, stretching from one corner of the room to the other, was a huge map of the entire world. The largest map he had ever seen. The sort of map he had imagined in the strategic headquarters of military superpowers. Instead of magnetic disks that might signify fleets or squadrons or divisions, he saw the national flags of some of the countries pinned into their respective nations. There was no organised pattern it seemed to him. A concentration of flags in Europe and Africa; fewer in Asia and South America. He drew out the flag from South Africa. It had a name and a date on it. 'Saul Prentiss'. The date was more than sixteen years ago.

There were a ring of flags in the countries round South Africa—Mozambique, Namibia, Zimbabwe, Angola and Zambia. In all cases a name and a date.

There was no flag through India.

He put the flags back into the pinholes they had made in the map.

He sat on the bed to await her. He heard the clapping from the floor below; the shuffle of feet emptying into the street. A few words in French, too muffled and far away for him to understand.

He heard her come up the stairs, into the corridor and up to the door, every footfall magnified by the silence around him. Telling him precisely who she was and where she'd be. The ever-increasing sound reached the door. His footsteps had been clothed by the clash of cymbals; hers were bare.

She came into the room, almost without seeing him. The red dressing gown, thrown carelessly round her body, was half open at the top. Held by a cord at the waist. Her thighs broke through with every step as she walked in.

She stopped abruptly when she say him; stopped, turned around as if to make for the door.

"Forgive me, Madame," he said softly, "for being in your dressing room without your permission. May I be pardoned the intrusion?"

She held the door open for him.

"Strangers are not allowed in my dressing room, M'sieu. I have no wish to be rude to a foreigner, but I must ask you to leave."

"Even a close friend of Saul Prentiss?"

"I do not know anyone by that name."

"It is very important to me, Madame, to talk to you. Please! If you will only give me a few minutes of your time? That is all I ask of you."

"Will you leave, M'sieu, of your own free will, or will I be forced to have you thrown out of this room? I would prefer you to leave in one piece."

"Madame," he begged, "in order to be in your dressing room at this moment, I have had to forgo the pleasure of watching you complete your act. Surely that must tell you how important it is to me. To be here. Please, Madame! I only wish to talk to you. About a matter that was very important to both Saul and me."

She seemed to soften. A smile formed on her lips. The hand clutching the dressing gown relaxed a little. He saw her hand slide to her side.

"Most men, M'sieu, flatter me by telling me how exciting they found the conclusion of my act. How the mere anticipation of it aroused them. Uncontrollably! How they would lay all their wealth at my feet to watch me complete it. Yet you are telling me you could quietly slip away from it—to talk to me? That is a new line, M'sieu, and, I must confess, it amuses me."

She closed the door behind her. Did not bother to lock it. She moved to the dressing table and sat on the padded stool facing into the mirror, her back to him. The smile still played on the lips. Saul had adored her, and Joshua could see why. She was ravishing, the oval face highlighted by the high cheek bones framing large eyes and lips. The auburn hair tied in a massive bun at the back of the head, was adorned with paste jewellery that winked and twinkled at him with every movement of her body.

She undid the pins in her hair, and it cascaded around her. She reached for the cleansing cream on the table, rubbing it all over into her face and neck, her shoulders, and sliding her hands over her breasts. A fragrance emanated from her.

She watched him, watch her, in the mirror.

When he noticed, he jerked his eyes away from her. She permitted herself to smile again.

"What did you say your name was, M'sieu?"

"Joshua. Joshua Samuelson. I really was a friend of Saul."

"Your are a doctor? Why, yes. He spoke of you sometimes. I feel as if I know you a little—through him.

So you were unable to see the completion of my act, Joshua? Because you wanted to talk to me? Well, I should hate to feel that any one of my customers, paying good money to see my act, was not fully satisfied at the Coq D'Or. Especially a friend of Saul."

He did not understand, until she stood up from the padded stool.

She allowed the dressing gown to fall away from her, facing him, unhurriedly, unashamed; then almost as if he was not in the room, languidly, reaching for a nightgown from several in the closet near the bed, raising her hands high above her head, holding them there, poised, for more than a few seconds, finally allowing the nightgown to fall over her.

"Have you nothing to say, Joshua?" she said. "No word of applause? No comment? Perhaps criticism?"

"What can I say, Madame? You are indeed a queen."

"Where are you from, Joshua? Not where you were born, but the country you can call your own?"

"India."

"Ah! L'Indie! A beautiful country. Though I have never been there. I would like to go there sometime."

She walked over to the map on the wall to point it out to him, tapping it with her forefinger. She opened the drawer of the small table below it, searching within the flags it contained until she found the flag of India. She placed it on the table.

"I was in love once, Joshua. Sixteen years ago. And the man I loved, adored me. I will always believe that. We were going to be married. We spent so many hours in bed, not just making love—anyone can do that—but talking to one another. Feeling the love, not just making love.

I told him all about myself, my family, even my great-grandmother who spoke Afrikaans and came from his part of the world. From Cape Town. I thought he would have been pleased, I could trace, in my ancestry, some part of his people."

Joshua touched her on the cheek, feeling the hurt through his fingers, trying to caress it away.

She held his hand to her face, grateful for the comfort it gave her.

"I know how you feel, Madame. I know the places you have been. Even the road seems dreadfully familiar."

She dropped his hand.

"He told me about you, Joshua. But that was all a long time ago. A very long time ago. We have to keep ourselves alive—you and I. And do you know the best way to do it? Shall I tell you?"

"Please."

"It is to have a goal in life. Any sort of goal. However trivial it may be. It allows one's life to be full of expectation. Of some achievement still unattained. Without a goal in life, one is a dead person, M'sieu."

"Almost anyone would agree with you, Madame."

"Shall I tell you mine?"

"If you wish."

"You will not laugh?"

"I promise."

"My goal in life is a simple one, Joshua. Perhaps because I am a simple woman. God did not make me intelligent, or witty, or talented. But he gave me a body and he filled it with desire. I live within my limitations. I live with a goal that fits my abilities."

"Nothing could be more sensible, Madame."

"Please, will you call me Simone? That is my name. My goal before I die, Joshua, is to put a flag of every country into my map. Then every people on Earth will have had a part of me!"

"A worthwhile goal, Simone, I can hardly fault it."

"I'm glad you think so. There are some who would not understand. Did you say you wanted to talk to me? What did you want to talk about? Here, come sit by me."

Joshua obeyed.

"About Saul. A few questions about Saul. May I ask?"

The marine-blue eyes, with the touch of green, smiled mischievously.

"I am a simple woman, Joshua. Satisfied, the truth comes to me very easily. Unsatisfied, I find myself telling the most outrageous lies!"

She got up from the bed; beckoned to him with her forefinger.

Joshua smiled for the first time that evening. His face relaxed; so did the doubts and anxieties of the evening. Suddenly he felt as if he'd known her for a very long time. He was not going to make love to her for the truth, though that is what he had come for. He was going to love her for herself—because she had once belonged to Saul? Or was it because he saw Saul, naked, on top of Julia's naked body poised for entry? A chance encounter between them could have been easily forgotten. But she'd been his mistress—if Laura was to be believed—for a full year! How many times, in that year, had he violated her? How many times had she curled up with him, stretched herself for him, trembled with excitement for him, given herself to him, and taken him?

That is what Laura had said. All that would be left for him would be Saul's leftovers. Is that how people looked at each other? As leftovers? Was he someone's leftover? And Julia? Was she too Saul's leftover? He had never thought of people that way, even with au pair girls. Each time it had been a person.

Like Simone.

He undressed, standing beside the bed.

She did not undress.

He did not understand; looked inquiringly at her, ready to apologize if he had misread the signals. And in doing so, possibly offended her as well.

He reached for the clothing on the floor beside the bed.

She stayed his hand.

"Tell me, Joshua, would you like to be my male partner on that floor below us? In a dance? For a few moments? Cavorting around me. Waiting for the right beat of the music and the roll of the drum when you will tear my clothes away from me?"

"I must confess, the fantasy excites me."

"It is not a fantasy. Here, take the sleeve of my nightgown. We had one such tableau a while ago. They are all nearly the same—these tableaus! This was a stage prop we used for it. Feel inside the sleeve. Do you find a little loop there? Put your finger inside it. And pull. Et Voila! I stand, naked, before two hundred people, as I do before you. Could anything be more satisfying?"

Could this be happening to me, Joshua thought, as he watched her glide round the side of the bed, the firmness of her body barely quivering in the subtle movements of her thighs. She was a trained dancer; he could see that.

She slipped in between the sheets, and patted them invitingly.

He found her strangely exciting. And liberating. He felt a sense of relief from the doubts that had plagued him since last night. That night he'd spent with Laura. And it had come close to being disastrous. She had saved him—by angering him. How could one love that way? On a sustained basis? That was hardly a good reason for love. And Laura had been someone he'd known and loved for fifteen years.

The Frenchwoman beside him was a total stranger. He had not known her until a few minutes before—though he had heard of her before then. She had revealed her name—her real name—in just those few minutes, and asked to be called by it. Yet, here he was, willingly, wantingly, urgently making love to her. It was in the feeling, he decided, the difference lay. The touch of people wanting each other. Each knew of the other, and both being rejects brought them closer to one another. Seeing her eyes light up in delight at his desire—and the passion of it—made it all the more satisfying. One could not love unless one is really loved.

She lay with her head on his shoulder, breathing warm air onto his chest, passing her hand over his nipple, playing with it, even toying, occasionally turning onto her back so he could do the same. Only to come back to him.

He rubbed her back.

"You were very good, M'sieu," she said, half asleep.

"Thank you. I'm not too young anymore. I've lost fifteen years somewhere—as you have too—and still quite don't know why? Now it seems I am free to start all over again. Perhaps, you can too, Simone?"

"I doubt it, Joshua. But I am happy for you. My life is set in irrevocable fashion. The walls are too steep for me to overcome them. But within those walls, I seek my goal, and I am not unhappy."

"Will you tell me about Saul? Will you talk about him?"

"What is there to talk? What is there to tell? He was my lover; now he is dead."

"You called him six days ago. Why?"

"Did I?"

"You promised, Simone! The truth!"

"Yes, so I did. I called him six days ago. And he came at my bidding."

"Why? Why did you call him here?"

"I felt I owed him something, Joshua. For having loved me at one time. And I really do believe he loved me. So, if any trifling bit of information came my way, I shared it with him—and then I was free to pursue my own goal. Have you felt that way before? With someone you loved? So you gave something, so you would feel less guilty when you were with someone else? Must we continue to talk about Saul? At a time like this? Oh! You were so good, M'sieu! Again, perhaps?"

She squeezed him tight. With her eyes closed.

"What did you tell him when he came down here to see you? That evening? What was so important, you brought him up here from Nice?"

"I couldn't know whether it was important or not, Joshua. But I was able to wean him away, gently, from the English girl he was seducing down there. For his sake. Not mine, you understand. It mattered little to me who he seduced. I gave up a long time ago trying to keep track of all his lovers. But he could not make her fall in love with him, and it was upsetting him! She belongs to the upper class in England. Her body he could have, but her heart, M'sieu, that she would not give—and he couldn't bear it. I saved him some agony. Was that very wrong?"

"But what did you tell him when he came?"

Joshua's insistence only seemed to make her more drowsy and quiet. He brushed the hair back from across his chest and away from her ear and, very gently, he tugged it.

"Maybe it is better you don't know, Joshua. Maybe he died because he knew. I don't want you to die as he did, Joshua."

"I will most certainly die, Simone, if I don't know. Will you believe that? Please!"

She opened her eyes at the panic in his voice.

"Tomorrow. I will tell you tomorrow. Go to sleep now, Joshua. It is almost two o'clock in the morning. We will talk about it after breakfast. I will cook you a nice omelette for breakfast. Oui?"

"Non! Now! I must know now! Why did you phone Saul that day? What did you find out that was so important to him? Tell me now!"

He shook her in bed. She squeezed him again in delight.

"You are so persuasive, Joshua. I like strong men. You are very strong. I sleep with a lot of men, I ought to know. Anyone who has the courage, to ask it of me, is welcome to it. Men of all races and nationalities—I love to love them all. The previous night, I had a man from his part of the world. An important person. I don't discriminate. Politicians, royalty, generals, even stockbrokers, have lain beside me. He was shopping with the Defence Ministry, here in Paris."

"Black African?"

"Yes. From Mozambique. A display of his own power—to be able to tell me something only he knew. They are all that way! I don't know why. I had an architect, once, who offered to remodel the room for me, and a doctor who gave me a physical. Why they should think it impressed me, I'll never know. I didn't even ask for it, and he kept telling me. We weren't even talking about his part of the world. In fact, if I remember rightly, we weren't talking at all, about anything, and then suddenly he let drop a date.

The names of three or four places that meant nothing to me."

"What was the date? The places?"

"I can never remember such things, Joshua. So I always write them down. Then I don't have to worry if I forget—and I always do. I don't remember, here in bed."

Joshua got out of bed and dressed rapidly, his shirt hanging out of his trousers while he put on his tie, knotting it crudely before reaching for his shoes. He stuffed his socks into his pockets.

"Where are you going, Joshua?" she said, sleepily. "Come back to bed, my love. Can't it wait till morning? I will find it for you in the morning. I promise."

"I have to go, Simone. Oh! You're so beautiful. But you've heard that before. I am not the only one to tell you so. I have to go.

You don't need to give me anything. I understand. I will always remember you."

He sat on the edge of the bed, bending over, kissing her long and hard, holding her by the shoulders, while she put her arms round the back of his neck and pulled him close to her. It was goodbye, and they both knew it.

She held his arm as he arose from the bed, but he pulled it away slowly, and she let it slide.

"It is on the map," she said. "On the flags. Take them. They're not any use to me—now that Saul is dead. Such information will never be of use to me. You are welcome to it."

He went to the map and drew out the flags of all the countries in southern Africa, except South Africa. That belonged to her. He put them away in the torn lining of an inner pocket. Deliberately slit.

She watched him from under the arm that was thrown over her head, the bedclothes drawn right down to her waist.

It was the way he would remember her best.

He took the Indian tricolor, with the spinning wheel in the middle of it, that she had placed on the table in front of the large map and at the foot of it—and drove it in through Bombay.

The sound of Joshua's footsteps receding down the corridor, activated the shadowy figure waiting patiently in the darkness of the washroom at the other end of the corridor that led to La Reine's dressing room.

One hand drew the gun with the silencer attached to it. Victims would try to run! The temples throbbed, setting the eyeballs ablaze; the pupils dilated in the darkness. A smile lurked at the corners of the mouth, frothing with the drops of saliva that oozed from within.

The other hand, holding it firmly at the centre of the short shaft, clutched the machete.

Chapter 16

Donaldson telephoned Julia.

"I've lost him, Miss," he said contritely. "I'm sorry. I really am!"

"What do you mean by 'lost him'? You went with him to Paris, didn't you?"

"Yes, I did, Miss. Word of honour, I did."

"And?"

"Well, he spent the day drinking on the sidewalk with the Frenchie who owns the place. Then, at night, he went to the Coq D'Or. It's a small nightclub in Monmartre, on the Rue de la Bruyere. The late, late show, Miss. I was very tired."

"Did you see the show, Donaldson?"

"Actually, yes, Miss. Not my type of thing—or yours. Men and women taking it all off. Sometimes together. Most unappetizing. He seemed to enjoy it though."

Julia could not resist a smile, in the intimate privacy of her bedroom. She imagined dignified, staid, little Dr Samuelson, with his eyeballs popping, and she could not help feeling amused.

It would do him good. Make him more relaxed with people. Bring him back into being himself again.

"Never mind all that, Tom," she said severely. "You seem to have been living it up yourself. Then what happened?"

"Well, Miss, just at the very end of the very last act, he disappeared! I looked for him everywhere when the lights came on, but he wasn't there."

"You mean he skipped the good part to give you the slip? While you were ogling elsewhere?"

"You could say so, Miss. I'm really sorry, I haven't anything to report. I hung around there for a couple of hours or more, in the hope he might be around inside somewhere, but it was very, very late—so I left."

"What did you do then?"

"Me?"

"Yes, you. What did you do then?"

"I went back to the hotel and had a bath, Miss. Freshened up a bit. I was travel-stained. I checked up on him at the hotel in the morning, but he'd checked out real early. They wouldn't know where he'd gone, or wouldn't tell, so I took the next flight back to London."

Julia bit her lip as she tried to imagine a crestfallen Donaldson at the other end of the line. She could hear his slightly heavy breathing come over the line. Whoever Donaldson was, she concluded, he wasn't all that young. With a touch of asthma, brought on by excitement?

"Donaldson," she said firmly. "I want to meet you. Compare notes and all that. Did you check with Dr Farnsworth?"

"I did, Miss Julia, and he left it all up to me. I really don't think it would be wise. We are both safer that way—particularly you. Please, Miss!"

"I will be at the Evening Star this evening at eight, Donaldson. Either you be there and show yourself to me—or consider yourself fired. Do I make myself explicitly clear?"

"Harsh words, Miss," the voice said over the telephone. "I was quite beginning to enjoy our little telephone chats. How will you do without me?"

"I'll get on just fine, thank you. I mean it, Tom. Either you're there at the Evening Star this evening—at eight—or don't bother to phone me again. I'll get Dr Farnsworth to assign someone else to work with me."

"Seems I have no choice, do I, Miss?" he said, and her eyes lit up with the moroseness with which he conceded defeat.

"None whatever, Tom. Come on, cheer up. I'll even buy you a drink."

"That's kind of you, Miss," he said with a sigh, as he hung up.

When he reached London, Joshua went directly to his flat, letting himself in with the spare key under the doormat. After late night, heavy drinking, he'd forgotten where he'd put his keys so often, it was safest to have a spare outside the front door. It was still very early, but traffic had already started to move on Fitzjohn's Avenue, from Hampstead down to Swiss Cottage and then on to Central London.

He checked his mail. There was an urgent and panic-stricken note from Amelia.

Dr Clayborne, she wrote, had been murdered. Brutally murdered, she repeated. And he—Joshua—was missing. The police were asking questions. They'd been around three times already, and she'd told them, each time, she didn't know where he was. And what was she supposed to tell the patients who came around to the surgery? She'd sent them all to Dr Stevens on Primrose Hill. And she'd put a sign on the door, saying the surgery was closed, indefinitely, until further notice, due to the sad demise of Dr Clayborne. But please, please, would he contact her as soon as possible?

Poor Amelia! Trust her to be able to cope with everything. Without realising it, and inspite of her panic.

There was an enclosure with the letter. The post mortem results on Mr Prentiss were in, and knowing he'd want to see them right away, she was enclosing them.

They were more detailed than he'd expected. More conclusive than he thought they'd be. The body had been badly charred, in some places right down to the vital organs. Part of the report was speculative—but not the cause of death.

A massive air embolus lodged in the blood vessels of the lung. Boko had not been lying. A man of Saul's height and build was hardly likely to stand by idly and allow himself to be injected with a large syringeful of air in a vein on the forearm. Unless it was his doctor who did it—and Clayborne was dead too.

Which raised new questions.

Why?

Why had Saul committed suicide in such a bizarre way?

Particularly when he was sitting on information that was very valuable—no matter which way he took it.

In his flat, Joshua took out the flags of Mozambique, Zimbabwe and Namibia, laying them in front of him on the dining table. Behind each flag was a date—the same date. Barely a month away.

And behind each flag was a name but they weren't the names of people. They were the names of places. He opened the atlas to Africa, searching down to the south, finding the enlargements of the areas he was interested in. And he found them. Two of them on the Limpopo River; one on the border between South Africa and Mozambique; the other on the border between South Africa and Zimbabwe to the northeast. He had difficulty finding the third town—it was such a small one—but he found it eventually. It was on the Orange River, on the border between South Africa and Namibia.

He put the flags back into his coat pocket, in the slit lining. But first he removed the pins so they would not stab him if he was hit in the chest. They came out easily, sliding along the edges of the flags. He disposed off the pins carefully in the trash can, wrapping them first in a piece of felt.

The dear old landlady, who cleaned out the trash and looked after all the flats, had a soft corner for him. She was suffering from arthritis, and the curling fingers had some trouble carrying the trash away. She suffered from a bad back as well, and she always consulted Joshua about it, often on the stairs on his way up. She baked him cakes for his tea—not in payment for his services; she made quite sure he didn't take it that way—when she was baking cakes for herself. Baking two cakes was just as easy as baking one.

He had a slice of the cake, made himself a cup of tea, and thought it over for a long time. For a very long time.

He knew what he ought to do.

He wasn't quite sure it was what he wanted to do.

He'd made such decisions often enough, but even with patients who were almost surely going to die, it was never easy.

Finally he decided he would do what he ought to do.

He made a phone call.

"Meet me," he said tersely.

"When?"

"Now! Say an hour."

"It's that urgent, is it?"

"Yes."

"Where?"

"Same place," Joshua said. "On Hampstead Heath. The south corner. I trust the bench will still be there."

"I see no reason why it shouldn't be there," the voice said. "Can't you tell me over the telephone?"

"No. I can't tell you over the telephone. I'm not even sure, I'll tell you when you come."

There was a silence. He could hear the drumming of fingers at the other end.

"It's like that, is it, Joshua?"

"I'm afraid so. See you in an hour," Joshua said, and hung up.

He thought of phoning Julia; then decided against it.

Something would have to be done about Julia. It just couldn't go on in this way, much as he wanted it. Leading her on. He had no rights on her. But the information Simone had given him made his heart sing. Not the date and the places—they didn't stir any emotion in him—but that Julia had never been in love. She had tried very hard to protect him, and he was still alive.

He owed her something for that.

Should he share his information with her and trust her good judgment?

That was where the problem lay. Good judgment. Good for which set of people?

Would it please her? To have the information? Would she then promptly pass it on, against his wishes? Would being told make her feel inadequate? That she was still searching for it, while he had stumbled on to it in barely a day. And how on Earth was he going to tell her how he'd obtained it?

Where did they go from there? Or rather, which way would she go?

Saul's death had an answer to it now—if no reasons. They were two different things—answers and reasons. One was a statement of fact; the other was always ambiguous. He had an answer; no reasons.

And in that respect, he was still as much in the dark as Julia was. The reason for Saul's suicide still evaded him. Was that because reasons came differently to different people? With the same answer? Two people like Saul and Julia—both lily white—would view his information differently.

How much more difficult for someone who was black or brown?

There was only one way to find out the reason for Saul's death.

He had to enter Saul's mind.

Chapter 17

Colonel William Farnsworth asked the chauffeur to stop the car at the top of Hampstead Road leading to the heath.

He would walk the rest of the way, he said. It would do him good. He felt sedentary.

He took his umbrella—you never knew when it might rain in London—tapped his bowler firmly on the almost bald head, and disappeared from view into the crowd of children thronging the ice cream van parked at the edge of the heath.

He rounded the raised mound that hid the dip from the view of the road and plunged into the gorse that lined the path, growing wild where it was permitted to grow by the absence of feet. The gorse had grown wild around the abandoned bench, but he knew where it was.

The rusty metal creaked dangerously as he sat at one end of it.

"Nice day, Colonel Samuelson," he said, touching his bowler.

"Fine day, Colonel Farnsworth," Joshua said, tipping his felt.

Farnsworth waved his umbrella in the air. "They're expecting rain though. Later. The weather people said so."

"Did they now?" Joshua said, looking up at a cloudless sky. "Is that why you brought your umbrella?"

"Yes. I thought it would come in handy. At least, then, we would have one between the two of us—since you absolutely refuse to do the sensible thing and carry one."

"My dear Bill, after having lived through the rains of Bombay and Ranchipur, I don't see how you can possibly call English rain

'rain'. A prelude to a show, if you like, that never takes place. Or the opening notes in an opera. But rain?"

"Shall we walk," Farnsworth said.

"I think it would be better."

"So you found out," Farnsworth finally said, prodding at the gorse with his umbrella, which also functioned as his walking stick.

"Yes."

"Oh? What?"

"Vladimir didn't talk."

"That's impossible! That's not what I heard."

"I know. That's what we all heard. And that's what makes me see how cleverly it was done. We were pressured into Operation Canard—as a distraction."

"From what?"

"Andropov doesn't really want Slagter. They don't give a damn what happened to Vladimir. Sentimental rot! It's out of character for them to make such a fuss about what happened to him. British Intelligence might have and Indian Military Intelligence might have—but the bloody Soviets? Do you think they'd care?"

Farnsworth was silent. Thinking hard. He struck at the offending gorse bushes, slashing away at the branches that intruded into his path.

"Slagter couldn't make him talk. If he had, the matter would have been over. The invasion would have been aborted. But it isn't, Bill, it isn't!"

"How interesting? We live and learn. All the time in this business. Just so long as we don't pay for our own mistakes. So we've been seemingly trying to protect our agents in Eastern Europe, when they were never in any danger? You'd better be sure, Joshua, or we may have to withdraw all of them in a hurry from there—or risk them going down the drain. It was you who said so. You who made such a fuss of it. Brought my ceiling down too making such an issue out of it. You owe me a few pounds on that one."

"Look, Bill. Vladimir gets killed. Horribly mutilated. Now that was a mistake you made. One night with Julia and he was willing to tell all. But no! Sweet, young, pretty, English girls—your very words—weren't meant for Russian agents—even if they weren't virgins."

"Point of principle, old boy. All right. So I made a mistake."

"I'm not so sure about that now, Bill. It's one I can live with."

"We won't argue the point—whether it was or wasn't a mistake," Farnsworth said generously. "Then what?"

"Vladimir doesn't talk. Andropov knows that. Saul, covering up for Slagter, tells us he did talk. So we assume the invasion has been aborted. But it hasn't. It's right on schedule. Only this time there's going to be no goof up on their side. They're going to keep us busy—chasing bloody decoys they don't give a damn about. So Andropov sends word to you—through me. Deliver Slagter or he knocks off half a dozen of our known agents in Eastern Europe. And we fall for it."

Farnsworth stopped to tie his shoelaces. Joshua could see him play for time. He was loath to make up his mind. When he had tied the one, he undid the other and tied it again.

"But Andropov doesn't come to you. He comes to me. There's nothing unusual about that. IMI and the KGB have close links. The KGB agent in New Delhi is an old friend of mine. You know him. Shanker, Indian Medical Corps."

"Do I?"

"He knows you. He was stationed in Calcutta during the war over Bangladesh."

"Ah! Bannerjee?"

"That's right. But Andropov doesn't go to him. He comes to me. And do you know why, Bill? Because he wants me to sell you on the idea. He knows of my interest in Slagter. He knows how close Gangoly was to me, and how I felt about the way he was butchered in Bombay! He knows I've had Slagter tracked by our people in every place he's killed. Like Saul was doing for you.

Andropov used me, Bill. God! The bloody swine used me to get to you."

"What language," Farnsworth said, rolling his eyes in mock surprise. "I would never have thought it of you. You're actually upset. You are so alike the two of you. I told Julia the same thing. Revenge is never a suitable motivation for what we do. It impairs the judgment; makes us vulnerable."

"You wouldn't say that if you'd seen Gangoly the way I did. The way he ended up. Even now, after almost four years, I see, still, the ravaged look in his eyes and the terror in his face."

"Do go on, Joshua. You're fascinating when you're excited. Do you know that, Joshua? You wave your arms as weapons! There is a circle of danger around you, within which I run the risk of being clobbered."

Joshua stopped. Lowered his arms to his sides.

"The rest is easy," Joshua said, more quietly. "To a point, that is. Saul, you and I are under orders from our respective governments to cooperate in handing over Slagter to Andropov. Even Pretoria agrees that Slagter has overstepped their bounds of ethical interrogation—though I would question that rightly—and orders Saul to reveal who Slagter is. They're quite willing to eliminate a crazed killer who is fast becoming an embarrassment to them—you could hardly expect them to have any loyalty to him seeing his usefulness had come to an end. And then we have a problem."

"Yes. Extraordinary! Because Slagter is a freelancer. And even Saul doesn't know who he is. He has a complex series of drop operations to get his messages across to Slagter, and the same in reverse. Or so Saul says. So we play it the long and natural way. Saul sends a telegram to South African National Intelligence, as he would normally do—a RED ALERT—that you must be made to talk. They contact Saul in the normal way for passing the message on to Slagter. Everything done as natural as possible to avoid arousing Slagter's suspicions that this was anything other than a normal interrogation. Make sure Samuelson talks. He is the only one who knows! And all this for our friend Slagter's benefit—in case he has any other contacts in South African National Intelligence who might give the game away to him."

"Now, go slowly, Bill. Here's where it goes wrong," Joshua said, coming to a dead stop.

"Ah! I wondered if you'd notice. The telegram?"

"Precisely! The telegram. The wording of it. Why did he say 'Only Samuelson will know' instead of 'Only Samuelson knows'? Maybe he made a mistake. He, too, was under stress. He was agreeing to deliver Slagter to the Russians—and Slagter had served his government well all these years. Maybe he forgot the wording when he went to the post office. But he repeated it again in his letter to Boko. And then he commits suicide. Why?"

"That was suicide," Farnsworth agreed. "Did you see the results of the post mortem? Massive air embolus in the lung."

"No doubt about it, Bill," Joshua said, as they resumed their meanderings through the heath. "Boko found him leaning up against the banister, the syringe beside him, and I'll bet it has Saul's fingerprints all over it. And there's the suicide note to Boko. But why?"

"Never mind the goddam whys!" Farnsworth said, displaying rare emotion, the sweat drops beginning to appear beneath the rim of his bowler. "Just stick to what we know. That's difficult enough without you throwing in the whys. My muddled brain can't handle too much at the same time."

"All right. So we stick to the facts. Slagter was supposed to come after me, and I'd be waiting for him. To make it seem all very natural to our friend, you assign Julia to keep an eye on me, and she, poor thing, gets that crazy Welshman Donaldson, as a back-up. I feel sorry for her."

"Feel sorry for me, Joshua! How do I explain to the top brass at MI-6, that instead of Slagter going after you, Clayborne and Shari get hit. Shari was expendable, but Clayborne was not. He wasn't active in MI-6, but we need such doctors to look after the practices of active agents—such as us. God knows, doctors aren't the most sympathetic of people when it comes to working for British

Intelligence. And yet who could be more qualified? To obtain information from the proper patient laid out on a couch? How's the practice, Joshua?"

"There isn't any. Amelia's been sending patients to Stevens. She's filed an urgent need request form with MI-6, for another doctor to hold things down while I'm away, but they're difficult to get. Maybe they ought to try some of my countrymen. They run the health service; they ought to be good enough for MI-6. I was good enough for them."

"You're different, Joshua. You were educated here. You're one of us."

They had circled the heath, coming back to the rusty old bench behind the mound, hidden from the view of the road. They sat on it gently, testing it for weight. Farnsworth's end creaked in protest; Joshua's hardly moved. It was a fine day for flying kites, Joshua thought, looking up at the sky.

"There's something about all this, Joshua, that still mystifies me."

"Only something? Nothing seems to make sense! Saul knew the date of the invasion, and the places where the initial thrusts would be made. He got them from La Reine—as I did. But he doesn't pass on that piece of vital information to South African National Intelligence. Why?"

"How can you be sure, he didn't? He was a loyal enough agent to have done so. I'm sure they know all about it. The matter's over."

"No, Bill! No! He didn't! That is why South African National Intelligence diverts Slagter to obtaining it. Don't you see? That is why Clayborne and Shari were killed. Saul had a weakness. Everyone knew it. Slagter knew about it. We all did. He confided such information to his lovers in bed. For the thrill of it. In the telegram he tries to protect them by saying only I would know. But Slagter isn't buying that. I'm a difficult target and I'm expecting him. So he goes after Clayborne and Shari. If he gets the information from either of them, that's the last we'll hear of him. He'll retire to South Africa, assume a new identity and disappear. If not, he'll come for me. You can count on that. It's what I'm counting on."

"I'm not concerned about Slagter," Farnsworth said. "We've just decided Andropov was bluffing, and we'll call his bluff. There's going to be a bloody confrontation in southern Africa. When? What's the date? Where?"

"I won't tell you."

Farnsworth took the bowler off his head, placing it on the bench between them. He lit a cigar, puffing the smoke out towards the gorse, away from Joshua. "What do you mean, you can't tell me? Why can't you tell me?"

"I didn't say I can't, Bill. I said I won't. Do you know how long I agonized over the simple act of making a phone call asking you to meet me here?"

"You're not playing fair," Farnsworth said. "This is Operation Canard. There is an article of agreement between MI-6 and IMI in the matter—or have you forgotten? An understanding between us. You can't hold back now. You've committed yourself."

"You're wrong, Bill. This isn't what we started out with. This isn't Operation Canard, any longer. That was to deliver Slagter to the Russians—and we're not even talking about Slagter anymore."

"It's all related, Joshua," Farnsworth protested. "You can't withhold information that came your way in the course of that operation. That's not fair! Not gentlemanly!"

Joshua laughed to ease the tension; patted Farnsworth on the knee. "Come now, Bill. This doesn't really concern us. Certainly it doesn't concern my government. In any case, I would have to check back with them. I could also be wrong. La Reine could have been wrong."

"Don't hedge, Joshua! You bloody Indians are always on the fence. Either you give me the date and the places, or the agreement we had on Operation Canard comes to an end. In which case I will be free to tell South African Intelligence, through normal operating channels, that there is to be such an invasion—and that both you and La Reine know the particulars of it. That ought to interest them."

"Blackmail, eh?"

"Friendly persuasion, Joshua. Look at it that way."

"It won't work."

"Why?"

"It's a welcome change to have you ask why. Shall I tell you why? Because they already know that Vladimir didn't talk. They know the invasion is still on. What they don't know is when or where. That is why Slagter knocked off Clayborne and Shari. That is why he will have to come after me."

"Or La Reine."

"She doesn't know, Bill. She doesn't memorize information. She put it on little flags that are stuck on a huge map that adorns one wall. Quite a map that! And she gave me the flags—for safe-keeping. She'd never remember."

"He didn't know that, Joshua. How could he have known that?"

"What do you mean?" Joshua asked, knowing the answer even as he asked it, feeling the softly spoken words settle apprehensively over him like some birdcage.

Farnsworth put out his cigar and put it back into his pocket. The upper outside pocket of his jacket. Behind his handkerchief. He patted it as flat as it could get.

"Henri phoned not long after you left Paris. He got to her. He was there when you were with her. The doorman went up to take a look when he didn't get the smell of frying omelette. It was a smell he'd been used to each morning, for many years."

"Dear God! In the same way?"

"I'm afraid so. It must have been very early in the morning—after you left her. Makes you wonder? How he knew? And if she talked, Joshua, he won't be after you."

"She couldn't have talked, Bill. She couldn't remember such things. She told me so. God! I wish she had. Death would have come quicker. But if she couldn't tell, because she couldn't remember, it must have been long in coming! God! The monster! What sort of a person is he, Bill? To kill in this way?"

"He's probably a very good agent," Farnsworth said, but he, too, wiped his forehead with his handkerchief. "Will you make a deal with me? Just the date. Never mind the places. That's good enough. Let Slagter be."

"No!"

"He's not important, Joshua."

"He is to me. And now doubly so! She was a fine person, Bill. Kind and very generous. I had never known her before and yet I felt I had known her always. You feel that way with some people. Give me twenty-four hours."

"I don't follow," Farnsworth said, as the first few drops of rain splashed on his bald head; others kicking up the dirt as they splattered at his feet.

"I'll give you the date—not the places—if you won't do anything hasty for twenty-four hours. He has to come for me by then."

"What makes you so sure? He's waited so long. Why must he come for you, now, within twenty-four hours?"

"Because Boko's two days are almost up. If Boko gets to me—as Saul advised him to do—he has blown it. I don't think he'll risk leaving it any longer. I might panic and leave town. Or Boko might know of the information I have and hit me earlier. Twenty-four hours, Bill! He will come for me in twenty-four hours—or not at all."

"And this time tomorrow, if I refrain from having the South Africans pull Slagter off you, you'll give me the date?"

"Yes. One condition."

"Oh?"

"You take Julia off the case."

"But why? In God's name, Joshua, why? Didn't you enjoy her company? Didn't you like being thrown with her?"

"I loved it," Joshua said quietly. "But she isn't cut out to be an agent. She's only risking her life—and I won't have it."

"Do I detect a note of tenderness in your voice?" Farnsworth asked. Joshua decided it was a nice day for flying kites. The sprinkle of English rain had stopped. The wind was still fresh; the hazy sunshine made it ideal weather for the sport.

"I do detect a note of tenderness in your voice," Farnsworth said.

"That's irrelevant, Bill. I'd say that for any girl in jeopardy. The only thing more tragic than a poor agent is a dead one. And that's what she'll end up being, if you don't pull her off."

"Don't underestimate, Julia. She has it in her. The stuff we're made of. And talking about Julia, you had no right to tell her about the little mix-up between Jane and Donaldson. That happened so long ago. Couldn't you have left matters alone?"

"Well, there you are. Only proves my point. She's so—so trusting! I felt I had to drop her a hint that in this business, we don't trust anyone. Yet, even after what I told her, she still trusted Donaldson."

"Did she now? Interesting. Maybe she finds him irresistible? For talking to on the telephone, that is."

"Be serious, Bill," Joshua said, almost hating himself for the suggestions he was making to Farnsworth about Julia. "Tell her to find another job. Something safe. Like a schoolteacher. With her connections, she could even go into politics. Marry a duke or something. Certainly she's better suited to cutting ribbons at country bazaars than looking after me."

Farnsworth was in no hurry to be rushed into agreeing. He leaned back into the bench, dangerously twisting the back of it into a warp. Joshua compensated by leaning forward, and the bench held.

It sprinkled some more. Farnsworth with an air of triumph opened his umbrella. He offered to share it with Joshua, who promptly and disdainfully rejected it.

"I knew it would rain," Farnsworth said mildly.

"Will you or won't you?"

"I'll think about it. MI-6 can hardly take dictation from Indian Military Intelligence on what it should do with its female agents. We are not as squeamish about using women as you are. But I'll give it serious consideration."

Joshua got up from the bench with a bound, nearly upending both it and Farnsworth, who wasn't expecting Joshua's sudden removal from the other end.

"No deal, Colonel Farnsworth! You must do as you please! I wish you a good day."

"Sit down, Joshua! For heaven's sake stop being so dramatic about it. Bloody Indians! Get all sentimental for no bloody reason. All right! All right! Don't make such a bloody issue out of it."

Joshua sat down.

"Who's making an issue?" he said innocently. "Just a suggestion."

"She hasn't done all that badly, Joshua. I gave her the job of keeping you alive, and seeing you're still here, she did very well. Wouldn't you say? A noble purpose too. Keeping you alive. And with only Donaldson to help her."

"I don't want her keeping me alive! Or protecting me! Or anywhere near me! Damn it, Farnsworth, do I have to speak Welsh to make you understand? He's in serious trouble with her though. Donaldson, I mean."

"Is he now?"

"Yes. Either he meets her in the Evening Star tonight. At eight. And introduces himself. Or he's fired."

"Is he going to meet her?"

"Tonight? No, not tonight. Definitely not tonight. Though he sort of gave her to understand, he might."

"Oh! Why?"

"Well, at least I know where she is, Bill. Safe. In the Evening Star where she can come to no harm. Joe will be there, and possibly Jomo, and they'll look after her. She may be disappointed but she won't be anywhere in a danger zone. Do you think she'll forgive me?"

"I hope not," Farnsworth said. "Do you want any other back-up help for tonight? A man outside? To check periodically with you?"

"And frighten Slagter away? No, Bill, no. Please! No one outside my flat. This time I'll be waiting for him alone. With a loaded gun."

They rose from the bench and walked towards Farnsworth's car parked on the grass verge, innocuously tended by the uniformed chauffeur. The sort any middle-aged businessman could well afford to have.

"You will forgive me," Farnsworth said, "if I don't come visiting tonight."

Chapter 18

Joshua did not return to his flat in Fitzjohn's Avenue—not directly. He declined Farnsworth's offer of a ride for the short distance between the heath and the flat, hailing a taxi instead.

"The British Museum," he said.

It was the safest place he could think of.

He wandered through it, touching a case that contained an Egyptian mummy or African masks, barely noticing them, trying to piece together disjointed facts while keeping a seemingly sleepy eye on other visitors to the museum. He changed rooms constantly, and satisfied himself there was no one face that appeared where he appeared.

There was no coherent pattern to what he did; as little as the facts he was struggling to connect.

I must be dense, he thought, because all the pieces are here, and they make no sense to me. It would need, he decided, someone looking in from the outside—and at some distance—to be able to see the close-fitting edges; all he could see were the facts, presenting him, mockingly, with no viable solution to his liking.

It was just past seven in the evening, when he slipped into the bench on the sidewalk of Fitzjohn's Avenue, fifty yards from where he lived, and across the street.

In all of the cases he'd studied, Slagter had operated in a set pattern. There was no reason to believe he would change it. He had always killed when he was sure he would find his victim alone. In Joshua's case, seven was too early, he would be out for dinner; eight might be too late, he would be at the pub. It would be some time yet before the sun set, the last oblique rays streaming down from the West, along and in between the long lines of gardens and terraces that ran on the other side of Finchley Road towards Kilburn.

At eight o'clock, he thought of Julia sitting in the Evening Star and waiting for Donaldson. At least he knew where she was. Safe. One less detail to worry about. Now that he knew her, he worried about her. His attention slipped from the double doors that marked the entrance to the building, as he thought of her. She was a fine person. They didn't come better than that—anywhere. He was not right for her. He must be more than a little mad to have had such thoughts about the granddaughter of the eleventh Earl of Bromfield. Her son would be the twelfth Earl—no matter whom she married. She mingled with royalty. She was royalty! She could trace the royal blood in her for centuries, into the grandeur of British history.

And he had thought of her as his 'Julia'?

Such a possibility—that she might care for him—seemed to him—sober as he was—to be both preposterous and absurd.

They came from differing backgrounds.

He didn't feel inferior to her—though many an Englishman of the lower classes might—but they must feel differently about different things. Not that his way of thinking was inferior to hers. In her presence he had certainly not felt that way. She had the charm to dispel any such fears.

But that didn't mean she felt the same way about him. She did not think of him as anyone but a commoner, and quite possibly a foreigner. Though she had never shown any such disdain. It was his fault; not hers. She had a charm and a caring feeling she, probably, bestowed on all she knew, and he—poor fool—was reading all sorts of meaning into the soft voice and caring eyes. It was her aristocratic upbringing that was leading him astray!

But of one thing he was sure. When this was all over, and if he came out of it alive, he would go away somewhere to start all over again. Maybe he would leave Indian Military Intelligence, resign from the Indian Army, and revert back to being a doctor.

No! He couldn't leave England. It was his home.

He saw the tall, black African walk down the sidewalk. He stopped outside the house, and opposite to it, as if checking the number with the one in his memory.

He was too far away for Joshua to see him clearly.

He left ten minutes later. His landlady, Mrs Thorn, saw him to the door.

Joshua remained seated on the bench. It was quarter past eight when he entered the building. He checked his mail, deliberately killing time in the hallway, so Mrs Thorn might hear him.

As he expected, she heard him and came out from her basement flat to greet him, at the foot of the stairs.

"I'm so glad you're back, Dr Samuelson," she said. "Did you hear about poor Dr Clayborne? The police have been here asking for you. I told them, quite distinctly, you had not given up the flat. They've telephoned twice since then to find out if you were back. No patience, if you ask me."

"How are you Mrs Thorn? How's the back? Did the samples I gave you help any?"

"Oh, yes! I don't know what I'd do without them. You aren't leaving the flat, are you Dr Samuelson?"

"My dear Mrs Thorn, there isn't a landlady the likes of you in the whole of England. Why would I give up the flat?"

She blushed with the praise being heaped on her, mentally resolving to bake him a cake. He lingered on the steps, as she hesitated at the foot of them, knowing she was forgetting something. Then she remembered.

"I almost forgot! One of your African friends was in a little while ago. Said he knew you well. He had a package for you. I told him you weren't in, so he asked if he might wait for you. I let him into the flat. He waited ten minutes, changed his mind, and left. I hope I did right?"

"Quite right, Mrs Thorn."

There was no one in the flat when he entered it. He made sure of that. He opened the windows wide; then searched for the package awaiting him in the flat. He found the brown wrapping paper that held it. In the waste paper basket. It was thoughtful of the man who had put it there. At least he wasn't a litterbug.

But he had to be very careful. Amateurs in this business, by their very ignorance, could be lethal.

It was under the bed, the low ticking sounds almost inaudible as it clung, with its magnetic base, to the steel springs of the bed. Inaudible, except for the ear that searched for them. He lay flat on his back as he worked on it. Above him. First he touched it gingerly, soft hands on hard metal, feeling for the button that made it operational.

There was none.

The dial on the clock facing him read the correct time; the alarm was set for two in the morning. No buttons, no ridges, no screws! God! Boko was getting better at this sort of thing. The bomb he'd exploded in Johannesburg, fifteen years ago, had been a crude affair compared to the silently ticking object above him.

He twisted the dial and leaned back in pleasurable surprise, as it unscrewed towards him. It came away in his hand, and, involuntarily, he braced himself for the impact of an imagined explosion.

There wasn't one.

He cleaned the moisture from his face and his fingers, and snipped off the hands of the clock in quick, motionless jabs of the long-nosed pliers from the tool box Jomo had given him on his last birthday.

The dial floated towards him. It fell onto his chest. Now he could see the explosive crammed into the back, the black, white and brown wires cuddling together in a tight curl before disappearing into the magnetic base. He slid the pliers in and cut all three of them. He leaned his head back into the shag carpet, easing the tension in his neck, and permitted himself a smile.

He reached forward to unstick the magnetic base from the steel springs of the bed, when the doorbell rang.

Insistently.

He slid out from under the bed and drew out the gun. He switched off the light in the bedroom; the living room was already in darkness.

The bell rang again as he eased himself into the padded armchair, facing the door. He rested his elbow against the switching button of the table lamp on the table beside him. He did his reading in that chair, when he couldn't sleep at night. He would see who it was, before he fired. And he would fire first. No sense in playing chivalrous games with a crazed killer.

The doorbell stopped ringing. There were moments of indecision—until he heard the key inserted in the lock.

Whoever it was had a key to his flat.

That couldn't be right? He saw the shadowy figure fumble for the light switch just inside the door. He seemed very familiar.

He knew who it was. The figure at the door. He had known him and loved him since early childhood. They had played with marbles in the hot dirt of a dirty street in Durban.

He lowered the gun as the lights came on.

"Don't you ever answer the door?" Joe asked. "And what are you doing sitting in that chair? With a gun in your hand. Is it loaded? Or were you just cleaning it? I didn't know you even had a gun. When did you buy it? And what are you doing sitting in the dark?"

"What are you doing here?" Joshua said, his throat dry. "Why aren't you at the Evening Star?"

"I could ask you the same question," Joe said. "You haven't been there last night and tonight. I got worried about you. Are you ill or something? Put that thing away, will you? You make me nervous!"

Joshua placed the gun on the table. Put the evening newspaper on top of it.

An agent was always an agent, he told himself, in self-defense. An agent didn't trust anyone—anyone at all—if he wanted to stay alive. And sometimes it ended this way. For one brief, horrible moment, that would haunt him all his life, he'd thought Joe might be Slagter. Against all reason, cold logic, or his love for a brother. He felt ashamed of himself. He went up to Joe, and embraced him.

That surprised Joe. "You're sick with something, aren't you?" Joe said. "Why don't you say something? What's the matter with you?"

Joshua snapped himself back into the room. Made for the kitchen. "Would you like a drink?"

Joe followed him through into the kitchen.

"Where have you been? Clayborne's dead! Did you know that? And the police want to talk to you. You disappeared without a word to anyone. They came to question me, and I had to tell them I didn't know where you were. Where were you?"

"Paris."

"Paris? What were you doing in Paris? That Israeli dish of Saul—what's her name?—was found all hacked up too. And the police want to question you about that too!"

"So they found Shari?"

"Yes. Laura did. She came down in the morning for something she wanted from the shop, and she threw a fit! Ran, all hysterical, into the High Street, in her nightgown too, screaming blue murder. Was nearly run over by a bus. They questioned her and she had to tell them, you were waiting for her the previous night when she came in and you'd spent the night with her. And you left early morning without waking her. It's all in the evening newspapers. Don't you ever read them?"

Joshua poured out two large whiskeys. He led Joe back into the living room.

"You can't blame her, Josh," Joe said. "Her husband gets murdered a few days ago. And then her shop assistant gets hacked up like you wouldn't believe! Don't blame her, Joshua. You could still get together with her. I think she still loves you. I think she'll always love you."

"I don't blame her for anything," Joshua said. "I tried last night to go back all those years, but it just isn't the same anymore. Time, sort of, seems to move only one way. Now, maybe, I can move along with it?"

"You wouldn't believe the number of girls who were in the Evening Star, last night and this evening. Asking for you. Just your luck not to be in."

"Really? Who?"

"Well, yesterday, there was this Italian dish who came in asking for you. I've never seen her before. Said her name was Lysa. Lysa Romano. I sort of took care of her, for you, with a few drinks. You don't mind, do you?"

"Not at all, Joe. I recall I've stolen a few from you over the years. I trust it was a profitable evening?"

"It's not like that, Josh! This one's different. I'm almost thirty years old. I'm getting tired of chasing au pair girls. I'd like to settle down. Maybe go into the restaurant business. Work for her father—if he'll have me. Why, one day, it might even be Romano and Samuelson."

"How does she feel about all this?" Joshua asked. "It's all very sudden, isn't it? Are you sure?"

"I took her straight home to Oxford Circus, when the pubs closed. We only held hands. I swear it! But when I asked if I might see her again, she said 'yes'."

"Look, Joe, you have my blessing for whatever it is you want to do. Do me a favour. Just finish your drink and go! I'm expecting a visitor—and it isn't you. Who else came to the Evening Star asking for me?"

"Ewa was in there last night. Asking urgently for you. She seemed upset you weren't there. She doesn't look too well to me, Josh. Maybe you better have a look at her. And then the English girl, Julia, was in there too. This evening, at eight, she asked for you; then came and sat with me. Asked a lot of questions about your schooling in Wales."

"Oh, crikey! She knows."

"Knows what? Did I do wrong?"

"No, Joe. You did just right. Maybe it's better this way. She'll never want to see me again."

"I bought her a round, and then she bought me a round. Insisted on it. And when she left, she kissed me on the cheek. English girls are not usually very demonstrative. Surprised me some. She's quite a dish, Josh!"

"But not for me. Have you finished your drink?"

"No," Joe said, "and I'm not likely to, unless you tell me what you're doing pointing loaded guns at me."

"I'll tell you one day," Joshua said, motioning his finger to his lips. "Trust me."

They heard the footstep through the open door.

Softly padded.

Like the noiseless tread of a lion in the African veldt, stalking a wildebeest near a water hole. Joshua pushed Joe into the kitchen, muffling his mouth, warning him with his eyes.

Then Joshua sat back in the padded armchair, his hand underneath the newspaper.

"Are you there, Joshua?" Jomo called out softly. "Can I come in?"

"This is a surprise," Joshua said. "Were you here earlier this evening?"

"Me? No. Why?"

"Someone was here earlier this evening. Left me a visiting card."

"Boko wants to see you tonight. Now!"

"Tell him, I'm busy tonight. I'm expecting company."

"Please, Joshua! As a friend, I implore you. He won't do anything to you while you're still talking. For my sake, come with me."

Joshua patted him on the shoulder.

"Jomo, you're a very good friend. The best I have. And I love you—more than I ever loved Saul. But you don't know Boko. I can't feel the way he does—and that makes him very bitter. We will change the world—you and I—without losing it. Or ourselves. Don't worry about me. I'll be fine."

Joe came in from the kitchen.

"Tell him, Joe! You're his brother. You tell him. Tell him to take a vacation. Get out of the country for a while. Is that asking too much?"

Joshua ushered the both of them forcefully to the door.

"Go!" he commanded. "To the Evening Star. And have two rounds on me. I'd offer you more, but it's bad for your health. Now will you go?"

They had all been brutal. Not just Slagter.

They were all capable of it—Boko, Saul, Farnsworth, even himself.

Would he have killed Joe if his brother had been Slagter? Or Jomo, if he'd been the one Joshua had been waiting for? The one but not the other? Making fine lines between people—those you knew and those you didn't—wasn't that also brutality? To feel for one and not the other? Never to trust. Was that any less brutal behaviour between civilised people?

Except Julia. And he had said she wasn't a good agent.

Except Ewa. More powerless than them all.

He would give up the business. He was getting too old for this sort of thing, he told himself. Waiting in the darkness of the night, holding a loaded gun, for a killer he didn't know to come through the door. Would he shoot the first stranger that entered?

He didn't care anymore. Whether Slagter came or not. Maybe La Reine had remembered. No! He was not going to think of her as La Reine. She was Simone. That was the woman he'd made love to in Paris.

He went into the kitchen to pour himself another whiskey. He didn't care about the door anymore—or who came through it.

When he returned to the living room, Laura was sitting where he'd been sitting. In the padded armchair, reading the newspaper.

The gun was in her hand.

She came to him as she saw him, flinging the gun back into the armchair, putting her arms around him, spilling his whiskey down the front of her dress, holding him tight.

He patted her back.

"Where have you been, Joshua?" she said, tearfully. "Shari's dead! He got to her. I'm glad I'm going away. Come with me, Joshua!"

He disengaged her gently, leading her back to the armchair she'd been in. He put the gun back in the drawer of the table; then he knelt before her.

"Laura, my love, why are you always so afraid? They're not after you—they never were. The nightmare is over for you. Go back to South Africa. As you planned. In a little while, Saul's death won't seem as anguished as it is now. And I will write."

There was nothing else he could say. She seemed so tired and worn out, he felt sorry for her. He stroked her cheek, drew her up to him, kissed her lightly on the mouth and lips. She smiled at him. "You're right, Joshua. I can only go back to South Africa. All this will soon be behind me. I know you can't come. So I came to say goodbye. I will never forget you, Joshua. You have made fifteen years of my life more bearable—just by being there. And I did, at least, try to be kind?"

"You were, Laura. Oh, you were! I can't wipe out fifteen years either. And in those years you will always be a part of me. But, for the both of us, the waiting has come to an end."

She got up to leave him. The vulnerable look had entered the eyes once more. The elegant posture, with the shoulders thrown back, banishing the tiredness he had seen, of late, so much in her. She folded Joshua in a warm embrace. She tightened her hands around his back and he felt her breasts crushed up against him. While she searched out his lips in a kiss she wanted to imprint in her mind. For future recall. He stood as motionless as she had been, allowing her to draw what she wanted from him.

Julia watched from the door.

"I was just leaving," Laura said, disengaging herself guiltily.

"Please don't go. Not on my account that is. May I come in?"

Joshua went up to Julia, uncertain of what he must do. Should he offer her his cheek? Or reach for her? Where had intimacy reached today? Was it different from the day before?

She made it easy for him. She opened her arms and he walked into them. Then she kissed him on the mouth, in a manner that left him speechless. For the lack of inhibition in it. Long and hard, unhurried, soothing his fears, until he responded in the same way.

"I think, I'm intruding," Laura said. "May I wish you both every happiness? I'll have to find a hotel for the night. I've given up the flat in South Kensington."

This time it was Julia who disengaged herself from him.

"Let me come with you," Julia said, "In a sense, I am intruding too. He is expecting a visitor, and he doesn't want me around when he comes. I have a car downstairs. Perhaps we can talk for a while in it, and then I'll be happy to take you wherever you wish."

Joshua collapsed into the armchair when they had left.

The evening had turned out quite different from the one he'd imagined. His apartment, that day, had been like a hotel. Or a railroad station! With all the traffic that had moved in and out of it. First Joe, then Jomo, now Laura and Julia. If Slagter had been watching the place, he'd be a fool to try anything.

Joshua went to the window and drew the curtains, peering into the street, almost indecently shadowy under the faint lights that had now been turned on. A party was on in the house opposite; he could see the shadows of dancing forms on the thin curtains.

Down below, in the street, the Bentley was parked—as it had been for most of the evening. After eight thirty.

He saw the well-dressed figure turn into the house. He heard the exchange of a few words with Mrs Thorn at the bottom of the stairs, inquiring whether he was in, and the gentle laugh of relief on being told that he was.

He heard the footsteps climb the stairs.

He put away the gun, from the drawer in the table, back into its place in the closet. Then he went to the door to greet her.

She carried the overnight bag, which she dropped at his feet, as she brushed past him into the flat. One hand lightly moving across his shoulders, then holding him by the hand as she drew him back into the living room with her.

"I'm glad you've come, Ewa," Joshua said. "I've been expecting you."

Chapter 19

He reached for the overnight bag as he went in with her, letting her lead him to whichever corner she wished. He dropped the bag beside the armchair; looked inquiringly at her.

"I've left home," she said simply. "I don't care if he's my eldest brother and the head of the house. I can't stay with him anymore."

She was dressed very differently from the last time he'd seen her. The suit she was wearing fitted her as if it had been custom tailored for her. The short coat was open. Underneath he saw the lacy white blouse buttoned up to the neck. The matching skirt came to just above her knees. The pastel shade of light-brown and beige was so becoming to the richness of her that his eyes lifted appreciatively.

She dropped the coat on the sofa; kicked off her shoes.

"May I stay here for the night?" she said. "I'll look for lodgings tomorrow."

"Of course. Why must you ask? You're the only niece I have. Joe's not married, though that might change soon, and Susan is with Mother in India—and shows, yet, no interest in boys. You will always be first with me. Stay as long as you wish."

She took the overnight bag into the bedroom to change. When she emerged from it, she was wearing a very English nightgown that covered her from her neck to her toes. The front of it was laced and scalloped. She had untied the scarf from around her head. She sat on the arm of his chair, and he put an arm around her waist to steady her. She kissed him on the head, cuddling it against her breasts, feeling warmth without desire, desperately longing for his closeness. The sat that way for a long time, hardly speaking, content with each other, and gradually they both relaxed from the tensions that had plagued them all evening.

"I sometimes think, Uncle Josh, that you and I are the only two sane people in the whole wide world."

"Find room for one more," he pleaded. "Another as fine a person as you are. Way above me. More loving and warm and caring than I."

For the first time that evening, Ewa broke into a laugh, as she cuddled him closer, tousling his hair without respect, pulling his head back towards her, so she could brush the hair away from his eyes.

"Why, Uncle Josh," she said, "you're in love."

It was almost one in the morning when they went to bed. They tossed a coin to decide who should have the bedroom. Joshua offered it to Ewa, but she said 'no'. She could curl up on the sofa in the living room and be just as comfortable.

So they tossed for it.

It came heads, and gave Joshua the sofa; Ewa the bedroom.

She blew him a kiss, standing in the open door to the bedroom, smiling enigmatically; then she closed the door behind her.

It was one minute to two o'clock when the telephone rang in the passageway near the entrance to the flat. In the short corridor that opened into the kitchen on one side and the living room on the other.

Joshua let it ring for five rings, hoping whoever it was would hang up. It was hardly the time for anything—except sleep.

When it had rung thrice more, and he was fully awake anyway, he got up to answer it, cursing soundly in Hindi as he stumbled towards it. He stubbed his toe on the protruding leg of the chair with the wicker back, and that didn't help any. The passage light wasn't on; neither was the light in the corridor outside the flat, which might have thrown in a faint beam from under the door. To guide him.

He knocked the receiver off the saddlebar, groping for it, half-asleep, as it dangled on the other end of its short cord.

It was Boko.

"Is my sister there?" he said.

Joshua, now coming to his senses, wasn't quite sure whether to say 'yes' or 'no', so he cleared his throat instead. And did not answer.

"God, damn you, Joshua! Is she there or not?" the hysterical voice yelled, impelling his attention.

"Yes, she is. In the bedroom. Asleep. Do you want to talk to her? I'm not so sure she wants to talk to you."

"Get her out of there! For God's sake, Samuelson! There's a bomb under the bed!"

"I know," Joshua said, stifling a yawn. "I found your little present. The one you left for me earlier this evening. Naughty! Naughty! I disconnected the internal clock mechanism. I've snipped the wires. Go to bed."

"Please, Joshua! Get her out of there! God! Damn you! Wake her up! The digital quartz mechanism is in the magnetic base. Please! Get her out of there!"

He heard the futile screams as he dropped the receiver and turned to race towards the bedroom. The three steps he took were the last towards her. He heard the roar of the explosion as it blew open the bedroom door. He felt the wave of hot air hurl him against the far wall of the flat, in the kitchen, where he slithered to the floor.

He smelt the acrid smell of toxic plastic, burning rubber and human flesh.

The flames surged outwards from the bedroom into the living room, the wave of fire igniting the curtains with dense crackling sounds, the leaping firebrands reaching upwards to the ceiling. He felt the blood run down his cheek and arm, and the stabs of released pain, as he wrenched slivers of broken glass from them. The ceiling had started to disintegrate. The plaster, expanding with the heat, found no place to go, erupting downwards in chunks to be engulfed in the flames that swept, majestically and methodically, along the carpeting towards him.

He stumbled to the door. The hiss of a bursting pipe told him the walls of the kitchen had ignited.

The receiver dangled from the telephone.

No point now in answering it. No point at all. He threw one last glance to the bedroom, where the inferno raged unabated. Almost by force of habit he reached for his jacket on the coat rack as he walked slowly down the stairs, the heat and the smoke driving him down each step, mocking him as if toying with him, never quite overtaking him, yielding him up with derisive roars, to the front door.

Or so it seemed to him.

He saw the other tenants, of the flats two to eight, clustered in dressing gowns and robes, on the sidewalk. He heard the sirens of the fire engines and plaintive whine of an ambulance, as he walked slowly up the road, at that time in the morning, each faltering footstep unsure of its reception when it reached her door.

He stood outside it and knocked. She answered it almost immediately, though she, too, must have been asleep at that time—unless the sound of the explosion had awakened her. The silken dressing gown she had thrown over her thin nightie, hugged her body, knotted tightly, as it was, at the waist.

"Dr Samuelson," she said, sternly. "I am not used to having strange men wake me up at two in the morning. Or should I call you 'Donaldson'?" But she held the door open for him.

"Couldn't you just call me 'Joshua'?" he pleaded.

She saw the blood on him, as he entered.

"You poor dear! Are you hurt? Shall I call a doctor? What am I saying? You are a doctor. Does it hurt, darling?"

He forced a smile, though it hurt in the ribs.

"I'll be fine. These are only minor cuts and bruises."

"Can I get you anything?"

"Yes. A strong whiskey."

When she came back he was curled up on the couch. Unconscious, or asleep. She checked to make sure he was alive, by sliding her hand through his jacket into his pyjama top and feeling his heart. He could not have been either, because he held her hand in both of his own and would not let go, playing his nightmares over and over again, mumbling to himself. She didn't know what she was supposed to do, so she pulled up the rocking chair to the sofa and sat alongside him, her hand between his.

When, half asleep, he released her hand, she took off his bedroom slippers, loosened the top two buttons of his pyjama top, and drew a light covering over him.

It was a warm night. He would not need much else to keep him comfortable.

She sat on the rocking chair, and watched him mumble some more, before he fell asleep. Not listening in. It wasn't necessary.

There wasn't much point in offering him the whiskey, so she poured it down the sink.

She locked the front door.

It was almost three in the morning when she went to bed. She did not close the bedroom door, in case he should need anything in the night and call out to her.

Chapter 20

"Twenty-four hours!" Farnsworth stormed, pacing in front of the bench, lashing out indiscriminately at the gorse bushes—those that intruded on the path and those that didn't—with his umbrella.

Joshua had his head in his hands.

"That's what you said. Twenty-four hours! Now what's the date?"

"I know, I did, Bill," Joshua said. "And I've told you what happened. Calm down, Bill, will you? Don't get so excited. Englishmen never get excited. Keep repeating that to yourself. Leave that sort of thing to us Asians. It was just bad luck."

"Bad luck? A girl gets killed—blown to bits and then cremated in your flat at two in the morning—and all you can say it was bad luck? The whole thing has gone too far."

Joshua put his head back into his hands, and closed his eyes. He did not need Farnsworth to remind him of Ewa's death. It was all too painfully fresh in his mind. In time, no doubt, solace would come, gradually, until she had mellowed to a loving memory, but now all he could feel was the closeness of her, as she had sat on the armrest of his chair and cuddled his head to her breasts. Sitting as he did, on a rusty bench on Hampstead Heath, his arm did not hold his head; instead it felt the strong waist it had circled the night before, and the touch of the pelvic girdle below it.

"You're right," he said softly. "You don't know how much I shall always regret Ewa's death. I will never forgive myself. I could have saved her, Bill. I should have removed the infernal thing and chucked it out of the window—and I would have if it hadn't been for Joe."

"He saved your life," Farnsworth said. "Our explosives people moved in almost immediately. I checked with them. If you'd have removed it from the steel springs, it would have gone up in your hand."

Farnsworth sat on the bench, tracing doodles with the point of his umbrella in the soft earth. It had rained some last night, but not enough to make the ground mucky. Just soft.

"Don't blame yourself, Joshua. You'll feel that way for some time. You've watched a bomb go off, cremating a friend in your bedroom; been hurled like a nobody against a blank wall—and you're still alive. The shock of it can be fearsome. But I kept my part of the bargain, and you must keep yours."

"You broke your part of it, Bill."

"Did I?"

"Yes. You promised to take Julia off the case. It was a condition I made. Instead of which what do I find? That my good friend, Bill Farnsworth, has filled her in on everything. We had a long talk this morning. Over breakfast. She cooks a fine breakfast. Did you know that? The toast was just right and the marmalade the best I've ever had. She broke the eggs turning them over, but you can't be fussy about such things. You broke the bargain, Bill."

"But I did take her off the case!" Farnsworth protested, his doodles in the earth becoming increasingly agitated. "Sure I told her about Jane's little mix-up with Donaldson, and how we gave you his identity. I had to. I felt I owed her some explanation when I terminated her connection with the case."

"That's not true."

"I don't know what you mean. Why would I lie to you?"

"She wasn't off the case. She was in a Bentley across the street, from about eight-thirty onwards, monitoring everyone who came into the building. Off the case, did you say?"

"Certainly not on my orders, Joshua. She's free-lancing it."

"I must admit I was happy to see her when Laura showed up. And she set some doubts in my mind at rest. And she was an absolute brick to take me in at night, the way she did."

"Do you realise," Farnsworth said, "that so many days later—I've lost count—and with three murders, and Ewa's death on our hands, we're still no closer to knowing who Slagter is? I think I'll retire, Joshua, and grow cabbages in my backyard. I'll be better at it than this."

"I have a theory, Bill. Want to hear it?"

"I'll clutch at anything—including your half-baked theories."

"Let's just say, for argument, that Slagter is the South African code name for two people—and Saul is one of them. We don't know who the other half is—and we may never know it. But Saul was the brains behind Slagter."

"I thought it might be Saul," Farnsworth said slowly. "He was so obvious. But there is nothing in the files to confirm it."

"Your files are filled with Saul's reports—and little else."

"I discounted his reports, Joshua, but you cannot discount the facts. It's true Saul was in Tangiers when Abdul was murdered. But in all of the other cases, and all of the other times—in Miami and Bombay, in Haifa and Paris, even Johannesburg—Saul wasn't anywhere near the place when the murders took place. And you know that too. Your men tracked him, and they filed the same reports with you, didn't they? I sent him there after the murders; not before."

"Yes, Bill. That's why I'm saying Slagter is two people. Saul gets his orders from the South African Government, and passes the information on to Slagter. He may or may not know who Slagter is. I think he did. Then he makes sure he's nowhere near the place when it happens."

Farnsworth snorted impatiently.

"He was there the first time. Why did he invite suspicion then? You haven't told me anything we haven't gone over before—and discarded."

"But after Saul dies, something changes. Saul gets valuable information from Simone in Paris, but doesn't pass it on. Instead he forces the South African Government to send Slagter after me in the normal way, for information I don't have. And Slagter knows I don't have it! So he goes after Saul's lovers in the hope that, true to form, Saul has passed it on to one of them. How did Slagter know I didn't have it?"

"So?"

"So Slagter must be someone who knows me very well—not as Donaldson, but as Samuelson." They lapsed into abrupt silence as they heard the sound of running footsteps on the gravel behind the mound. Joshua peered through the gorse. "It seems to be your chauffeur, Bill," he said. "He seems to be coming up here in an awful hurry."

"I told him we were not to be disturbed," Farnsworth said, the small eyes in the large face closing in perplexion.

The footsteps rounded the corner.

"I'm sorry to disturb you, Sir," the chauffeur said, "but there's an urgent message from Detective Chief Inspector Benton. They found the body of the African gentleman, Mr. Jomo Mbangeli. He's been hacked to death."

"Oh! Dear God!" Farnsworth moaned.

"When did it happen?" Joshua asked.

"Sometime this morning, Sir. The body is still warm. The landlady found him, and she threw a fit. He'd asked her to call him at ten, and when she got no reply, she went up to check."

"Jomo? Why Jomo?" Joshua asked aloud, and the answer hit the both of them simultaneously.

Because he had been one of Saul's lovers. It had been before them all the time. The set pattern, starting in Tangiers five years ago. And then the killings through the cities that had been the scenes of brutal interrogations.

And the change in the pattern when Saul died.

"Julia! My darling Julia!" Joshua cried. "How will I ever forgive myself? How could I have let you go through with this?"

"Stop that moaning, will you?" Farnsworth snapped, between gasping breaths, as they raced towards the car.

Even Farnsworth, with his portly frame, made good time. Joshua reached it first, and held the door open for Farnsworth, as the chauffeur slid in behind the wheel, bringing it to life with a roar that shook the frame.

"Drive, damn it!" Farnsworth barked. "Fifty-four Fitzjohn's Avenue. And drive on the bloody sidewalk if you have to!"

He reached for the telephone. Joshua punched in the numbers, his trembling fingers following the movements of his lips as he recalled them from memory, over-anxious with the dread it might fail him, and they would be unavailable to instant recall.

But he remembered, and his face flushed with relief, as he repeated them over and over again, afraid they might slip away from him, the relief fading into disappointment as the seconds ticked by.

"She doesn't answer," Farnsworth said.

He tried again.

There was a shattering noise. Then the line went dead.

Chapter 21

Julia finished her bath and dried herself on the mat. She towel-dried her hair, wrapping the towel around her head like the turban of some Eastern potentate. Of late, she'd found herself making comparisons more often to things from the East. She gave her breasts a quick check, then slipped into a pale-yellow dressing gown and sat on a padded stool opposite the dressing table mirror, while she brushed her hair. She used a blow drier to curl it into shape. Sometimes she used hot rollers, which took longer, but not today.

Today she couldn't be quite sure of the time she would have. And she wanted to look presentable.

Joshua spending the night in the flat had made a difference. Today seemed a little different from every other day. For one thing, she'd had company for breakfast, and that had been missing from her every other day. She'd found out how he liked his eggs—over-easy. But he'd eat them as solid rock, if that's how they came out, he'd said. It would be nice to have a husband who wasn't fussy about little things like that. Though with a little bit of practice, it shouldn't be too difficult to flip them over without breaking the yolks. Better buy a few extra dozen, she thought, when you decide to try it, in case the first twenty-seven refuse to easy over. She'd have to give up bacon though. Everyone had to compromise a little in marriage, she thought. It was a minor enough concession.

Does everyone in love think such silly thoughts? Or am I the only one?

She wanted to look her best. One never knew how the day might end. Take poor Ewa. All she had done was to sleep on a bed in the home of an old and trusted friend. Decided by the toss of a coin.

She had not met Ewa, but Joshua had told her all about the years he'd known and loved her in South Africa.

She went into the kitchen and made herself a pitcher of orange juice. She watched the crushed fibers settle, like sediment, into the bottom of the green jug made of Venetian smoked glass. She covered it with a cloth napkin, with the crest of the Bromfields engraved on it; then took the jug to the dining room in the alcove off the living room.

She sat on the rocking chair and waited.

Joshua had not told her when he would be back, and she had not asked. She just took it for granted he would stay awhile with her in the flat until he could return to his own. The explosion had made an awful mess of it, particularly the bedroom.

Would he like some fish for lunch? He came from Durban and he'd lived in Bombay, and both cities were on the coast, by the sea. There had to be good fish in the area. But what if he'd been forced to eat fish as a child—and hated it? She knew so little about him—his tastes, and aversions. Not potato chips though. Maybe a cheese casserole with boiled new potatoes, sprinkled with parsley. Thank God for Emma and the pottering she'd permitted in the kitchens at Bromfield!

No finishing school would ever help when it came down to the real thing.

She looked at her watch more often than seemed natural.

It could be a long wait.

It wasn't. When the knock came—a tap—it sounded very quiet. Subdued. Almost timid, as if the visitor were inquiring if she was in; hoping she was not.

"Come in, Laura," she called out. "The door's open."

Laura entered carrying an overnight bag with her. She sat on the cushioned sofa, placing the bag beside her. Sitting on the very edge of the deep, plush cushions, reluctant to be enfolded by it, or to be comfortable in it.

"I'm leaving this evening for Johannesburg," she said. "I've checked out of the hotel. I have a few hours to kill, so I thought I'd spend them with a few of Saul's friends. I've just spent over an hour with Jomo Mbangeli. Did you know him? He was a very close friend of my husband Saul."

"No. I did not know him. I knew of him, though?"

"Really? How did you know of him? Well, never mind. You don't have to answer that. I thought I'd spend a quiet hour with you. Talking. Before leaving for the airport and home."

"I'm so glad you did," Julia said. "I did so enjoy the talk we had last evening in the car. Was the hotel comfortable?

Several of my friends who've spent the night there, recommended it to me. And it's not too far away from here. Did you sleep well?"

"Very."

"May I offer you a drink?"

"No! I never drink when I'm on such visits. Besides it is too early for a drink."

"Of course. A glass of orange juice then, perhaps? I will have one too. I have orange juice all the time. So natural and wholesome."

Julia poured herself a glass. The jug was full and heavy and she was careful to avoid sloshing it.

"Will you have some, Laura?"

Laura hesitated.

Julia drank deep, half draining the glass, wiping her lips with the edge of the napkin, placing the jug back on the table, preparing to put the crest of the Bromfields on top of it again.

"Yes, I will have a glass of orange juice, my dear," Laura said, stopping her. "My throat gets so dry when it is all over. Perhaps half a glass?"

Julia stirred the jug, pouring the liquid jerkily into the glass she handed Laura, standing over her as she offered it.

They clinked glasses.

"I had to come and see you, my dear," Laura said, placing the empty glass on the floor beside her, while Julia rocked in her rocking chair, stretching out her bare feet to peer at her painted toenails. "Especially after last night. We talked so well. I felt I ought to know you better. It's amazing how honest two strangers can be. With each other. Will you be honest with me?"

"You wanted to talk?" Julia said gently. "I will be happy to listen. Tell me anything you wish. And if I can help you I will. I want to help you."

"Oh, you can! My dear, you can. By telling me the truth. Did he talk about me at all when he made love to you? My husband Saul, did he ever mention my name when he covered your body with is own?"

"Mrs Prentiss, you must not torture yourself in this way. Last night it became so clear how much you must have suffered, being married to Saul. But it is over. He's dead. He can't hurt you anymore."

"But he does, Julia! Even when he's dead he tortures me. It hurts every time I think of his lovers. How can you know how much it hurts? How will I ever forget all his lovers? They rampage through my mind like goring bulls. And when they do, I could scream and scream and scream and nobody hears me. Did he ever talk about me when he made love to you? Why don't you answer? It is a simple enough question."

"Sometimes, Mrs Prentiss. Not very often. Always with compassion. For a very cruel man, which is what he was, he was unmistakably tender when he talked about you."

"Lies, Julia! All lies! But you're right about Saul. He was a monster! Insatiable when it came to women. They had to love him. Men too. Did you know that, my dear?"

"Sort of. In a way. Not directly, he never told me, but I knew."

"And it didn't bother you? Didn't it make you feel dirty? When he made love to you?"

"I didn't love him, Mrs Prentiss. If I had, it would have bothered me very much. As much as it did you."

"Would it bother you if Joshua was that way?"

"I beg your pardon?"

"Joshua! I am talking about Joshua! He loved me once, and I loved him too, though I didn't know it then. I couldn't marry him, and when I could, you had to come along and spoil it all for me. Do you know that he loves you?"

"I know."

"Would it bother you if he played around with other women the way Saul played around with you?"

Julia did not reply.

"Wouldn't you be hurt? Wouldn't you want to rid yourself of such memories? Eliminate them. How do you fight a goring bull—except with a machete!"

There was no reply, Julia could give her. There was no simple answer Julia could make. Because there were no simple answers.

"Why don't you speak, Lady Julia? I can't hear you, Lady Julia. Wouldn't you be hurt?"

"Yes."

Laura leaned back into the sofa, for the first time, with an air of silent triumph. She unzipped the overnight bag beside her.

"My dear, you've been more than honest with me. And I appreciate it. Not like some of the others these past three days. Do you know that Shari even tried to deny it? She was most uncooperative. Clayborne and Jomo were just too ashamed of themselves. They were all over the floor begging for mercy. Only La Reine knew how to die. Simone. That is her name. See, I know her name. She was the only one who was as wronged as I was. I had to work myself into a real frenzy to kill her, because I felt very sorry for her. She looked so white, how could he have known she was coloured?"

Laura drew out the machete. Julia saw the light, streaming in from the window, gleam off the clean blade. It had been wiped clean, except at the handle, where the blood-stained fingers had gripped it. Laura took it by the shaft. "I'm going to leave this with you, Julia. As a gift. Would you like me to leave it beside you?"

Julia leaned forward, as if to accept it. Laura drew back out of reach. She edged the point of it underneath one of the buttons of the tufted cushion, snapping it off, testing the blade for sharpness.

They heard the telephone ring in the hallway. Julia got up from the rocking chair to answer it.

Laura drew out the gun.

"I wouldn't answer it," Laura said. "We haven't finished our little talk yet. About Saul. If you move, I will be forced to hit you in the kneecap—as he taught me—and it can be very painful."

Julia remained standing beside the rocking chair. Laura rose from the sofa. The telephone rang again and again. It stopped for just a few seconds, as if the caller had hung up, only to ring again. Repeatedly. Laura's eyebrows drew together in a rage at the interruption. She raised the gun, leveled it at the telephone and fired, shattering it.

"My aim is excellent," she said simply. "Because Saul gave me so much practice at it. Very rude of the telephone. Interrupting us in this way. Now we can talk freely again. About Saul."

"There is nothing more to talk about him, Mrs Prentiss. I have been as honest with you as I possibly can. I did not love Saul. I could not love him. I have never been in love, except these past few days with a not-too-tall, not-too-handsome, not-too-well built, little Indian, whose body crushed mine in the London tube. What can I say to you to ease the torture in your mind? You have suffered a great deal, but it can now be over. May I have the gun? And the machete?"

"Did you know he was married? Saul, I mean. The first time he made love to you?"

"The first time? No! It was a casual affair I now deeply regret. I will always feel ashamed of myself for it."

"Lies! All lies! You will gloat over the many times you stood naked before him—and he before you. Another woman's husband crawling to you for your favors. How it humiliated me! While you saw it as a casual affair?"

"Mrs Prentiss, you are a very sick woman. You need help. And I will do all I can to help you. If you will only let me. Please let me help you, while there is still time. No jury in the world would convict you of the crimes you have committed, but you cannot go on in this way. Please! I want to help you."

"It is you who will need help, Julia, my dear, but it will come too late for you. It came too late for all the others. Why should it be any different for you? But I will be merciful. I will make it quick and clean. Not like the way Saul taught me. If you will cooperate, that is. I won't disfigure you, as I did some of the others. One sharp jab, and it will be all over. Without much pain. You are luckier than I am. I will have to live with my pain. I can't bear pain! There are ways and ways to die, and I have been sentenced to the most horrible of them."

"You are almost as cruel as Saul was," Julia said, glancing at her watch.

"I learnt a great deal from him, Julia. You cannot live with a man for fifteen years and not be taught what it takes to be an agent of the South African Government. That is what we were. It wasn't easy, I can tell you. It didn't come naturally to me as it does to some. It was horrible that first time in Tangiers, when Saul taught me how to interrogate Abdul. See, I even remember his name. Quiet little fellow, he was. Saul took his time over Abdul, working on him long and hard just so I could learn the rules of interrogation. I can still hear his screams at night, and Saul's silent indifference to it. It might have been better if he'd laughed. I was sick all over."

"He taught you how to kill in that way, and you did not protest it?"

"It was the law. We were agents of the government. He made that so clear to me. Would you have had me break the law? Why do you keep on in this way? We had, both, given up the ones we loved most, to live within the law. Could we have been faulted for that? Would you have advised us to do otherwise? And when we became agents, we were above the law. Saul made that quite clear to me. You know that. You have a license to kill, don't you? You'd kill me right now, if you had a chance, wouldn't you?"

"No, Mrs Prentiss, I could not kill you."

"You're bluffing! All agents will lie, especially when they're being interrogated. Saul taught me that too. They have to suffer for the truth to be extracted from them. See, I know it now. I soon became very good at it. Saul couldn't do the interrogations any more, because they were all tracking him—Joshua's men and Farnsworth's too—as he knew they would after Tangiers. He needed me, Julia. I could not keep his love, but it was the only way I could keep him needing me. Wasn't that important? Tell me, Julia, tell me that it was. Please!"

"I don't know, Laura. Why are you telling me all this?"

"Because I have to talk to someone. And now there will be no one to talk to. Gangoly was the most difficult to interrogate. For me. I kept seeing Joshua's face on his. They were very close friends and it wasn't easy, but it had to be done, because Saul said it was for his love and trust. The rest were easy after that. They all begged to be allowed to talk."

"Except Vladimir."

"Yes. Except Vladimir. He died too quickly for me. Do you know he had a last request? He wanted me to send you a dozen red roses. From him. And I would have, if he'd cooperated. But he ran on my machete and died before I could talk to him."

She moved a step closer to Julia.

"Why did Saul commit suicide, Mrs Prentiss?"

Laura stopped. Her face changed. Julia thought she might start to cry, but she fought back the tears, using the hand that held the gun to wipe her eyes.

"Because of me. Because I failed him in his final assignment. He showed me instructions, Joshua was to be interrogated about the date and places of the invasion. In the same way. They were tracking him—and he couldn't do it himself. So I would have to do it. But I couldn't do that to Joshua. That night Saul took me out for dinner and dancing. He was so sure of himself; so pleased he was. We were on the dance floor when he told me about it. I felt his back stiffen when I refused. Anyone else, but not Joshua! His hand dropped from my waist, and he walked away from me, leaving me standing all alone on the dance floor. I followed him, but he pushed me away. That was the last time I saw him. For him, I had killed and murdered, and I would have done it as long as he wanted me to—but not Joshua."

She sat on the sofa, within easy reach of Julia, and sobbed. Julia did not move. Let her cry. The rocking chair squeaked as she leaned against the back of it.

"Did you know, Laura, that he had instructions from the South African Government to deliver Slagter to the Russians? Because of what you did to Vladimir. Farnsworth, Joshua and he met in Welwyn Garden City that afternoon. He was forced by all our governments, including yours, into Operation Canard—which was to deliver you to the Russians. Did you know about Operation Canard? Did he tell you anything about it?"

"What could I know about such things? I'm only a housewife who runs a novelty store. How could I have known what governments decide? I only did what I was told to do. What everyone said I had to do. Why do you ask?"

"He had no choice in the matter, Laura. He would have had to hand both you and himself over to Andropov in Berlin. They might have imprisoned you for life, but he would have faced certain execution. Wouldn't you prefer to think he committed suicide because he wanted to save you? He could not save himself. Will it not make you feel better? I think that is why he chose the way out he did."

"You are unduly charitable to him, my dear," Laura said, rising to her feet menacingly. "Because you were his lover. I knew him better than that. But I'm glad it's over. You are the last of his living loves. This evening I'll fly back to South Africa, and everything will be behind me. Sometimes I have wondered, in all this, where I did wrong?"

Julia looked at her watch, snatching a quick glance as she moved her hand away from the back of the rocking chair.

"You seem unduly obsessed with the time, my dear," Laura said. "Could it be that you are expecting someone?"

"At this time in the morning? Not likely. Did you know that Joshua spent the night there? On that very sofa. It was big enough for him. I made him breakfast this morning. He likes his eggs over-easy. Did you know that? And we talked. About a lot of things. And people."

Laura stopped once more.

"Did you talk about me? What did he say about me?"

"I'm afraid I can hardly tell you, Laura, if you keep waving that blade in my face. I will be happy to tell you if you will let me. You wanted me to talk, didn't you? Now you must listen. We are alone; the door is locked. You locked it when you entered. We have all the time in the world—to talk. Then, when you have heard my side of it, you must do with me as you will. Wouldn't you like to hear from me what Joshua had to say about you? The truth. You interrogated so many for it. At least hear it this time from me."

Laura seemed undecided. Bewildered. Uncertain of whether she should cut Julia off, or permit her to proceed.

She wavered; then the hard look came back into her eyes.

"Why should I hear it from you? What Joshua said. It isn't right for Joshua to take up with you. You're not right for him. He should marry some obedient, little Indian woman from Durban. Not you! And I'll set that right too. Would you take off your dressing gown? I have always asked my victims to undress. The mark of Slagter. But no sexual mutilation. That I insisted on with Saul. It was the only time he gave in to my wishes in the matter. Please take off your robe for me. I only wish to see, and admire, what Saul saw in you."

Julia undid the satin cord that held the robe around her body. It was a stubborn knot, and though the robe opened above it and below it, the knot held—a single cord around her waist. Laura jerked the machete sharply from under it, slicing the cord. The robe swung open, hanging around her body, half open at the front, held by her arms close to her sides.

Was this the way it was meant to be? She had ignored opportunities for escape, even simple moves of self-defense, in her anxiety to learn the truth from Laura. As no one else could tell her. What good was the truth if it could not be communicated to others?

She slipped off the robe, placing it on the rocking chair. It hung limply over the back of it. She stepped to one side, clear of it, throwing her head back defiantly, as she waited for Laura's jerky movements.

"Stand with your feet apart," Laura commanded.

Julia obeyed.

"Now put your hands on your hips."

Julia did as she was told, her fingers feeling the muscles in her lower back, her shoulders arched forward.

"Throw back your shoulders, Julia! Look at me. You are so beautiful. Such rich, brown hair! Don't be ashamed of it."

Julia threw back her shoulders. Raised her head and looked inquiringly at Laura.

The end was near.

Laura looked at the beautifully formed, statuesque body, mature and alluring, through Saul's eyes, and anger crept into them, turning to rage as she trembled uncontrollably.

The tremor passed.

"I stood that way once," Laura said softly. "On a lonely beach, twenty miles south of Durban, with golden sands beneath my feet and the waters of the Indian Ocean behind me. How I wish someone had been standing in front of me with a machete."

She raised the blade and lunged forward at Julia.

Chapter 22

The car did run over the sidewalk at the junction of Heath Road and Fitzjohn's Avenue, screeching past the corner like a crazed animal hunted by its own passion. Robert took the corner deep to avoid the traffic congealing at the intersection, and the sidewalk was inconveniently wide at that point. He cut sharply across the faces of homes that lined the roadside, between the forked roads, swerving back into Fitzjohn's Avenue, the squealing tires registering their protest at such socially unacceptable driving.

The line of shade tress reaching high over the avenue, flashed by the window like unwelcome memories being hurried into the past.

Joshua and Farnsworth, sitting in the rear, pushed against the seat in front of them, urging him on. Robert ignored them. He was too experienced a driver to permit them to rattle him. No sense at all in killing some innocent passerby on the street, just to save the life of someone they knew.

He'd drive carefully, he said to himself.

It didn't seem that way to the newspaper lad selling newspapers at the corner, who scattered himself into the doorway of the tobacconist's shop, as the unmarked Rover flashed by. Or to the old lady pushing the pram with the sleeping child, who shook her fist at it in anger.

Farnsworth swore back at her. Robert's ears went red. He was grateful for the glass partition that sealed the two of them away from him.

It was downhill all the way from the heath, past the lines of stately homes that had seen horse-and-buggy days. Traffic was light at that time in the morning. The office rush had ended; the rush at lunch time had not commenced. Robert was grateful for that too. He could drive in the middle of the street without raising too many eyebrows.

Fifty-four was even. It had to be on the left side of the street going towards Swiss Cottage. Not that it would have bothered Robert any. The street was wide enough for him to make a U-turn without reversing—if he took both sidewalks into account.

But it was not necessary. Fifty-four was even. On the left side. The whole crazy world could drive on the right side of the road, but, for this one time, England had to be right!

At least Joshua thought so, as the car screeched to a stop.

They rushed up the stairs, taking the steps with unaccustomed agility, made frantic by fear, seeing only the door to her flat at the very top of the stairs, at the very top of the house, Joshua ahead of Farnsworth, Robert not far behind.

The door was locked. Only one sound came from within.

The gentle squeak of a rocking chair. Joshua fumbled for the key Julia had given him that morning. Farnsworth pummeled on the door to distract attention.

She was sitting on the rocking chair. Rocking gently. Her head leaned against the high back. She wore a pale-yellow dressing gown, and she did not even turn her head to greet them as they broke into the room.

Laura lay sprawled at her feet, the machete still clutched in one hand. The gun lay beside her, where it had fallen when she fell.

Joshua dropped to his knees, beside Julia, and put his arms around her, kissing her wherever he could, murmuring, incoherently, words that Julia concluded were words of endearment.

Farnsworth was busy examining Laura. Taking her pulse.

"She's alive," he said. "But asleep. What happened?"

"I will tell you, Dr Farnsworth," Julia said, "if you can persuade Colonel Samuelson, who is on his knees, to at least permit me to breathe."

Joshua recovered himself, and released her.

"I'm sorry. The relief was too much for me. I had such horrible visions of you stretched out here—naked and dead."

"What is it that bothered you more?" Julia asked innocently. "That I would be naked or that I would be dead?"

He forgave her the remark. She, too, had been under a fearsome strain. He drew his arms from around her and would have risen from the floor beside her, but she put an arm around him, drawing him back into her.

"I didn't say I didn't like it," she said.

Chapter 23

They sat, the three of them—Farnsworth, Samuelson and Spencer—at a small round table on the sidewalk outside Joshua's favourite hotel, just off the Place de la Republique, sipping expensive French red wine, with a plate of Danish pastries between them.

Henri had sat with them for a while—the bottle was with his compliments—but the pressures of running the hotel in the busy season—not to mention the dirty looks that his daughter gave him—had finally, and regretfully, drawn him back into the foyer of the hotel.

"I could sit with you all day," he said. "Such a pleasure! With the intellect of the gentlemen and the lady, which made for fine conversation, and with the added pleasure of Mademoiselle Julia's charms, I could sit with you all day on the sidewalk and never feel the need to move. Good wine is wasted unless it is consumed in fine company."

Joshua offered the Danish pastries round the table.

Farnsworth declined.

"Not for me," Julia said. "Thank you, but I've got to watch my figure."

"Not as hard as some of these French gigolos have been watching it," Joshua said. "I've never been with a woman who had so many wolf calls. And you're just sitting there, looking perfectly innocent. What's going to happen to them when you start to walk?"

"You're not upset, are you?"

"No, of course not. Anyone may watch. That was not a crime, was it?"

"None at all, my darling," Julia said gently.

"When do you reach Berlin?" Joshua said, topping off Farnsworth's glass and Julia's, before emptying the bottle into his own. He peered down the empty bottle and sighed.

"I leave at twelve-thirty from De Gaulle. A private commuter jet. It's been cleared with the Russians. Andropov meets me later this afternoon, but I don't know where, and I won't know where, until I get to Templehof. These Russians are paranoid about their safety. I'll be glad to get rid of her. Not that she's much trouble, though. With the sedation she's under."

"Quite right, Bill. Keep her well sedated. She's in good hands. After all she's travelling with her physician and his nurse. Is Jane with her now?"

"Yes."

"What will they do to her?" Julia asked.

Farnsworth took his time replying, lighting a cigar before he answered her. "I don't know. Andropov isn't talking. At least he wasn't willing to tell me over the phone. I will ask him, I promise you. They aren't all that bad, you know. Certainly not the way they're made out to be."

"But what do you think will happen to her?" Julia persisted.

"My guess is a lifetime of hard labour in Siberia," Farnsworth said. "That will make her very old, very soon. People just disappear into that vast hinterland of theirs. I doubt we'll ever hear from her again."

"And the pity of it is she just can't stand the cold." Joshua said.

"Does it shock you, Slagter was half a woman?" Julia asked.

Joshua said no.

"It surprised me just that little," Farnsworth confessed. "I'm rather sorry. Ruined my appetite for marriage—if I ever had any. Poor Jane! Imagine being wed to one of them. Present company excepted, my dear. Goes without saying."

"Quite all right, Dr Farnsworth," Julia said. "Men have been butchering each other, and a lot more, for years, and it doesn't seemed to have dulled our appetite for them. We seem to love them more than ever."

"You're right, my dear. Quite right. May I ask a question? How did you do it?"

"Ah!"

Julia drained her glass. She held up the empty bottle for inspection, turned it over and shook it, watching the last few drops hesitatingly, reluctantly, splatter into her glass, unwilling, so it seemed to her, to leave the comfort of the bottle that had held them for so long.

They took the hint.

Farnsworth took out his wallet with a groan. Joshua imitated him with an even louder one, which prompted Julia to inquire, solicitously, whether he was having the hiccups, offering him a sure fire remedy to arrest them by pinching his nose and standing on his head. On the sidewalk.

They pooled their francs. Farnsworth went off into the hotel to buy it from Henri.

Joshua watched his back disappear into the lobby; turned hastily to Julia, holding her hands quickly in his own.

The urgency startled her.

"Darling," he said. "If I were to ask you to do something in a hurry, would you do it?"

"Yes. If you wanted me to."

"Without asking questions?"

"If that's what you wanted, yes. Is it important?"

"Very. To me. Promise?"

"I promise. If I can't trust you now, I never will."

Farnsworth came back with the bottle.

"Now, my dear, seeing you've bled us both dry, we deserve some answers. I have to fill in my report to MI-6. How did you do it?"

Julia poured herself a glass of wine. A full glass.

"I prepared a jug of orange juice," she said. "It was as simple as that."

"I can't believe she fell for it," Farnsworth said. "She learnt a great deal from Saul. You'd think he'd have taught her not to fall for that one."

"She didn't fall for it right away. She was most suspicious. I had to drink from it first. Almost as if I was tasting it for her. Like Indian kings of old had their cooks do, in front of them, before they ate. And I did drink from it. A full glass too. That seemed to reassure her. Except that the chemist at MI-6 had given me what I asked for—a strong barbiturate that was colloidal and looked and tasted like shredded fruit. It didn't actually dissolve in the orange juice; just settled at the bottom as all shreds would. And in a smoked, green, Venetian jug, even I had difficulty seeing them. I poured my glass out first, without sloshing the juice around. Since the jug was full that wasn't suspicious. Even drank from it to reassure her. When I poured out her glass, I stirred the jug."

"Clever."

"Not really. I don't give myself many points for it. She wasn't a trained agent—just a badly used woman. Who'd suffered a great deal. Twenty minutes! That's what the chemist said when he gave it to me. It would work in twenty minutes. God! It seemed like hours. And I kept thinking. What if he was wrong on the action of stomach juices on the shreds? Or he'd given me the wrong stuff? Or the effective date had elapsed? Or if she'd drink it without draining it, leaving the shreds in the bottom of the glass?"

Her had trembled as it slid round the stem of the wine glass before her. Farnsworth pretended not to notice. Joshua traced his finger along her arm, feeling the soft skin, barely touching it.

"And I had to keep her talking. At first, that wasn't difficult. She wanted to talk. But when I looked at the time twice, she became very jumpy. Fortunately Saul was not the only topic of conversation. There was Joshua. And at the end, when she made me undress, I admit, I nearly panicked. I considered making a dive for it out of the window, and taking my chances on the ground outside. Had it rained? Would it be soft? Are there bushes to break my fall or is there a concrete path around the back of the house? I didn't know the answers to simple questions—and I was a trained agent."

Julia drained her glass. Farnsworth wasn't drinking; neither was Joshua.

"You'd think I'd have checked on all these things. I did afterwards. There is a concrete path that runs around the back of the house. Edged with sharp stones forming a border. It would have been an equally bloody way to die—and in the nude too."

"I'm sorry, darling," Joshua said, moving his hand into hers. "You'll never know how badly I feel about the whole thing. And involving you in it. And Bill feels the same way too."

"I do. I do," Farnsworth said. "But you were expecting her. You knew before she came who she was. Half of Slagter. The murderous half! And you knew she would be coming after you—not Joshua."

"Yes."

Julia did not seem anxious to proceed. Having gone through it had been painful; reliving it was no less. She would relive it many times over, and in time, she would see it as an impersonal observer might, but two days later, it was as real and horrifying as it had been at the time.

"Must we continue this, Bill?" Joshua asked. "Can't it wait until later?"

"I'm afraid it can't. Forgive me, Julia, but I won't be seeing the two of you for some time—where is it you're off to?—and I do have to fill out a beastly report on Operation Canard. Commendations to you, my dear. Highly glowing language, I promise. But I have to have all the facts, and with Joshua distracting you, I am not likely to receive your written report for some time. Am I now?"

She nodded in agreement. "It was obvious to all of us that Saul was involved in some way. He was their only contact with Slagter. He was there for the first killing and then, for all of the others, he was there after the killing. At the very least, he knew who Slagter was. He admitted that much to me. In Nice. Agents from many countries—including Joshua's men—had tracked him after Tangiers, and he was nowhere near the victims when they were killed. So it had to be someone close to him, who could be there in the same places too, without exciting attention. And what better person than his wife? Who sometimes accompanied him on his travels—and sometimes preceded him there. Withdrawn into the background, living unobtrusively in his shadow. That was merely a suspicion, of course. When Dr Clayborne was killed the pattern had changed. And when Shari was murdered, it had been set, but the bells still didn't ring in my mind, the way they should have. I assumed—as you did—that rather than go after Joshua, who was a trained agent and waiting for him, Slagter was hoping to extract the same information from his lovers, taking the chance that Saul did tell his lovers choice bits of top secret information. In bed. Yet he didn't tell me. Forgive me, Joshua! I know how this must hurt. Forgive me!"

She leaned across to him, drawing him towards her, ignoring Farnsworth, covering his mouth with her kisses, wet with emotion and hungry with desire, passing her hand through his hair, her anger with herself communicating itself to him, helping him to bury his hurt of things past.

"I seem to be intruding," Farnsworth mumbled, as Julia, finally, drew away from Joshua.

"You might as well hear it all," Julia said. "Then La Reine was murdered—and sometime when we have more time to ourselves, and not doing anything particularly exciting, you must tell me all about her. You will do that, won't you, Joshua?"

She leaned towards Joshua again, but this time she held his chin in her hand, ruffling his beard wickedly, as she looked him in the eyes. Her laughter reassured him.

"Will you stick to the subject matter at hand?" Farnsworth moaned. "I don't have much time. God! Lovers! I'd banish the whole lot—or anyone who said he was one—to an island in the South Seas!"

At hearing which, both Joshua and Julia, simultaneously, offered to take him up on his offer, if their expenses were paid.

"You still haven't told me all," Farnsworth prodded.

"We all assumed that Saul confided to his lovers in bed. But, then, wouldn't Slagter have assumed he also told the woman he was in bed with most often? His wife. Or am I being naïve? Yet no harm came to Laura. One would have thought she would have been his first victim. So it hadn't anything to do with information. It was Slagter, all right, but he wasn't after information! I'm only sorry it came to me too late to save La Reine. I did try to save Jomo. I saw him in the Evening Star, and I warned him about Laura. I don't think he believed me. He was too preoccupied with what Boko was going to do to Joshua to worry about what Slagter would do to him. I even thought Laura might come for me before Jomo. I'm sorry she didn't. It would have saved his life."

Julia drained her glass. Joshua poured her some more. He moved the bottle towards Farnsworth, but it was politely declined.

"Then why were you outside my flat, monitoring it that night? You knew I wasn't in any danger," Joshua said. "Why?"

"Because, my love, I couldn't risk it. What if I was wrong? What if she'd decided, out of guilt, to carry out Saul's instructions? There I was wrong! She'd never have harmed you, Joshua. Never! And I think that is what drove him to suicide. After all those killings he had conditioned her into doing, and after all those years, he still could not make her kill you. But I couldn't take the chance, my love. I was terrified I might be too late. I couldn't come in straight away. That wouldn't have been right. She might have had legitimate things to say to you, and I would have been intruding. The overnight bag was outside the door, when I reached it. She hadn't bothered to take it in because she didn't need it. So I had a quick look. Not very nice of me—looking through her personal clothing—but I had no choice. And I found it. The machete. Neatly wrapped in a heavy skirt. After that it wasn't conjecture any longer. But if I had turned her in then, I wouldn't have learned the truth about her—or told her the truth about myself."

"Excellent, my dear," Farnsworth said, patting her on the back.

"I couldn't agree more," Joshua said warmly. "You've put us all to shame!"

"I don't know about that," Julia said, beginning to feel her old self again. "Joshua didn't really want to know. You were too close to her, my love, to see the changes in her. And everyone was looking for a trained agent to be Slagter—not a housewife."

She put her head on Joshua's shoulder, stroking his cheek and beard with one hand, the other encircling him.

"This is Paris," she said defiantly. "I am not in London."

"Well, I'll leave you two lovebirds to get on with it," Farnsworth said, looking at his watch. "I'll have to be going soon. But a couple of loose ends need tidying up. What is the date of the invasion? And the places where the first thrusts are to be expected? The British Government will want to know."

"I can't tell you, Bill," Joshua said. "I'm sorry about it. That was never a part of Operation Canard, and is no concern of mine. I have been in touch with my Government, and I have to tell you permission has been denied. If you wish to take it up at levels higher than our own, you are welcome to try, but I doubt the Indian Government is going to budge on the issue."

"Say no more," Farnsworth said. "But before I leave, one final question. If you have an answer that is. We know that Saul committed suicide, and we may even know why. But why in such a bizarre way? And why didn't he pass on the information he got from La Reine to South African National Intelligence? He was a loyal enough agent. So I always believed."

Joshua poured out the rest of the wine between the three of them. Draining the bottle. Raising the empty bottle to his lips in mock bravado, as if he'd drunk it dry.

"I can tell you why. But not definitively. I can only guess at it. He had to make it look like murder. At least for a few days. And he couldn't pass on the information to them, because they wouldn't have bothered with making me talk. He thought he could get Laura to do it. When he found out she wouldn't, he wanted me to be interrogated by other South African National Intelligence agents in the country—I can name at least one of them. If they needed the information desperately, it seemed a natural way to go. And as a final insurance, he advised Boko to do the same with me. And but for Julia, and the toss of a coin, he would have succeeded too."

Joshua spent some time kissing Julia, oblivious to Farnsworth's presence. She could feel his mind churning even in his kisses.

"Of course," Joshua said, in between kisses, "this is all conjecture. The answer is a lot more difficult. We have to enter the mind of a dead man, if we want the truth, and that, now, is impossible."

Farnsworth reached for his umbrella. He had insisted on bringing it. Sometimes it rained, even in Paris, in the summer. Downpours too. And these days, Julia was getting as bad as Joshua about protection. He tapped the bowler firmly back on his head and straightened his tie. He shook hands with them, touching his hat to Julia as well.

He had gone exactly three steps towards the hotel, when Joshua called out to him:

"Have a safe trip back to Johannesburg, Bill."

Farnsworth stopped. He seemed to freeze, the umbrella poised like a foil, the portly figure motionless.

"Put your hands on the table," Joshua whispered to Julia, urgently. "Open palms upwards. Do as I say. Please! You promised."

Julia put her hands on the table, palms facing upwards, open towards him. Joshua did the same.

Farnsworth turned around, the point of the umbrella firmly entrenched, for balance, in a crack in the sidewalk, his free hand in the inside pocket of his coat. Joshua smiled and twiddled his fingers to draw attention to their hands on the table.

There was one brief, long, moment of critical indecision; then Farnsworth smiled too. He drew his hand out from the inside pocket of his coat.

Empty.

He tipped his hat to them once more, and walking rapidly he disappeared into the hotel.

"Johannesburg!" Julia said. "You said Berlin. To hand her over to Andropov in Berlin."

"Julia, my darling, she's a very sick woman. Let her go. They would be foolish to let her out of the country again. She will be institutionalised for years and years. Probably forever. I hope not. But it will be warm—and she just cannot stand the cold."

Julia nodded her consent.

"Besides, my darling, you were expecting her that day. You could have killed her very easily. And you didn't. Why?"

Julia brushed off the question, answering it by playing footsie with his knee under the table. Somehow, she felt eighteen again. "I've resigned from the Service," she said. "You were right about me all the time. I'm not cut out to be an agent. Donaldson didn't think I had it in me—and he was right too."

"We must be more alike than we think," Joshua said, responding to the pressure on his knee. "I did the same. Resigned from Indian Military Intelligence and MI-6."

"And the CIA," she prompted. "You're going to give that up too."

"How did you know about that?"

"Ah!"

"Come on, Julia. Out with it. I won't be hurt. Where did I slip up?"

"Not you, darling. Donaldson, actually. He called when I was with Farnsworth. That was a mistake. Because it gave me Farnsworth's end of the conversation. It was very sweet of him though, warning me to check up on you before I was too deep in it. That endeared him to me. I couldn't really see him as a killer after that."

"Poor Donaldson. He can now finally rest in peace. I won't be able to use him again."

"Don't you feel ashamed of yourself, Joshua? Being a triple agent? That's terrible!"

"What's so terrible about it?" Joshua asked innocently. "Lots of Indian agents work for the CIA. We have so much contact with the Russians at governmental levels, we're very valuable to them. At a political level rather than a military one. Let's just say I worked for the Western world. But I don't any more. I'm an unemployed doctor! Looking for a practice. And that's not a nice situation to be in. How do I go about supporting the granddaughter of the eleventh Earl of Bromfield in my condition?"

"You sound like you had a disease. Come on, Joshua. Cheer up! Something will turn up. Don't look so sad. It's such a nice day. Too nice to feel sad. Perhaps Grandfather will help."

Joshua looked more downcast.

"And that's another thing," he said morosely. "What's the eleventh Earl going to say when he finds out you're marrying a wog—and an unemployed one at that?"

Julia let him wallow in his own misery for a while, the smile barely causing her lips to part, until she relented and touched him on the arm.

"I've already spoken to Grandfather about you."

"And?"

"He's known about you for a long time, Joshua. Don't ask me how, because I can't tell you—it's not mine to tell—but he approves wholeheartedly."

Joshua gave a whoop of delight, much to the discomfort of a passing lady, who shied away from him, crossing the street to the sidewalk on the other side, reflecting sadly that the streets of Paris were not the same any more.

"I had a long talk with Joe in the Evening Star," Julia said.

"Yes. He told me."

"I asked him a lot of questions about you."

"He told me that too."

"About your schooling in Wales."

"Blew my cover as Donaldson. Without realising it."

"Oh! I knew that already. No. That wasn't the reason I asked him so many questions about you. I felt I wanted to know you better, and who could be closer to you than your brother? He told me a lot about you; your childhood in Durban; your life in India; and I began to feel I knew you more. And then he let slip one very important detail."

"Nothing damaging, I trust?"

"You played cricket for your school in Wales?"

"Why, yes. I was their star spin bowler. Jomo and Saul were the batting stalwarts, but I dominated the bowling. My off-break was unplayable. I don't play much these days, but I do go to watch the Test matches."

"That clinched it with Grandfather. He loves cricket. He'd bribe me something awful to go with him to see the Tests. Even the county matches. And I went for his sake. When he found out he was to have a grandson-in-law, who loves cricket, he couldn't have been more pleased. There! Does that make you feel better?"

Joshua brightened, his sense of relief from the doubts that had been bothering him for so long lighting up his eyes, making him look years younger than he was.

Julia finished her drink. Joshua persuaded her to forget about her figure and share a Danish pastry with him. And she did. Warning him that if she put on weight, and he started to look around, he'd know who to blame.

"You asked me to put my hands on the table, without asking questions, and I did. Would you do the same for me, Josh? Trust my judgment, sometimes, even if you cannot agree with it? Because it is important to me."

"Try me."

Julia reached for the handbag, lying at her feet beneath the table. She snapped open the clasp, reached inside it, withdrew the brown, manila paper envelope, and placed it on the table between them. The handbag, considerably deflated, lay on its side in her lap.

He did not understand.

He looked inquiringly at her, not quite sure whether he was expected to reach for the envelope, uncertain of what such a thick envelope could contain that might be of interest to her. Or him.

"It's Saul's copy of the investment list," Julia said. "The only copy outside of South Africa. Will you agree to an exchange of information, Joshua? Give me the flags with the date and the names of the places from the torn lining of your coat pocket—and, darling, we'll go shopping this afternoon for a new one. You can't go around with torn linings like that. Besides you aren't going to need them anymore. Where was I? It's a much more humane way, Joshua. Publicise it at the right time and you will bring the mighty rand to its knees. And when the rand falls—good and hard—the miscegenation laws will go first! The Group Areas Act will take longer, but if the pullout is massive, it, too, will come down. Social justice, Joshua! As much money spent on a black child as a white one. All the hurt you've felt is my hurt too. But this is a much better way, darling."

He dared not ask it. But there were no barriers between them, and he wasn't going to erect new ones.

"And political justice?"

"Eventually. With complete integration. And trust. But I'm realistic, Joshua. That won't come easily. Like asking me to love Saul. Would marrying him have solved my problems? Or his? Please, Joshua. It will avoid so much bloodshed this way. Yes? And will you put your hands on the table—as I did."

He did not understand again. But he put his hands on the table before her, palms upwards, open towards her.

"So I can hold them, when I ask you again."

He laughed. But he nodded, opening his coat and holding the flap open wide, so she could search for the flags in the torn lining. He felt her fingers, gently inserted, touch his chest as they closed around the flags, drawing them all out together between her fingers.

"May I make a suggestion?" Joshua said.

"Please."

"I don't fancy going back to London from here. And the matter can hardly wait. Why don't you go into the hotel and telephone your grandfather from there?"

"I suppose, I could. Grandfather! You know?"

"I can give you the names of all the other directors too," he said gently. "When we are married, ask me when we're in bed together. I'll reel them off for you—for the thrill of it!"

"I don't want to know," she said.

Julia got up from the table. For the first time, she turned the flags over to read the writing, checking the pronunciation of the names with Joshua. He pushed the brown, manila paper envelope, still sealed, towards her.

"Keep it for me," he said. "I will use it when the time comes. But I'll leave it in your safekeeping for now."

She had taken three steps towards the hotel when she stopped and turned around.

"Aren't you taking an awful risk, Joshua? I have the flags and the list. I could easily go out the back of the hotel, quietly, and you might never see me again."

He laughed.

"True. That's very true. Aren't you taking an awful risk too? In the ten minutes you're gone, some passing French mademoiselle might walk provocatively down the street past me, casting one of those sidelong glances, invitingly, and you might well come out of the front of the hotel—and find me gone."

She thought about it for a few seconds.

"On second thoughts, I have more to lose than you have. Will you come into the hotel with me, Joshua, while I make a quick phone call to Grandfather?"

"Go!" he commanded, like some Eastern potentate, pointing with his arm to the hotel entrance. "I will be here when you return."

She came out ten minutes later, all fears behind her. The talk with her grandfather had been a stirring one. She was flushed with some sort of success. There was a crusading light in her eyes. The sort he'd seen when La Reine had talked about her map on the wall.

She was dying to tell him and she did.

"We will have to delete one of the names from this list, Joshua."

"Oh! Whose?"

"Grandfather's of course! You didn't think I was going to let the British Government have vital information without extracting some concession from him, did you now? Poor dear! I shocked him a bit. But he was an absolute brick about it. And he'll do it publicly too. Announce in the House of Lords he's pulling up stakes in South Africa. There! Aren't we off to a good start?"

He received the news with quiet satisfaction. Not bubbling over as she was. There was a lot he had to learn about her.

"What are your plans?" she asked. "I mean for this afternoon. It is such a nice day."

"I haven't any. Did you have anything in mind?"

"Would you like to go for a walk?" Julia said, almost timidly, not entirely sure as to his response. Did he like walking? There was so much she did not know about him. In the years to come, she would read his mind, as he would hers, but not today. Today there was a freshness to it all, and uncertainty was a part of it.

"The flowers at this time of the year are absolutely splendid," she continued persuasively. "In the Parc des Buttes Chamont. A little off the beaten track for tourists. It will be quiet—even lonely."

"I would like that very much," Joshua said.

He paid the waiter, adding a generous tip to the bill. Waved to Henri, keeping a discreet eye on their needs, at the entrance to the hotel.

She took his arm, holding him tight, pressing her breast against it, feeling the warm feelings that radiated between arm and breast.

He felt them too.

"Why do I feel, you're a little shorter today?" Joshua said.

"Because I'm wearing flat-heeled shoes. I bought them specially for walking with you. So much more exciting. They put my body at just the right height with yours. For our delight. Wouldn't you say?"

He had to agree.

They strolled down the street, arm in arm, towards the park that was some distance away.